Vicious Ink Publications

PRESENTS

MY MASTER'S BED

ISBN-13: 978-0-9961432-9-5

ISBN-10: 0-9961432-9-7

First Printing

Printed in the United States

MY MASTER'S BED

A Novel By

Amanda Lee

CHAPTER 1

As I gazed out the window in Starbucks, watching the rain pour down, I felt hot and moist down below. I started moving back and forward in my seat, feeling uncomfortable. Alex was an hour late. He knew I wouldn't dare leave because of our agreement with each other. We met online on this dating site and immediately became attracted to each other. Once we discovered that we both wanted a dominant/submissive relationship, we were inseparable. Even though he lived in Calgary, Canada, and I lived in Atlanta, Georgia, we had to be with each other.

"Excuse me, miss, I see you are alone. I was wondering if I could join you," this deep-voiced, sexy man spoke as he moved a piece of his dark brown hair from his skinny face.

"That's not a good idea, because I am waiting on my boyfriend to show up," I replied as I glanced up and put my head back down staring at my now, cold cup of cappuccino.

"It doesn't seem like he is coming. You have been sitting here for two hours now."

"No, I haven't been sitting here for two hours. It's only been one hour. Are you a stalker? Why are you watching me anyway?" I snapped back hoping he would go away before Alex appeared. Alex was a very jealous man and wanted me all to himself. He didn't like to share. And me talking to another man was obscure to him.

"You don't have to be mean. I just want a little conversation," the strange man stated, before he took himself a seat at my table without permission. I jumped up quickly and gathered my things.

"I guess you can't tell I don't want to be bothered. And would you please move," I snapped again as I sat back down. My heart was beating so loud and so fast. The palms of my hands were sweaty and slippery. The moisture in my panties was even wetter. I need to calm the hell down before I explode.

"You want me here because your loser boyfriend isn't going to show up." He joked and gave out this funny laugh. The way he smiled caused me to smile back.

"He's definitely not a loser. Late, but no loser." I smiled as I sipped on my cappuccino. We both laughed and then, I looked up to see this blonde, muscular built man walking towards me. He looked like Alex, but I wasn't for sure. Alex was a brunette. The demeanor on this man's face was like stone. Everything in the room stopped. I heard no laughter, no people talking. Absolutely nothing as this man approached us. The stranger sitting at my table turned around trying to see what had my attention. He turned back to me and saw my face as it went from smiling to a blank stare. This blonde-haired man and I stared at each other until he approached the table abruptly.

"What's rule number one?" he questioned as he hit his fists against the table very hard, shaking it and spilling my cappuccino.

"Alex?" I asked as I stared into his face. He looked different than on webcam or Skype. He looked younger in person, and his hair was brunette. This guy in front of me could not be my Alex.

"What's rule number one?" he yelled, pounding his fist hard against the table again, scaring me and then looking to the stranger sitting at the table. He continued as he looked back to me, "I won't ask you again."

"Rule number one is never talk to another man unless it is dealing with business," I mumbled with such a low tone he didn't hear me. I glanced over at the stranger, hoping he didn't hear what I said, then placed my eyes back on Alex.

"Repeat it louder, I didn't hear you," he spoke again, but this time with not so much attitude as he pointed his finger in my face.

I stared directly in his eyes and repeated a little louder, "Never talk to another man unless it is dealing with business."

I was kind of embarrassed because I didn't think our first meeting would be like this. He told me that he would catch me off guard again and indeed, he did.

"Is this business?" he queried with such a calm voice.

"No sir, it's not but I tried to tell him to leave and..." Before another word came out of my mouth, Alex quickly punched the dark-haired man in the face. He snatched him up from the table and the two began fighting. I froze in my seat as Alex beat the crap out of this man I didn't even know.

After several Starbucks' employees broke up the fight, Alex snatched me up by my dress and we rushed out the door. I never looked back at this strange man or how trashed the place was. I was scared to go with him at first, but then I just went. This was the man I had fallen in love with.

"I can't believe you have embarrassed me like this. You keep breaking the rules and I can't deal with that," Alex barked as we walked out in the rain with no umbrellas.

"I didn't mean to embarrass you, master," I politely spoke as I tried to keep the rain out of my face. The second week we'd talked, Alex insisted I call him master until he tells me otherwise. I was a young black woman from the country and it sounded good on the internet.

"Don't talk to me until we get to the hotel. Tonight, you will be punished. This being disobedient has to stop." I noticed his lip bleeding. I touched his lip and he knocked my hand down. We began walking to the hotel at such a fast pace, I couldn't catch my breath.

As we walked in the rain, I couldn't help but to stare at Alex's body. He was more toned than I imagined. All I could see were the muscles piercing through his white tuxedo shirt. It hugged every muscle in his back. My pussy pulsated just thinking about how he would ravish me from the back, or choke me as he pounded my pussy hard. I felt myself starting

5

to drip. I almost had an orgasm as I walked behind him, admiring his sexy body. Damn, I'm ready to fuck.

ALEX'S THOUGHTS

As we walked in the rain, I didn't know exactly how I was going to punish Siam. This girl is different. She is the second black female that I have encountered. The first one was too weak and couldn't handle my authority. She ran back home to her mother talking about I was too tough, but reality was, she was weak. The other five girls I dealt with were weak too. I had two submissives at one time. Maybe, I should have a submissive for about a year or two, then, add another. These girls had o be trained properly if this dominant/submissive relationship was going to work. Especially, someone who has never been exposed to the lifestyle.

I must treat Siam different. My father told me to stop abusing these girls. I don't think it's abuse, but more so me being the dominant as I read in many books. There are so many ways to dominate your partner. Who says I only wanted to have a submissive partner in bed? I wanted a woman who was submissive all the time. I knew that I had to teach Siam, she was one of those psychologically submissive women. I have to teach her that she isn't going to be the boss, period. She will follow my lead and do exactly what I tell her to do. I won't embarrass her in public, but she will know before I take her back to Canada. I don't want all my friends and family to see that this girl is out of control. I had her somewhat where I wanted her to be, but she still was

6

disobedient at times. I can't punish her too
badly tonight, because she might not come back home with
me.

    As I looked back at Siam and the rain fell against her
beautiful, silky, dark-skinned face, I knew she would be
perfect. She was there to serve and obey. Turning back
around to lead her to our destiny, she squeezed my hand,
assuring me that she wanted to follow me. I walked a little
faster because I couldn't wait to get her back to the hotel to
punish her softly. A year had been too long not to have met
before now.

CHAPTER 2

As we approach the Four Seasons Hotel Atlanta, I felt embarrassed. Our clothes were soaking wet, but Alex didn't care. He was indeed angry and disappointed in me. Feeling bad, I tried to straighten myself up but the short dress I wore kept clinging to my body. As we continued walking around to the back side of the hotel, greeting us with the back door open was a tall, bald headed man standing there holding two white robes. He held the door as we stepped in.

"Take off all your clothes and put on one of those robes. You will warm up faster," Alex demanded as he stood there, watching me like a hawk about to attack his prey.

"Right here in front of this man?" I looked at the tall, bald headed man.

"Here we go again, with you not following instructions. You really need to be trained the correct way. It's a big difference from me telling you what to do on webcam to in person, but you will learn to do everything I tell you to do and it starts tonight," Alex proclaimed as he snatched my dress and helped me pull it off. I stood there in my bra and panties. He stared at me as if he was waiting on me to pull off the rest. So I didn't ask any more questions; I began pulling off my bra and panties, standing there naked as a jaybird in front of them both. Alex handed me one of the robes and I immediately covered myself as I put my head down in shame.

"Thank you, Castro," Alex spoke as he undressed too and put on his white robe. Castro gathered our wet clothes, putting them in a bag and walked away.

We walked around the corner to get on the elevator. Luckily, no one was on the elevator and it made me feel kind of comfortable. Alex continued to hold onto my hand. As we exit the elevator and continued down the hall to a suite, an older man standing outside the door waiting on us. He opened the door for Alex and me to enter the room. Alex stopped me dead in my tracks, turned towards me, and put me on the spot.

"Are you ready to start a new beginning as my submissive?"

"Yes, master, I am ready for a new beginning with you as your submissive. I need you in my life," I replied with a huge smile on my face. I had been craving this dominant/submissive relationship for so long. This BDSM lifestyle was introduced to me when I was eighteen and I desired it ever since. People might find it odd of me, but I craved for that special person to be in control of my life twenty-four seven, taking my body every way possible and making me want it.

"I am dead serious about this, Siam, because once we enter through these doors, there is no turning back. I will be your master. You will do any and everything I tell you. I am done asking you to do anything. I think you're a big girl and you can handle anything I do to you. Again, are you sure you're ready to become my submissive twenty-four seven? That means you're moving to Canada."

I looked into Alex's big beautiful blues and answered softly, "Yes sir, I am ready for you to control my life, twenty-four seven. I am here to serve you, master."

It sounded so good coming out of my mouth. I had practiced saying that line for years now and I finally had a chance to recite it to a real person, and not my mirror. My heart beat so loud and hard, it felt like an adrenaline rush. I knew that once I walked through those doors, my life would change forever.

"Let's go, Princess. Remember, I own you," he announced, as he took my hand and led me into the hotel room. I was so wrapped up into Alex, I forgot the older man standing there, until he closed the door behind us. Here we are, alone for the first time.

Turning around to face me, Alex asked, "You claim you have slept with only one man, correct?

The question startled me. I figured he was about to kiss me and make love to me right there. I didn't want to answer, but I did.

"Yes, I have slept with only one man. That was when I was eighteen. It's kind of embarrassing, because I haven't experienced much."

"And you're twenty-three now, correct?"

"Yes master, but it was only that one time. I was curious how it would feel," I softly spoke. "No, I didn't enjoy it, because he didn't want to hold me down. He wouldn't do it how I wanted him to. I wanted him to be my master and he thought I was crazy."

"I am glad I met you. It's hard to find someone like you. I

11

love to be in control. You will see when we move back to Canada," Alex stated as he took off my robe. He stared at my body as my nipples rose. Chills spread all over my body as he squeezed each one of my breasts gently. I damn near came on myself. His hands were soft. He turned me around and told me to bend over. Alex got on his knees and opened my pussy. He looked thoroughly at my pussy and then, brushed his thumb gently over my anus. I jumped before I realized it.

"Sorry master," I apologized, as I assumed the position again.

"It's okay, just don't do it again. I like the fact you haven't been penetrated in your ass. I promise, you will learn to love it," he uttered as he stood up and took off his robe. His dick was huge. My mouth fell open and he smiled. It was hanging, all eleven inches of it and possibly about three inches thick. The only thought that crossed my mind was, *how am I going to take all that in my anus*? My knees began to shake. *What in the hell have I gotten myself into*?

"Can I please take a bath?" I requested; I felt dirty and sticky from the rain.

"No, you can't take a bath right now…no, you can't use

the bathroom right now…no, you can't do a damn thing right now, other than get on your knees and put your hands on your thighs." Alex walked up to me and put his dick in my face. It was very hard and pretty, but I knew I could not touch him until he told me to do so. My body was very anxious to experience the eleven inches he was going to give me.

Alex stood in front of me, stroking himself slowly as I watched. I could not keep my eyes away from it. He continued to stroke and stroke until I thought he was about to explode, so I lifted myself a little off the floor, almost touching it. My mouth opened, wanting him to ram it down my throat but he just stopped.

"Please, master, let me take you into my mouth until you explode and I swallow every drop of you. Please, I need you," I begged as I took my hands off my thighs to grab him.

"No, don't you ever attempt to touch me again until I tell you to. Remember, you are on punishment. In case you forgot, you cannot follow instructions. You cannot do what you are told. You have to learn to do as I tell you and not what you want to do. If you want to be a submissive, then you will have to learn the hard way, because I see now that your head is hard." Alex grabbed me by the hair and slapped me in the face with his dick.

He then walked away and left me there on the floor, kneeling and looking stupid. He took a shower and then returned to see if I had moved. He grabbed me by the hair roughly. I crawled on the floor as he led me over to a chair. Pulling upward on my hair, he forced me to stand then sat me down kind of hard. Alex walked over to the bed, sitting down on the edge and stared at me. The stare was intense making me feel like a little kid who has gotten into trouble. I couldn't help but bow my head in shame, scared to look up at him. After staring at me with this stone look, he retired to bed, leaving me in the chair all night watching him sleep.

When I woke up, Alex was sitting on the edge of the bed again, staring at me. I didn't hear him get out of the bed. I jumped up and straightened myself in the chair.

"I apologize, master, I was just so tired and could not stay awake."

"If you keep apologizing and not doing what you are told, I'll have to replace you. I know we have a year between us but I will replace you immediately." Alex threatened me as he stared at me with no expression in his face.

"I promise I will do as you tell me, just please don't replace me, master. Please, don't do this to me," I begged again.

"Come over here and suck me right now," Alex ordered. "Crawl, don't walk."

Getting on my knees, I crawled over to him and placed both of my hands on him. It was so fat that I could not put my fingers around him. I opened my mouth and began teasing the head, sucking as much as I could. I tried to deep throat him, but I couldn't put all of it in my mouth. Sucking the head, I eased down slowly on each side of his dick, making sure that all of it got attention.

"I am about to cum," I let him know in between the sucking and licking.

"Don't you dare come right now, just keep sucking me and hold that pussy. Don't let a drop hit the floor because you will anger me. And I don't think you are ready to see that side of me yet," Alex growled. I gripped my pussy very tight, hoping that I didn't come. I tried to concentrate on something not related to sex, but I couldn't help it, because his eleven inches that had my throat jammed up.

Finally, he picked me up and placed me on the bed. Licking my pussy, I squirmed, not trying to explode so fast. He licked a few more times and then pulled on my clit, as two of his fingers slid in my pussy. It was too much to hold back and I exploded in his face. He continued pulling on my clit as I screamed out loud with joy. This felt so much better than me playing with myself every night until I was tired. I exploded in his face a second time, thinking about how big his dick was. Alex got up and mounted me. He entered my pussy and rammed himself deep. It was already sloppy and wet, so that helped me take all eleven inches of him. My pussy opened up and Alex went deep within me, again and again. I could actually feel him in my stomach as I held his body tight. He fucked me so hard. All you could hear was watery splashing noises as he pounded me. Alex bent my knees back towards my breasts as he put both hands on my thighs, holding himself up and pounding himself into me over and over, until my legs began to shake and I exploded several more times. He fucked me all that day and then half the night. We ate, rested, and plowed back at each other again.

Three days passed by with us fucking and sucking each other. The only exception was when it was time to eat. I had to wait until he started eating first, and then I could eat. I knew that my family had to be worried about my black ass because my cell phone kept going off and Alex was getting furious about it. They just knew because we met online, he was a murderer. If they only knew that I had committed my life to him twenty-four seven from that day forward to be his submissive. I am now owned by my dominant, my master, Alex Thompson Tremblay.

SIAM'S THOUGHTS

That night, sitting in the chair as I watched Alex crawl into bed with a limp dick, I just knew the first time we met it would be straight, raw fucking. But instead, I am sitting up in the dark, in a damn chair watching my supposed-to-be-man sleep by himself. I should be disobedient and do it anyway, but there would be consequences. What I have learned in the last year of communicating with him is to not disobey. I have seen him on webcam tossing and tearing up his house, screaming like a mad man because of something I had done. He snapped so badly on me the first time I went to the club without him or asking permission; I would never forget that. But afterwards, he calmed down and we had webcam sex.

As I smiled to myself, I looked at Alex lying in bed. He let out a soft moaning sound. I knew he was sound asleep so I

17

stood up by the bed admiring his sexy body. He had a light tan, with blonde hair and big beautiful blue eyes. This was my first time ever in my life being with someone outside my race. When I started talking to Alex, I didn't think he would want to be involved with a black woman. But, we started talking and hadn't stopped. It was like we couldn't get enough of each other. It made me feel good that a man wanted me for me and not just wanted to fuck my brains out.

I continued to stare for a few minutes and sat back down. His body glowed as the moon shined in from the big hotel window. He didn't close the curtains and I was too scared to wake him. I looked up to the moon and mouthed, "Thank you, God, for sending Alex."

This was the day I had been waiting for, but this wasn't how I thought it would be, sitting in a damn chair alone. I took another look at Alex and pulled my bra up over my breasts. I began pulling my nipples hard and grinding in the chair. Putting my finger in my panties, I imagined Alex shoving his dick down my throat. He was pushing it deep, as I tried to stop my teeth from scraping his dick. I didn't want him to know that I had no experience at sucking dick.

Listening to Zoey talk about it all the time, I knew it wasn't a problem. Just put the dick in your mouth and suck; how hard could that be? As I rubbed my clit and got my pussy wetter, Alex let out a snort; then the sound stopped. I looked up and he was looking at me. He didn't say a word, just stared. I removed my fingers and straightened up. I sat up straight as I put my hands on my thighs and stared back.

Soon, Alex went back to sleep. My eyes were so heavy, I could barely stay awake. I turned around in the chair, placing my legs over the arm and laying my head back. I was going to take a nap for a few minutes. Alex would never know if I had been to sleep or not; at least, that's what my mind said anyway. My body said otherwise. My ass was more tired than a mutherfucker.

CHAPTER 3

That weekend was very long. It was not as much fucking going on as I wanted it to be. He did pound my pussy, but I wanted more. His brain was stuck on training me what to do and what not to do. I wasn't thinking about that shit; I just wanted to feel him between my legs, serving me.

Monday came and it was time for me to return to my tiny two-bedroom apartment. I was kind of scared to take him home because my family and friends were probably going to pop up at my house. I didn't know how he was going to act. I didn't know how my family was going to act. Shit, I didn't know how I was supposed to act. All types of things crossed my mind. What if he wanted to fuck with one of my friends? I would lose him if I didn't cooperate. The dreadful thought crossed my mind; I might have to be prepared to give him up. Or, let him fuck my sister or friends.

As I heard the shower turn off, I immediately grabbed one of the bath sheets and waited for my master to step out of the tub. That was one of my daily duties, to dry him off whenever he exit the shower. I had to stand there from beginning to end until I was invited to join him.

As I wrapped the towel around him and began drying him off, he inquired, "Did you get my luggage out so I can show you how to pack my clothes? This will be my first and last time showing you, Siam. I need you to be a fast learner and a quick thinker."

"Yes, master, I will learn how you want everything. Is there anything else you would like for me to do before I clean the bathroom?" I asked as I stood there facing him. Alex gave me a kiss on the cheek and nodded his head no.

He took the towel from me and continued drying off. I guess I had to do a better job. I cleaned the bathroom, then placed his dirty clothes in a yellow plastic bag. Finally, after he taught me how to pack his clothes, we were off to my apartment. I was more nervous than a whore in church.

Arriving at the apartment, I didn't want to open the door. My mom and my best friend, Zoey had a key to my apartment. They always showed up unannounced. Opening the door, there was quietness; nobody was there invading my privacy.

"Smells real good in here. I see you are using the products I sent you. Nice, Princess," Alex stated as he looked around my apartment. He went from room to room, investigating like a detective.

"Of course I used the products you sent me. I didn't want to be disobedient. Plus, they smell so different. We don't have anything around here in Georgia that smells like that." I stated, as I felt comfortable in my own home. I carried the luggage into my bedroom and placed them on the bed.

"I am happy that you were being obedient. Maybe you need to apply that to other things that you need work on. There were times when I was at home in Canada, I really wanted to hurt you, because you didn't do what I told you. And that, Princess, is a no-no in our relationship," Alex added, as he stepped into my bedroom.

"Master, I apologized for those things in the past and I will apologize again; right now if you want. I really didn't know how to take the relationship at first because I had no knowledge, but now I know. I have read many articles on the internet, I have looked at many videos, and of course, the teaching you have taught me this past year," I responded as I walked over to him and got on my knees.

"I see you are learning fast and yes, you can apologize

again." He added, "Strip down right now. I need to teach you a lesson for those mistakes."

"I apologize, master, for all of the wrongdoings I have done in the past. I will correct everything I have done if I can."

"You can just apologize because there is no correcting the mistakes you have done in the past. You have been a bad girl and now it's time to teach you a lesson. I wanted to teach you a lesson in the hotel, but I was afraid you would scream too loudly; but now that you are comfortable in your own home, I will punish you like you should have been months ago," Alex boldly stated as I took off my clothes. There I stood in my birthday suit once again.

Those words didn't seem right to me and I felt like the punishment was not sex. As I stood there in my birthday suit, Alex took off his belt and demanded that I lay on the bed on my stomach.

"I apologize for being bad, please don't punish me, master. I promise to be good," I playfully spoke as Alex struck me with the belt very hard across my back. I almost jumped off the bed because of the stinging sensation.

"Turn your black ass back over and lay flat. You can lay there yourself or I can tie you down and teach you the hard way. Which way do you prefer? Either way, you will be punished severely," he instructed as he hit me with the belt again. Alex whipped me about four hard times across my back. I jumped and started crying like a baby.

"Please don't punish me anymore, master. I promise, I will do right. Please," I begged as I heard a knock at the door. Whoever it was began pounding louder on the door. Alex looked towards the door then put his belt back on.

"I will stop for now. Next time I won't be lenient on you. Go get in the shower, I will answer the door," he replied as I rushed off to the bathroom to jump in the shower. I was scared to death it was my mother knocking on the door. I couldn't risk her seeing me like this.

Turning the water on, I rushed in immediately. Lathering up the soap on the towel, I began scrubbing. The soap burned the whelps across my back, but I knew I had to bathe quickly but thoroughly. I sat down in the tub and began to cry. That damn belt hurt. I hadn't felt like that in such a long time. The last time I got an ass beating with a belt was when I snuck out of the house to go partying with Zoey. We had so much fun, I forgot to go home and my dad beat the hell out of me.

Suddenly, I heard loud noises. Zoey was in my bedroom, talking loud as usual. "Siam, where you at? I haven't seen you all weekend," Zoey called out as I stood up and stepped under the shower, putting water on my face. I didn't want her to see me crying.

"Zoey, is that you? I'll be out in a second," I answered as I stuck my head out the shower curtain to see if she had come in the bathroom.

"You need to hurry up before I attack your man. He is too sexy. I asked him if there are any more Canadian men up there that he could introduce me to," Zoey joked. I hurried up and jumped out. I didn't want this shit to turn into a threesome. I didn't want to share my cock with Zoey.

"Leave my man alone and stop being a whore," I remarked as I jumped out the shower and quickly dried off. I ran in the bedroom and put on my clothes before Zoey could see the whelps on my back.

"I am not being a whore, I am telling the truth," Zoey yelled back. After getting dressed, I rushed into the living room to see the two of them sitting on the couch talking.

"Hey Zoey," I greeted as I rushed over to her.

"You are glowing and shit, looks like you got some dick this weekend. It's about time you got the dust off that pussy. I didn't think you were ever going to fuck again." Zoey laughed as she lightly touched Alex on the leg.

"Seems like your best friend is very friendly and speaks her mind. I like that in a woman," Alex smirked, but I knew that was a lie. I smiled but wanted Zoey to get her ass out of here.

"Zoe, stop being so ratchet. I don't want you scaring Alex off." I smiled.

"You know better than that, Siam, it is very hard to scare me off and furthermore, I am really liking your friend. She would probably be a fun fuck," Alex advised as he moved his hand higher and patted Zoey's thigh.

"I see you are a shit talker too. I like you, Alex. You really need to bring me one of them Canadian boys here to Georgia. I heard y'all have them big juicy dicks." Zoey stated, as she batted her eyes at Alex. She smiled from ear to ear, looking at me then back to Alex.

"Do you want to see how big my dick is?" Alex asked Zoey. He didn't look at me once. He was focused on Zoey.

"Pull that mutherfucker out. Don't think I don't want to see." Zoey commanded as she sat up on the edge of the couch. Alex stood up and he was already hard. He pulled down his pants and Izod underwear. His eleven inches stood there exposed. I was breathless at first. The first thing that came across my mind was, why he wanted to show Zoey his cock. It belongs to me and not her. I know her; she would want to fuck him.

"Do you like what you see?" Alex queried as he made his cock move up and down.

"Hell yeah, I like it. Siam, you took all that dick? Damn you must have a big pussy," Zoey implied as she looked at me. I gave her that "stop fucking around" look. She added, "Let me stop messing around, Alex. I can see it on Siam's face she doesn't like it. I don't want her to be mad at me for weeks." Zoey went on as she sat back on the couch and crossed her hands.

"What look do you have on your face, Siam? Are you offended by what is going on? Please apologize to Zoey. Tell her that you don't mind her touching my cock and you don't mind her fucking your man," Alex demanded as he gave me that stone-faced look.

Putting my head down, I did what Alex wanted. "I apologize, Zoey. Go ahead and touch it.

"And what else did I say?" Alex addressed.

"Zoey, you can fuck my man if you want. I won't be mad at you," I managed to say, while Alex stared at me with an evil look on his face.

"What the hell is really going on? Siam, I am surprised at you. This is not like you. This man has changed you and I like it. I knew you were a freak," Zoey replied as she sat up and grabbed Alex's dick, stroking it; her fat fingers molesting him. Alex moved closer to her and directed her head to suck him. Zoey began sucking Alex, as I stood there frozen. Alex grabbed me and began kissing me.

"Siam, I think you need another shower," Alex insisted as he pointed his finger towards the bathroom. That meant get the fuck out of here. I didn't say a word, but walked towards the bathroom.

Looking back, I watched as Alex sat on the couch as Zoey undressed. She sat on his big cock, riding him wildly. Alex grabbed her by the shoulders, shoving her down on him roughly. She was so busy fucking my man, she didn't see me standing in the bedroom door. I watched as they fucked. Alex put Zoey on her knees and took her doggy style. He waved for me to walk over there when he noticed I was watching and not taking a shower like he ordered me.

"This is how you take a dick. Just open up the pussy," Alex briefed me while almost out of breath, as he put Zoey's head in the couch and lit into her like he never had pussy before. Zoey was screaming out as Alex rammed his cock hard in her pussy. I watched as he put every inch deep in her. He pounded and pounded; and I could see her white cum all over his cock. It turned me on in a way.

After Alex took out his cock and came on her ass cheeks, he demanded, "Suck me until I get hard again." Zoey got down and began sucking. He looked at the expression on my face. "Get the fuck out, Siam. You don't look happy. You better get fucking happy, Princess, because this will happen all the time. Don't make me punish you again." Alex said as he fanned me away like a fly. I walked off and slammed my bedroom door behind me.

It was silent for a few minutes, then I heard Zoey screaming again. I got up and cracked the door open. Alex had her lying flat on her back. He was giving it to her hard, stroke after stroke. Her fat ass enjoyed it. I knew Zoey, she just loved a good fuck. Alex took out his cock and yelled out for me. "Siam, get your ass out here."

Opening the door wider, I slowly walked over. "Yes master."

"Suck me right now. I need to feel your lips," he commanded me as I stood there with my arms crossed.

"Really?" I said before I realized it. That wasn't being submissive. My mouth was about to write a check my ass couldn't cash.

"Fuck! Suck me, Siam," he demanded again, as he slapped Zoey's pussy with his cock.

Zoey yelled, "Suck it, Siam. My pussy clean." She thought the shit was funny. She always joked about sharing her men, but I never thought she was serious. That is, until now when my man's cock is all in her pussy.

"I'm not sucking nothing," I smarted off. As I was about to turn away, Alex snatched me back quickly and pulled me to him.

"Suck me now, Siam. I won't ask you again."

"Fuck it, I'll suck your dick," Zoey volunteered, about to turn around.

"You keep that pussy in the air. I want to ram this mutherfucker all the way to your throat. I like thick girls. They can take dick, unlike skinny bitches," Alex remarked as he let go of my head. Easing my head down, I began sucking. I slobbered on that cock like a kid with their favorite lollipop. He rose quickly as I spit on it and kept slobbing on it. Alex grabbed my hand and put it to Zoey's pussy. I tried to pull back, but he gave me that stone look again. He ordered me, "Do it now."

Tears fell down my face as Alex entered Zoey's pussy again with his juicy dick. Alex directed my hands so his hands were on top on mine. We stroked her clit together as he slow stroked her. I looked at him with shame and jerked my hand back. Alex pushed me backwards. I walked over to my chair and watched him as he finished fucking Zoey. As he released, she jumped up and began sucking all the cum out his cock. Alex's legs got so weak, he almost fell over on her.

I didn't want Alex or Zoey to see me still crying. Running to the bathroom, I ran water in the tub and put bubble bath in it. Sitting down in the tub, everything got quiet; too quiet because I fell asleep.

Suddenly, I felt water being splashed in my face. "What the hell?" I yelled as I tried to get out the tub. As I opened my eyes, Alex pushed me back in the water.

"You need you to cool the fuck off, Siam. You have embarrassed me once again. What's rule number twenty-three? Have you fucking forgot? Rule number twenty-three states, 'Master is allowed to own more than one slave. I will accept that and live with it.' Alex yelled as he tried to push my head under the water. I started bucking and kicking, trying to get away from his grip as he held me tighter.

Finally, he let go of me. Standing there as the shower head spit water in my face, I was coughing and choking all at the same time. After a few minutes, I got my composure and stepped out of the tub. "What are you doing?" I sighed as I looked at him. Alex dragged me by the neck and held me against the wall. As he talked, I felt his cock starting to grow as it lay between my ass cheeks.

"What is rule number twenty-three? Think Siam, think. We have been over this for a year. You should know these rules by heart. It's only twenty-five of them."

"Rule number twenty-three is master is allowed to own more than one slave. I will accept that and live with it. Basically, I don't own him, he owns me," I recited. I had to memorize that fucking twenty-five-rule book over and over the first three months we got together.

"Good girl. You didn't remember the rules when I fucked your friend. Things like that will happen again. If I penetrate another woman, you better be prepared to eat her pussy and fuck her too. You belong to me. Don't ever forget that." Alex's hard cock pressed against my ass. He began fiddling with my pussy and entered me right there by the bathroom wall. I placed both of my hands on the wall above my head and lifted my ass up. Alex began choking me softly as he fucked me slowly. After I came, we walked to my bed. Alex handcuffed me to the bed and then, pulled out his black belt again.

"Wait, Master. Please, don't hit me. Please. I'm sorry. Please," I begged as I got louder and louder.

"So, that's how you want to scream out. Okay then, we will play the game your way." Alex threw his belt on the bed and walked over to his luggage. He pulled out a roll of gray duct tape. He tore off a piece and then walked over to me, placing it on my mouth.

Alex began swinging that belt like he was angry. I kicked and bucked trying to turn but he had me spread out. Each lick sounded horrible. He beat my ass and my back. I screamed through the duct tape as loud as I could. Finally, he stopped. "There you go, twenty-five licks for my twenty-five-rules. Whenever you forget, this is what you will get."

Alex took the handcuffs off me and demanded I sleep on the floor. I cried silently to myself until I fell asleep.

ZOEY'S THOUGHTS

Picking up my clothes, I got dressed and sneaked out the front door before Siam awakes. Alex had put a fucking on me that I won't ever forget. It just shocked me that he had a huge dick. I have never seen one so big like that before in my life. I got carried away and now, I am looking like a jackass.

Getting in my car, I put my head down on my steering

wheel and sat there for a few minutes. "Damn it, Zoey, you knew better than to fuck Alex. What in the hell have you done? Siam talked about being in love and wanting to marry this man, but you fucked him. Damn it," I yelled out as I turned the switch on and drove off.

So many things crossed my mind. Did Siam really mean for me to fuck Alex? Why did he show me his dick and tell me to touch it? Siam knew I was weak for dick, why she didn't stop me? "Come to think about it, why didn't she stop me?" I said out loud. That was very odd for her, sharing a man she loved. Someone she wants to spend the rest of her life with. He obviously had her under his control. Siam sat there looking stupid in the face as Alex fucked me. He told her to get out and she did with no lip. He told her to shut up and she did that too. I knew he controlled her life just a little bit, but now he is here in the flesh, I saw it for myself.
She used to tell me all the weird things he wanted her to do. And, of course she did it and had never met the guy before. Siam had me curious about this dominant/submissive relationship stuff. Her parents would die if they knew that's what she was committing her life to. The thought of it excited me, but I just wanted to fuck. I wonder if Alex would hook me up with a big-dick man like him.

As my brain went in all kind of directions, I remembered the expression on Siam's face when Alex was fucking me and telling her that's how he wanted her to take it. Siam is a skinny chick. She can't take dick like me. Most of my fat blocked me from being hurt while a man rammed me hard. I encourage it a lot because most men were small. I needed to

35

feel that pressure.

When Alex fucked me, I hid my face from Siam because I didn't want to see the expression on her face, but after she told me to do it, I just said fair game. Something told me that she didn't approve of it, but I had to be a whore like always. Just selfish, always thinking of myself.

It felt good though, because I got a chance to experience fucking a huge dick, but I felt bad because of Siam. Well, it's over with now, I shrugged as I shook my head driving home. I could still smell Alex's cologne all over me. It smelled so good, it made me crave more of him.

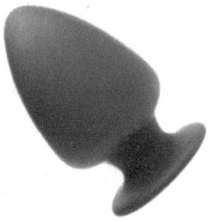

BUTT PLUG

CHAPTER 4

I woke up the next morning, smelling bacon and eggs. I didn't realize I had gotten into the bed. Slipping back on the floor before Alex caught me, I wrapped up in the thick comforter he had provided for me the night before. But before I could pretend to be sleep, Alex stepped in the room.

"Get up, Princess, and come enjoy this beautiful breakfast that I have prepared for you," Alex demanded as he kneeled down on the floor and kissed me on the forehead.

"Thank you, master," I replied, as we both stood up and faced each other. I didn't realize how shiny and blue his eyes really were. I wanted to kiss him, but it was forbidden at that moment.

"Today is going to be our Safe Day. I am allowing us to be free today. It doesn't have to be the dominant/submissive or master/slave stuff today. You are allowed to say and do whatever you want to do," Alex notified me as he kissed me passionately. My body responded to him immediately. He hugged me so tight, I thought I was going to stop breathing.

After our passionate kiss, Alex smiled widely. He was like a totally different person. Before he could say another word, I slapped him across his face very hard. His face went from a smile to stone cold. "How could you do me like that? I can't believe you treated me that way." I cried as fell to my knees crying like a baby.

Alex tried to comfort me, but I pushed him away. He fell over, looking at me cry and began to cry with me. I cried for a long time. Alex even shed a few alligator tears. It didn't feel like he cared last night when he beat my ass with that belt.

"I'm so sorry, Siam. I didn't mean to hurt you like that," Alex apologized as he touched my thigh. He added, "I wasn't going to start out like that, but when I saw you with that idiot at Starbucks, it triggered something inside me that I couldn't control. It's been a year for us and I come here, just to see you with another man. I was furious. And, you're lucky you didn't get it too that night."

"I tried to get him away from my table before you came, but he wouldn't go away. I never thought I would ever see you so angry like that, but you were like a totally different person. What happened to your hair? I thought you had brown hair," I managed to say as I looked him in the eyes.

"I know, baby, and I didn't want you to see me like that yet. I do have anger issues, but I told you that already. Sometimes, I can't help but to punish when I'm angry." He sighed, then added, "Blond is my natural color. I changed it to brown and decided I didn't like it, so I changed it back to my natural color."

"You didn't have to punish me like that. Why did you whip me with that belt like that?"

"I should have told you as I punished you, but I couldn't speak. All the anger from over the past year crossed my mind. Out of the twenty-five rules, you have broken twenty-one of them. What did you expect when you saw me in person? Just forget what you did? You said you wanted this dominant/submissive relationship. Either you deal with it or you can leave. Rule number sixteen? Do you remember that?" Alex asked calmly and more caringly.

"Rule number sixteen, I am free to leave my master at any time without the fear of permanently losing him. I know the rule book like the back of my hand."

"I know you do, princess. I just want you to be happy with our relationship. If you want me to go, I can go now.

It's not a problem, if that is what you really want," Alex stated as he stood up to leave.

"I don't want you to leave, but I don't want marks like this on my back either. Look at this," I said as I stood up and looked at the whelps in the mirror. Alex put his head down and a smirk came across his face.

"I apologize in a way, but you need to do what you are told. I shouldn't have to keep telling you the rules over and over. I worked hard teaching you the rules I command, and you need to follow them. I refuse to keep telling you," Alex barked as he walked off and went into the kitchen.

I marched right behind him and continued, "And what about you fucking Zoey? That wasn't right at all. You being with any other girl wouldn't have mattered, but my best friend? How can you say that you love me and did that to me?"

"How could your friend fuck me? If she is your best friend, then maybe you need another friend. I just wanted to see if you would obey. That girl wanted to fuck me when she first laid eyes on me. I wasn't even thinking about doing her until she wanted to see my cock. Don't blame all this on me.

You need to blame her too." Alex fixed my food and handed me my plate. I snatched it out of his hand, almost knocking the food on the floor.

"I blame the both of you. Maybe, I should just call her right now and tell her about herself. Or then again, maybe I should just shut up and eat," I mumbled as I looked at Alex face and it had that stone look. He scared me when he looked like that. Seems like some evil shit was going through his mind at that time.

"Baby, please don't be mad at me. Remember, we agreed that I would be sleeping with other women whenever I felt like it. We talked about this."

"No, we didn't agree, you told me this was what I was going to do. I really don't care to suck on another woman's clit. I've never done that before."

"I know you haven't and trust me when I say this, once you do, you will enjoy it. It's just like me licking on that sweet pussy of yours." Alex giggled. His smile was so bright and shining. His teeth looked perfect and white. I couldn't be mad at him anymore.

"You're silly, Alex. You know that I really do love you."

"I love you more, Siam. If only you knew how deep my love is for you. I would kill before I let another man have you. You are mine forever. Don't think I'm crazy, but I'm never letting you go. Not ever," Alex announced as he put his head down to eat. Those words sent chills down my spine. The hairs on the back of my neck stood up. He added, "Another thing, I thought I told you to quit that police job. I don't want you as a cop anymore. That's what's wrong with you now; you won't listen to me."

"I did quit my police job; three weeks ago. When you first told me, I put in my resignation that same day. My parents thought I was nuts for doing so. I wasn't even sure if it was the right thing to do. The thing is, I was wondering if I would ever see you. Would you really come here and get me? So many things crossed my mind, which caused me to have doubt," I replied as I ate my breakfast and drank my orange juice.

"You should never doubt me, baby. Once I tell you something, you better believe me. When I saw that you wanted the type of relationship I wanted, I became obsessed with you. The truth is, I have been here in Georgia for about a week just watching you. Making sure you did the right thing."

"And what if I hadn't done the right thing?"

"Then once I did introduce myself to you, you would have gotten beaten worse than what you did. I don't play when it comes to my property. I want my submissive to submit. Don't just say it, but be about it." Alex spoke with a little more bass in his voice.

After we ate breakfast, Alex laid me on the countertop and ate my pussy. He pushed my legs back and stuck his tongue in, darting in and out. He pulled on my clit with his fingers, making me swell. In a way it hurt, but felt good at the same time. He finger-fucked me until I cried out, "Please, master, take me. I want to serve you. I want to do whatever you desire of me. Please, master, take me right now."

"Yes, princess, I will take you however you like," Alex replied as he took me to the bed and laid me on my stomach. He knew I liked it like that. He mounted me and inserted himself into my already, sloppy wet pussy.

"Damn, princess, you are so wet for me."

"Yes, master, yes. I want to feel all of you," I called out as

43

I thrust back on him, trying to make him fuck me hard like he did Zoey. I rotated my hips to every stroke. He kept slow rolling me. He was indeed trying to make love to me.

"Do you like that, princess? I just want to take my time and make love to you."

Alex turned me over and mounted me from the front. We stared at each other as he moved in and out of me slowly. His relaxed face made me feel so comfortable.

"Master, I'm about to explode. Please, fuck me harder." I squirmed as he stood on the tip of his toes and rammed me.

I folded my legs all the way back as he pushed all eleven inches deep. I felt like I had to vomit but kept that under control. Stroke after stroke and then, I exploded. Alex jumped up and ate my pussy as my body jerked from the orgasm. My pussy actually squirted; I could see my cum on his face. Wiping his face with my hands, he continued to suck my pussy as I tried to remove his head from down there. I yelled out with laughter as Alex jumped up and banged me some more.

"Fuck me like you did Zoey. Show me that control you seek of me. Punish me, master, for being disobedient," I harshly spoke as I lightly slapped him on the face.

Alex jumped up and put his dick in my mouth. He tried his best to push all of it down my throat. I gagged until he finally gave up. Alex put me in the doggy style and stroked me good. He put his foot on my head as he kept fucking me. He was very flexible.

"You dirty fucking whore, open that fucking pussy wide. Get it wider and stop gripping my dick. I want it making all kind of noises as my balls slap against that pussy," Alex ordered me as I tried to release my pussy grip and let him do what he loved. I kept tensing up because he was hurting me. Being put in the doggy style, I felt every single inch of him. I really didn't see how in the hell Zoey took all of it like she did. She bounced back on it like it wasn't hurting her. The image of Alex screwing Zoey caused me to open wide as ordered. I was turned on by that image. My body jerked each time Alex went all the way out and then inserted harder. As he hurt me worse, I kept moving up further and further on the couch. Alex chased me as his dick flopped out and he shoved it back in. I had cum so many times, it started to hurt me real bad.

"You're hurting me. Please stop, it's hurting," I jumped up

45

and his dick fell out. He was still hard.

"It was getting good, baby. I need some relief, please don't stop now." Alex said, as he looked with sad eyes.

"I will try riding you, but that doggy style ain't no joke. I don't see how she took you like that. Have you realized you are bigger than normal size?" I joked as I stood up holding my stomach and putting my lips on the head of Alex's cock, he laughed.

"Well, when you come to Canada, you will see that we all think this is normal size. Just about all of us have big ones." Alex laughed out loud. He had the cutest laugh. I hopped on him and began to ride slow. He stroked to my strokes and it was wonderful. My stomach didn't hurt as bad. I guess it was because he was just ramming me before and now, we were making love.

After we finished for about two hours, we finally headed over to my parents' house. I was kind of glad that Alex gave me a safe day. I wouldn't have known what to call him or how to act in front of my parents. My dad would have thought I lost my mind. Especially being submissive to a white man; he would have definitely flipped out.

We walked up to my parents' front door, and mom opened the door wide as she invited us to come in. "So, this is the young man who has my daughter not calling her parents to let us know she is alive." Mom joked as she gave Alex as big hug.

"About time you showed up. We have been waiting on you all day," dad stated as he walked up and hugged me tight.

"Sorry about that, mom. I apologize for not calling my parents," I sarcastically replied as I gave her a hug. Once she hugged Alex, she acted like she didn't want to let him go.

"I apologize too that she didn't call home," Alex said to my dad as he shook his hand. My dad grabbed him and hugged him tight too. Alex seemed surprised. He thought my parents wouldn't like him because I met him online.

"Well, come on in and let's eat dinner." Mom took Alex by the hand and led him to the kitchen table.

"I am hungry. The food smells real good," Alex complimented my mother.

"I hope you enjoy it. Siam told me what your favorite

foods were and I prepared them," Mom replied as she looked at dad.

"I wish I could get her to make me dinner like that. You are some kind of special," dad stated to Alex.

"Where is everybody else?" I asked as I looked at my mother and father.

"I didn't want all them fools over here messing up my house. I wanted your mother and I to enjoy our future son-in-law. Well, I hope he is anyway, since he made you quit your job and is trying to get you to move to Canada." Dad laughed as he looked at Alex. Mother gave him that "don't start no shit now" look.

"That's exactly what I plan to do, sir. I didn't spend a year of my time for wasting. I love your daughter dearly and I promise to protect her. And far as marriage, it will happen." Alex smiled. I smiled at him as he planted a kiss on my cheek.

"That's what I wanted to hear. So, Siam, how soon are you planning on leaving?" Dad asked. I looked at Alex because he hadn't told me anything yet.

"Alex?" I spoke as I raised my eyebrow, hoping he would answer dad's question.

"You mean, you don't know?" Dad queried as he frowned at me.

"We are leaving in a week," Alex replied as he smiled.

"A week. That's not enough time to say goodbye to everyone. You have to see your brothers before you go," mom replied as she ate some of her asparagus.

"I think that's plenty of time to say goodbye," Alex remarked as he continued to eat his food, not looking up at either one of us. I looked at mom and shrugged my shoulders. Dad just shook his head. He excused himself from the table and walked off. Mom frowned at me.

"What's wrong with him?" I asked as if I really didn't know. He didn't want me to go to Canada, but I was going with my master whether they all accepted him or not.

"Siam, he is upset about you moving to Canada. We are concerned that you are moving too fast. We don't know anything about him," Mom added as she tried to finish her food quickly and not offend Alex.

"You can ask me whatever you like, Mrs. Wilson. I will answer anything you want me to. I'm not a serial killer. I'm just a businessman who has his own company. I travel all over helping people with their business solutions. You can look my company up on the internet. You can call my office. I will give you the number to my home and give you my address. You and your family are welcome anytime you want to visit. I will pay for all expenses," Alex revealed, giving out details.

"I'm not saying you are a serial killer. This is my baby girl and you have to understand, she has never been away from home like that. I don't know about this moving to Canada. It's so far away," mom replied as her face looked worried.

"Mom, it's going to be okay. You're acting like I am never returning. Alex already told me that when he has to travel out of the country, I can come stay with you and father," I assured her as I got up and gave her a big hug. I added, "Please don't be worried about me. I will still have my cell phone, so you can reach me at any time. I will call and text you every day."

"She will definitely have her phone on her at all times.

And I will make sure she keeps in touch with her family," Alex stated as he finished his food and drank all of his tea.

"Okay, Alex, I am going to trust you with my baby. Just take care of my love," mom mumbled as she got up and placed a kiss on Alex's forehead. She walked out to find father. I didn't realize how upset he was about me moving to Canada. I guess he didn't believe me until Alex showed up.

"Do you trust me, Siam?" Alex asked.

"Yes, I trust you. I wouldn't be moving to Canada if I didn't trust you," I answered back.

"Yes, you would. You would go even if you don't trust me. I don't think you do trust me. The look on your face tells me that you doubt me. Don't forget the rule about lying to me. That won't be tolerated once we get to Canada," Alex stated as he wiped his mouth and stared at me. That stone-faced look was on his face again. I knew then, that our safe day was over.

SIAM'S THOUGHTS

As Alex drove us back to my apartment, I had to prepare to leave for Canada as soon as possible. I knew I was going back but not this quick. I figured he would let me say goodbye to my brothers, my friends, my cousins, or my co-workers. I wanted to ask him what day we were leaving, but was too scared to open my damn mouth. Ask him stupid, I said to myself. No, don't ask him, just let him tell you when and you just go. Don't fucking mess this opportunity of a lifetime up because you want to ask questions. Looking over at Alex, his mind was locked on the highway. He was driving like he actually knew where he was going. I didn't have to tell him how to get back to my apartment.

I began to think about how my dad had walked out. He had thought it was crazy for me to be dating a man online anyway. I had told him and mother over Sunday dinner one night. They both looked at me like I had lost my mind.

"Siam, are you that desperate for a man?" my dad asked as he slammed his glass on the dinner table.

"No dad, I'm not crazy or desperate. I have plenty of sense. We have been talking for about three months now, and I thought it was time to let you and mother know who I was dating. And yes, we have decided to date each other long-distance," I replied as I picked up my plate to rush off to the kitchen. It didn't go as well as I thought it was going to be.

"Siam Wilson, don't you dare leave this table while your father and I are talking to you," Mom interrupted as she walked over to me and pulled my chair back out. That meant for me to sit my black ass back down and finish the conversation.

"Who is this guy? What does he do?" My dad questioned,

as I tried to answer the first question.

"His name is Alex. He lives in Canada and he is a business consultant," I stated.

But before I could say anymore, dad mumbled, "You mean to tell me that you couldn't find a man in Georgia? You had to go to Canada to find you a black man?"

"It's not like that and plus, Alex is white. He isn't black."

"Oh Lord, this girl is dating a white man online. He's going to kill her," dad blurted out as he grabbed his chest, acting like he was about to faint. He was being extra right now.

"A white man," mom repeated with a disgusted look on her face.

"Don't start that color bullshit with me." I snapped before I knew it.

"Girl, you have gone crazy cursing in my house," my dad yelled as he motioned towards me. He was probably going to slap the shit out of me, but mother stopped him.

"I apologize, dad. It's just that you and mother should accept what I want to do. If I want to date a white man, so be it. If I want to date an Asian, so be it. It shouldn't matter who I date or marry. I'm just tired of everyone trying to tell me what to do and how to do it. Now, after I got out of high school, you wanted me to become a police officer. I did that. And now, I'm twenty-three years old and I want to do something I want to do," I explained as I picked up my plate again and walked out. I didn't want to hear anything else they had to say.

From that day forward, my parents didn't say anything else about Alex until I showed up at the door with him for dinner. Dad seemed like he didn't want any part of Alex. Shit, he acted like he didn't want anything to do with me after that. I had always been daddy's little girl, so it was difficult for me to see my father unhappy. I talked to my mother over the months about Alex, but she never talked against him since that day at the house. They both had to learn that I was grown, I had become a woman.

As Alex pulled into the apartment complex, he looked at me and gave me a kiss on my cheek. My smile was humongous. The man I fell in love with is here in the flesh. I was ecstatic.

ALEX'S THOUGHTS

I really didn't know if Siam's parents were going to try to convince her to stay here in Georgia or not. I was hoping that they didn't go against me, because I was taking her back to Canada regardless. Her old ass father looks like trouble. I will be able to convince her mother. I bet they all thought I wasn't a real person until I showed up here. Now that I'm here in the flesh, I want my prize. Siam belongs to me. I had been prepping this entire year for what her life was going to be like with me. She knows what I want and what I don't want. I'm scared to expose her to a lot of things that's going to happen to her, but she will learn once we step foot on Canadian ground.

I really didn't know what to say to her. I had to hurry up and get her away from Georgia. I wonder if she really wants to be with me. One day I will make her my wife, but I have to train her first. I didn't want to bring her home and she is a disgrace to my family. Or that she would try to send me to jail like my last couple of submissives. Things had gotten out of hand with one and I almost killed her. That secret must never be told, or she would never be with me. It would be hard to get that ass on Canadian soil if she knew the truth of how dangerous I really am.

CHAPTER 5

We arrived at the Calgary International Airport around 6 p.m. My eyes lit up as we exit the airplane. Looking up at the beautiful sky I noticed the air felt crisper. High in the sky, flew the red and white Canadian flag. Alex grabbed me by the hand and led me to gather our luggage, which was located on the arrivals level at the information booth. We had six bags altogether. Alex said I didn't need all my clothes, because he already had some already at his home. It's a good thing I had already told him earlier in our relationship my dress, pant, shirt, and underwear sizes. Let's not forget shoe sizes; that was a must know for him. And I knew this because he showed me everything he bought when we were on webcam. I hated my toes being out but if that's what he wanted, then I must obey.

As we gathered the luggage, I noticed how huge the airport seemed. It looked like the ceilings were much higher than the airport in Atlanta. I saw that they had dining places like Subway, Chili's, BK Whopper Bar, Taco Time, and Chick-fil-A. I don't know what made me think that they ate different types food than we did in the U.S.

I smiled to myself thinking about how naïve I was. I

failed to realize, we are all humans. Smelling all that good food made me hungry and my stomach let out a small growl. I tried to swallow my spit, hoping it would go away. I forgot neither one of us had eaten because of the excitement of me moving to Canada. My stomach growled louder as Alex hurried me along, taking huge steps with his long legs. I saw a store called Purdy's Chocolatier, looking like elegant chocolate, such as the Godiva Chocolate stores we had back home. Elegant chocolate prepared in many different ways, on many different things. Licking my lips, I wanted to ask Alex to stop, but his actions seemed like he was in rush. He wasn't playing around, trying to get out of there. A thought crossed my mind for a second, *was he ashamed to be seen with a black woman or was he really in a rush to get out because it was so many people*? I didn't think that many people traveled to and from Canada like that.

Anyway, that thought went away quickly as my luggage got heavier. My luggage, with my shoes and handbags were the heaviest of the three. I had to double my steps to keep up, but then I slowed down to peep into Purdy's Chocolatier for a few seconds.

"Come on, princess. We have no time to stop by there

now. I promise to bring you back later. We just need to get out of here before it really gets crowded," Alex advised as he kept walking in long strides. I thought, *this is already crowded to me. I'd hate to see it get more crowded, we wouldn't be able to move.*

"All that chocolate looks so delicious. We definitely have to come back. My stomach is growling so badly and you know I love elegant chocolates," I replied as I tried to catch up.

"I know you do. Now keep up before I leave you," Alex joked as he took off running then stopping as he laughed out loud. His laugh just made me melt.

"Wait," I yelled out as I tried to take off behind him like a little kid. It felt good to hear him laugh like that.

"There is the iStore over there. I have one by my house too. We will go there for your phone services. I don't want your father coming to Canada trying to kill me," Alex spoke as he nodded his head to the left.

"Can we go there now? I need to get my services up so I can contact my parents and let them know we arrived safely," I replied as we rushed right on by. I acted like he didn't say he had one near his house. I wanted to go to that one before it was too late.

"Not now, princess. We have to get going. My father is waiting for us outside. I asked him to pick us up."

"It is like the Apple Store back home, right?" I asked, before feeling like that was a dumb question. Of course, it's like the Apple Store.

"Yes, princess. Now come on, my father is waiting."

"Your father is picking us up? Well, glad you prepared me for this," I sarcastically laughed.

"I didn't know I had to tell you our every move," he laughed out loud again.

"You have jokes," I replied, hoping he didn't say anything about me talking back. I was fairly surprised because we were having a normal conversation like a normal couple. Not a dominant to submissive type demanding conversation.

"Can we go there too?" I asked as we rushed past this store called Artizan. It looked like it had clothes, jewelry, and elegant handbags. I love matching shoes and handbags.

"Later, princess. Stop asking me questions and come on. You already getting on my nerves asking all these damn questions," he shot back as he wrinkled up his nose at me like a little kid. I wrinkled up my nose right back as we exit the airport.

"There is Father," he yelled back to me as we headed towards this black Mercedes Jeep.

I rushed behind Alex as my heart started racing. I didn't think I would meet his father so soon. Better now than never, I guess.

This older man with gray hair, and a gray beard stepped out of the black Mercedes Jeep. He was tall and lanky like Alex. He was a little chubby though. He had many wrinkles on his face and under his neck.

"Alex, my boy, you are home. So happy to see you, and who do you have here?" his father stated as he took the luggage from me and load it into the vehicle.

"This here is my girlfriend, Siam. That's why I traveled to the United States; to bring back my queen." Alex announced as he loaded his luggage too. Closing the back door of the vehicle, his father directed to me, "Glad to meet you, my lady, Siam. Very odd name for an African American lady."

"That was my mother. She had a friend who died and she named me after her," I responded as Alex took me by the hand to enter the jeep.

"Sweet name. You can call me father too, but my name is Jason. Father or Jason is fine. I will answer to both." He giggled with such a deep voice.

"Yes sir," I replied. They both turned around quickly and looked at me. So, I turned around quickly too thinking something was wrong.

"You can say yes or no, Siam. Only address me as Sir," Alex ordered as he and his father turned around facing the front.

"Yes Sir. My parents always taught me to say, yes sir, no sir, yes ma'am and no ma'am, to my elders. Sorry if I offended you, Mr. Jason."

"Call him father, Siam," Alex snapped again.

"Yes Sir. I apologize, father, if I offended you in any kind of way. It's just a habit." I apologized while looking out as we started rolling down the highway.

"That's a habit you will break," Alex harshly spoke as he looked back at me with that stone face again.

"Don't be trying to punish her, Alex. Teach her first, then go from there. You can be an extremist at times. I think you got that part from your mother," his father stated as he also looked at me through the rear-view mirror.

"I wouldn't call it an extremist. I just like to make sure everything is in order." Alex smiled. I was thinking maybe he was bipolar. He was happy one minute, then crazy the next.

About fifteen minutes from the airport, we pulled up in this community called Arbour Lake. It had so many big beautiful houses. I was glad they were not so close together. Pulling into this driveway, there was a nice two-story brick house. I say it was about 2500 square feet. But of course, I hadn't gone in yet to investigate.

"Princess, we are finally home," Alex acknowledged as he looked back at me and smiled so big.

"Is this where you live? Such a beautiful home," I replied.

"Yes, this is our home."

"Well, I will help you two unload these bags. Your mother will be worried if I don't come back in an hour. She can be crazy at times," his father joked as he jumped out the jeep like a teenager to help carry the bags.

"Mother won't be stressed too bad. She is probably glad you're gone," Alex laughed.

"Knowing her, you're right," they both laughed as we carried the luggage into the house. Alex pulled his keys out and unlocked the door. I thought it would blow me away with unique furniture, big chandeliers, and expensive paintings, but it was plain. Reminded me of my parent's house. I immediately felt comfortable as I entered.

"Welcome home, princess," Alex announced as he hugged me and I squeezed him tight. Finally, my dream had come true.

"Well, I am leaving you two lovers alone. Nice meeting you, Siam," his father spoke as he rushed out the door. As soon as he closed the door, Alex locked it quickly.

"I finally got you here in Canada. I have been waiting for so long to do this."

As I stood before him, he pulled down my pants and pink panties. Staring at my pussy, he began to caress it with his lips. I couldn't help but to moan out loud, because it felt so good; him trying to push his long tongue in between my pussy lips. I tried to pull off my left shoe, so that I could come out of my pants leg to open wider for him. Alex tugged on my pants leg, pulling it off. I took my right shoe off so that way, I could balance myself on the floor as he ravished my pussy. Alex forced his face deeper as I grabbed the back of his head, pushing him further. Lifting my left leg and placing it on his back, his tongue went deeper within me as I cried out for more. Alex began taking off his pants and exposing the eleven inches that I loved so much. He pulled me down on the floor and mounted me in the missionary position. I placed my arms above my head, hoping that he would grab my breasts before he entered me. He entered my wet pussy and then reached for my arms above my head, holding me tight as if he was holding me down. We began rocking our hips and catching every thrust between us. My pussy cummed repeatedly as he kissed me all over my neck and my breasts. I wanted Alex to fuck me harder.

He grabbed me by my shoulders, pulling me to him as he slammed his dick inside me, my pussy making wet noises.

The house was so quiet that him fucking me, was all you could hear. It echoed through the entire house as he pushed my legs back, standing on his tiptoes and rushing within me. It didn't hurt me at all because I was so hot and ready for him.

Finally, he began to shake and pulled out, leaning back on his knees as he grabbed his dick and began to ejaculate on my bald pussy. As he exploded, I squirmed all over the floor. Alex looked at me and we both began laughing hysterically as he fell on the floor next to me. This was the man that I wanted to see every day, all the time. Just to hear him laugh made me happier than he could ever imagine.

After we laughed at each other, we showered and he prepared us food. I really didn't know how to take him at that particular time because he was doing things for me, instead of me doing it for him, since I'm the submissive. He didn't treat me as if it was a dominant/submissive relationship. He treated me as if I was just a normal girlfriend. That's definitely not what I was looking for. I wanted to him to dominate me. Back home, it seemed like he was a totally different person from what I was experiencing now.

"Now that are we are alone, I can tell you what I expect

from you. Don't think of me as an extremist like father said. He thinks I take things a little too far. Sometimes I do, sometimes I don't. It all depends on you. If you become the sweet submissive woman I know you can be, then we have no problems. When you start to act stupid and disobedient, then I beat your ass. I will never punch you or anything like that, but I will whip your ass with a belt like I did," Alex explained as he ate his sandwich and chips.

"I understand completely what you want me to do. That whipping me with the belt was extreme."

"Well, if you follow the rules, it won't be another episode like that. Just remember, it's up to you how you want to be treated."

"What exactly do I call you whenever we are out in public? I know behind closed doors, I need to address you as master, but it has bother me when in public what to call you." I asked because it had me confused at one time what to say.

"You can call me sir. Don't ever address me as Alex unless it's during our safe day. And with other men like my father, it is yes or no. Whenever you fuck another master I choose for you, you address him as master and nothing else."

He watched the expression on my face about fucking other men. I saw it on the movies and read about it in the books, but he never told me that I would be actually doing it. I just figured it came with the relationship.

"Well master, I didn't know you wanted to share me, immediately."

"Of course. We both will get fucked by other people, immediately," he explained as I finished drinking my glass of water.

"Oh okay. And the rules you had me to learn still applies."

"Yes, those rules will never change. There are many more you need to learn. I just felt like those were the most important to me. I wanted you to learn them all before you move here with me. The other rules will come later. You do know that you will never move back to the United States," Alex replied with a blank expression on his face.

"I won't be allowed to visit my family either?" I asked as I started to feel down and unhappy. I can't go on without seeing my parents.

"You will visit them whenever I am out of the country. I

said you wouldn't ever move back. I didn't say you could not visit."

"You really scared me. My heart fell to my panties." I laughed as relief came over me.

"I usually go out of the country maybe four times a year. But it depends on you. If you start talking stupid about leaving me and never returning, you won't ever leave."

"I understand, master. I don't ever want to leave you. I am here to stay forever, if you will have me."

"Maybe."

"Why maybe? You know I love you deeply," I replied as his "maybe" stuck in my head.

"I am just saying. After six months, many women have left me. You're probably like them. If only you knew what you have gotten yourself into."

"I know exactly what I have gotten myself into and that it's what I want. You can't compare me to those other women; I know exactly what I want." I stared him in his eyes.

"Wonderful, I am so glad to hear that. Since we have finished eating, let me give you a tour of the house." Alex and I jumped up and he grabbed me by the hand.

We walked back in the living room and he showed off his pictures. His mother and father looked more like his grandparents. They were so much older. Alex was only thirty but didn't look like it. I had already toured his big kitchen with the huge island in the middle of the floor. It didn't look like he ever used the stove. I guess that is where I will come in handy.

We continued on through the house on the second level. There was a huge master bedroom with a luxurious bathroom. "Wow, this bathroom is breathtaking. I can only dream of a home like this." I gasped between breaths as I walked around, admiring everything.

"Dream no more, princess, because this is your home."

"Thank you, master. I appreciate you sharing your home with me. It's so gorgeous."

Alex had to drag me out of the bathroom to look at the rest of the house. He thought I was crazy for admiring a bathroom. As we continued with our tour, he showed me the laundry room, which was located in a big room next to the garage. Moving along, we headed upstairs where he showed me the rest of the house. There was another master bedroom upstairs and that's where he slept. His bathroom wasn't that big, but I liked it. His queen-sized bed was nice.

"I always thought that the dominant and submissive slept in different rooms," I said out loud as Alex looked at me and smiled.

"You watch too much television. Don't say you have been watching *Fifty Shades of Grey*," he joked as he pulled me downstairs.

"I have watched it more than I should have, but I couldn't help it. That's what I'm looking for, but more intense."

"Well, you don't have to look anymore, because I'm here, Siam. And, I'm not going anywhere. We have bonded together for life. The only way you leave me is death," Alex threatened as we proceeded back in the kitchen.

"I don't know about death, but I'm never leaving you, master."

"I know you're not." Alex took me to another room on

side of the laundry area.

"What room is this?"

"This is where all the action happens for me and the other masters that come into my home. I bought a few items over the years." He opened the door to this bright, white-colored room.

"Wow, it's so bright in here," I said as I looked around. Alex let go of my arm as I walked around to investigate each sex toy.

"Are you afraid, Siam?"

"No master, I'm not afraid at all. In fact, my pussy is very excited. I'm ready to experience whatever you want me too. I have no boundaries towards you, master," I affirmed. It sounded much better than I rehearsed. A lot of the stuff I had rehearsed over and over. So, it felt right for me to actually say it to someone. A real live, talking person.

"I'm glad you're not afraid, princess. Maybe not now, but you will be," he stated. Chills ran down my arms, raising goosebumps as the hairs on the back of my neck lifted.

"What is this one?" I asked as I sat down on the black

71

chair with black leather straps. The wrist cuffs looked comfortable and not like regular police handcuffs.

"That's what I call the *bondage chair*.

BONDAGE CHAIR

You will experience it tomorrow night. I have my friend, Master Charles and his submissive, Linda, coming over. They are going to help you get comfortable. Just imagine what the arousing anticipation of me restraining you is going to feel like. They are going to have you squirming with pleasure, you won't know what to do," he explained in a sexy voice.

Alex already had me ready for tomorrow night.

"I'm ready, Master. I want it so bad I can actually taste it."

"Calm down, princess. You will definitely taste her pussy too. It always tasted like strawberries when I licked it. Her pussy is pretty, but not as pretty as yours."

"I have to eat her pussy? I thought it was them going to do me and that was it," I stated as I looked like a deer caught in headlights. I had never eaten a girl's pussy before. How in the hell was I going to do that?

"Yes, you have to eat her pussy, just like she has to suck your pussy. This isn't a, 'you receive the pleasure all the time' kind of shit. You will have to give it too."

"Yes, master. I didn't know."

I stood up and began rubbing the chair, feeling that it was solid oak. Many thoughts crossed my mind about how many women or men had been in that chair. I was definitely going to be next. Tomorrow night, I have to put on my big girl panties. "I already know that this is a *pink and black silicone ball gag.*

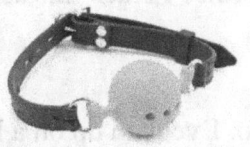

PINK AND BLACK SILICONE GAG BALL

I've read up on these items. Whenever you play in hot, erotic bondage, it helps to keep your partner nice and silent. Something I am looking forward to one day, but I like to moan and scream out showing my emotions," I added as I moved on to the next item.

"You may like to moan and scream, but a lot of masters don't want to hear that shit. Most of the women are so loud and fake. We'd rather go ahead and have our way without all the noise. That is irritating and brings your dick to a limp," Alex explained as he grabbed a black and blue item off the shelf. He continued, "And this here is a *suede flogger*.

THE BLACK SUEDE FLOGGER

I guess you know about this too. You won't mistake the impact it will bring. Once I crack this across your breasts, you won't forget it."

"Yes, master, I do. I've read up on a lot of things since I found out you were into the dominant/submissive relationship. I wanted to be prepared for anything and not be dumbfounded when it came to the sex toys."

"Good, now take off your shirt," Alex spoke in a deeper tone than normal. Pulling off my shirt and bra, my big breasts were exposed. My nipples were flat and now standing in attention. Alex walked over and pulled my nipples. He pushed me against the wall and said, "Place your hands above your head."

I didn't hesitate to do what master wanted. "Oh master, please don't hurt me," I pretended to beg as Alex cracked me across my breasts with the suede flogger.

"That's right, beg, you little bitch. I'm going to teach you a lesson." Alex said, as he started to get into the role-play. He hit me repeatedly on my breasts. My body began to squirm with pleasure as my breasts began to swell even bigger. I had never felt that pleasure before.

"Yes, Master. I've been a bad girl. I'm sorry. I won't be bad again." I begged some more as Alex hit me again with a little more force. That time it stung. He hit me continuously until I took my arms down. He rushed me, quickly grabbing my breasts and squeezing tight. He began to kiss my neck as he still held my breasts tightly.

"You're going to be the best submissive I've ever had.

Keep that up and you'll get whatever you want out of me," Alex whispered in my ear as he let go of my breasts. It hurt a little, but felt so damn good.

"Don't stop, master, please don't stop," I begged as I wanted more.

"No, princess, not tonight. I have to prepare you for tomorrow," Alex replied as he began to walk out of the room.

I looked around and asked, "Master, I don't know what this is?"

I held up this sex toy. Alex walked over to me and took it out of my hand. "This is called a *prostate stimulator*.

VIBRATING SILICONE COCK RING & ANAL
STIMULATOR

I can't believe you didn't know what this was."

76

"Believe it, because I really don't have a clue."

"This prostate simulator is something like a finger up your ass, but for men. When I get my dick sucked, I like for a finger to go in my ass. This item here is for when I'm getting myself off; this end here goes in my ass and massages my prostate. The cock ring fits snug around my dick and balls to make me more sensitive. It makes me harder and last longer. I don't get myself off often, but I love using it while I fuck. My throbbing dick with the veins popping out will make both of us feel great. While fucking anyone, this part here will vibrate my prostate with every movement; that gives me intense sensation. You wouldn't understand," Alex stated as he stared off into space. He had fell deep into thought, talking about that prostate simulator.

"When are you going to try it?" I asked as I stepped closer, feeling his hard dick through his pants.

"Slow down, princess. All of these toys will be used on you. Some you will enjoy and others, you won't. I think you really better slow down. Now, let's get out of here and go to bed. We have a long day tomorrow, preparing you. Your day will start at six."

77

"You mean six a.m. in the morning," I fretted, as I followed him out the door. He closed it and smiled.

"Yes, princess."

"That's early."

"Well, get used to it because that's the time you will begin your day, every single day, except for on Saturday and Sunday. I will let you rest one Sunday out of a month, unless you act up; then you get no free days."

"I think it's time for bed," I joked as I grabbed Alex. He hugged me back. We rushed off to bed without any sex. Damn, I at least wanted the dick one more time before he sends me off fucking other men.

SIAM'S THOUGHTS

I lay in bed next to Alex as I thought about the room with all the sex toys. I was dying to find out what the rest of them were. Alex doesn't want me going in there without him, but I'm tempted. If I disobey, then he would consider me as bad. I surely didn't want to be whipped by the belt again. I will wait until he takes me back in there. Me being anxious was going to send me over the edge.

As I tried to remember everything in the room, I thought about what Alex had said. He basically said we were going to be together until death. So, that means one of us has to die before we split up. Looking over at his fine ass, I snuggled up against him. I turned around and backed up to him. He threw his arm around me and squeezed me tight. I just let the thought go of us separating by death. That was what men used to trap the woman, by threatening her with death. I wasn't falling for that shit.

CHAPTER 6

Up early this morning, feeling tired. I should have gone to sleep than lying in bed thinking about all the sex toys in that room. First, I had to wake up ten minutes before he did, so my time actually starts at 5:50 a.m. every morning. Putting his slippers next to the bed so his feet wouldn't get cold when he stepped on the floor, I had to kneel by the bed and stay there until master got up. He took his time and my knees were like, *hurry the hell up.* As he sat next to the bed trying to gather himself, I was still kneeling with my head bowed down. He rubbed the top of my head and spoke, "Good morning, princess."

"Good morning, master," I replied with no other words. Today was the day that I learn to serve. It was all about acceptance, which wasn't fair but equitable. Going down this road in my dominant/submissive relationship was going to be hard, challenging, and probably confronting.

"Are you ready for whatever we go through in this relationship? Things aren't going to be easy as we start our journey together. Don't think down of yourself or think anything is wrong with you once we start. Always remember that I will never do anything to hurt you and I will not let anyone else hurt you."

"Yes, master."

"Do you trust me?"

"Yes, master, I trust you to protect me. If we don't have trust, then we don't have anything. I hope you believe me when I say that I do trust you one hundred percent and you want the best for me," I announced, because I really did trust him. I remember he said before that I didn't trust him. There is no way that I would have come all the way to Canada away from my family if I hadn't trusted him. A year of talking and being dominated over the webcam gained my trust. We had talked every day all day, even with us both working. That's why I had to quit work because he couldn't get in touch with me when he wanted. I didn't have to worry about money or bills, because he had control of that.

"I'm happy to hear that you trust me. Now that we are here together in the flesh, it will be better for us. I promise not to hurt you unless you are bad. I don't want to punish you like I did before, but don't push me."

"I understand everything."

81

"You do know that a dominant/submissive relationship is more than sex?" Alex asked me as he smiled.

"Yes sir, I do know that. I know that I have to sacrifice. I have to give up many things to pleasure you in every way possible. That way we both can have a deep submission and nurturing dominant/submissive relationship," I smiled back. I added, as I crawled on my knees in front of him, "I give you the power to own me. Everything that once was my rights becomes privileges, I know that."

"Do you really know that? Privileges like what, because I want you to understand what they are. And yes, I know we have talked about this over and over, but I need to know that you truly understand," Alex stated as he looked into my eyes.

"Privileges such as sexual gratification, privacy, pleasure and pain, my pride, the shame and anything that is considered as my sense of self," I remarked as I remembered the first time he presented it to me.

"Glad that you know that. You will also be given tasks. I will show you everything. I would start off small, but you know how I want everything done. Do you remember everything I told you about giving your hundred percent in everything you do for me?"

"Yes master, I remember that you expect me to put in my maximum effort and do my best at everything you expect of me. If I have any questions, communicate with you and be honest about it." I quoted from his small book that he had given me. That book was like my bible. I had to learn every single thing in that book before we met in person. If he asked me something, I damn well better answer quickly and know what I'm talking about. It took me a year, but I learned the entire thing.

"You're right, princess. We both have to be patient with each other as well. The truth be told, I have messed up in the past because I was too rough on those girls, but you are different. There will be many obstacles in the road for us and many, many mistakes will be made by both you and me. If I get too rough or out of hand, communicate with me. Don't just sit back until it's too late and you want to go. Remember, leaving me is not an option. I'm not letting another submissive go," Alex replied as he got up from the bed and began to walk towards the bathroom. I quickly jumped up and walked behind him. Alex liked to take showers so I prepared the water for him.

After he urinated, I had his toothbrush ready for him to brush his teeth. After he finished with that, he rinsed his mouth and hopped in the shower. I had to stand right there until he finished, so I could dry him off once he exit.

After he showered, Alex stepped on a soft white cotton rug until I dried him off. This time, I had to make sure he was dry completely. Even though I did, he still took the towel and went behind me. "Thank you, Princess. Now you can take your shower. You will showers is in the mornings before we do our morning exercise."

"Yes, master," I remarked as I stepped in the shower to clean myself. He had some type of honey and milk shower gel I had to use every morning. As I showered, I thought about how I really needed to dedicate myself to just pleasing him and doing whatever he wanted. It was going to be hard since I had been a cop for a long time. I was used to giving orders, not taking them. But it is what I have wanted to do since I turned eighteen, so he shouldn't be a problem. The journey was going to be long term. I had to stay true to the relationship. I might suffer doubt and despair, but it would be all good. This was a commitment that failing wasn't an option. I knew that I had to serve and obey. Turning off the water, I realized that this shit is real. There is no turning back now.

After we showered, we went to the gym. Alex was very intense with his workout. I damn near passed the hell out, trying to keep up with him. I wasn't in shape as I thought I was. We worked with a personal trainer. He tried his best to not work me hard, but I was determined. After that, we did a three-mile run. My legs were beginning to feel like Jell-O. How in the hell am I supposed to be having sex later and I'm tired before I get started? What in the world was Alex trying to do to me?

"How did you enjoy your workout?" Alex asked me as we walked up the driveway.

"It was great. I thought I was in shape, but you showed me different. This workout was crazy."

"Well, this is the routine we will do every single day, except for Saturdays and Sundays. Those are the days we either visit other couples, clubs, or parties. We have to stay in shape. That is a pet peeve of mine. I don't like lazy people hanging around me."

"Yes, master, this is our routine and I understand that," I

acknowledged.

"After I shower and you take a bath this time, I will show you the clothes you must wear. Those few clothes you brought with you probably won't be used much. I have certain things I want you to wear, even around the house," Alex stated as I opened the front door and let him step in before me.

"Yes, master."

"I almost forgot the most important part. When you walk through these doors, you need to put on your collar," Alex said as he reached on the small wooden table next to his office and picked up this black leather collar with steel spikes.

I didn't say a word, but put on the collar immediately. It had me all excited. My pussy became hot and bothered. But before he walked off from me, I had to ask, "Have you ever been to a bathhouse?"

"What do you know about a bathhouse?" he giggled.

"I've read many, many articles and books. Plus, my cousin named Tony says he goes all the time on weekends. I was just curious to know if you go there."

"I have been on occasions." He continued to walk off. He didn't go into details, but I knew what that meant. I wondered if he let another man fuck him or did he fuck another man? Did the man suck his dick or did he suck another man's dick? All types of shit started going through my head then. I knew that most bathhouses were for gay men. I wondered if Alex was telling me everything.

Again, I waited until Alex got out of the shower to take my bath. Drying him off, he stated, "Clean the tub, then take a bathe. You will soak for thirty minutes, then get out. We have a long day ahead of us."

"Are you going to work today?" I asked.

"Not today, princess. Don't forget that I work for myself. I'm my own boss. And today, I'm off," Alex replied as I rushed along and cleaned the tub for my bath.

Sitting in the tub did wonders for me. It felt so good that I almost fell asleep. Suddenly, I heard a timer go off. Alex had set it for me to get out. My thirty minutes was up fast. "Damn that was quick," I said to myself as I got out and dried myself off.

87

Putting the towel around me, I heard Alex yell out for me. I put on my house shoes and ran immediately to him. He was in the master bedroom downstairs. "Don't forget to bow every time you approach me."

"Yes, master," I said as I got on my knees and bowed my head. Then I looked up at him to stare into his eyes. That was one of his main things, to look him straight in the eyes.

"Here are the clothes you will be wearing. Over here, is your box of collars." Alex handed me a pink box with different collars to go around my neck. I jumped up off the floor to retrieve the gifts. They were personalized, fun, adult fetish collars. There were names on them such as bitch, whore, master's slut, slave and so on…

There were so many different colors. There was a rainbow collar that said, "Fuck My Slut". It made me smile as I picked it up. Alex added, "That one there is special. You will see one day soon."

"Wonderful. I'm looking forward to it." I happily spoke as I closed the box and continued to look through all the clothes.

"This one here is a sexy, black, fetish wear, gothic cat

suit, with a muzzle on the mouth. Many Masters' will want to fuck you once you show up in this. I can't wait for you to try it on."

"Can I try it on now?" I asked.

"No, the clothes are to be worn when we go out to the parties. This is not an everyday outfit," Alex smarted off as I raised my eyebrows.

"Sorry, master. I just wanted to make sure that it fit. I didn't mean any harm," I apologized as I bowed my head.

"That's okay, princess. Just remember you can't wear anything in here until the day of. You can try it on that morning though and that's the only time."

"Yes, master," I said as he moved on to another outfit that caught my attention.

"This one here is a black fetish top, with the breasts exposed and the matching strap-on. This outfit here is when you go to fuck other women or fuck me. All the strap-on's must be cleaned thoroughly, no half-ass cleaning them."

"Very interesting outfit," I said as I tried to ignore the fact he said, *when I fuck him*. So, that means I was probably

89

going to fuck him in his ass too. Well, if that is what he wanted me to do, his wish was my command.

"Did you just understand what I said, princess?"

"Yes master, I understood what you said. You said I would fuck other women or fuck you with this strap-on. I'm following the conversation closely."

"Good. Glad you caught on. Of course, I have to have you wear the slinky schoolgirl bedroom costume. This outfit is my favorite."

"I love this outfit," I stated, as my eyes got big. It was a slinky set that featured a plaid panty-skirt with a white waistband, white bra top with plaid trim, and a bow. I liked the matching mini tie choker around the neck, with plaid hair ties and suspenders. Alex had the white thigh-highs with it. This was a neat costume. He had good taste.

"Glad you like it. Here is another one you might like as well. This is a nurse's outfit. The G-string teddy has red leather straps that crisscross around the body and the back. Here is the matching hat to go with the sheer cups."

"This is a very nice outfit. And yes, you are right, I do

like it. There are so many outfits that I like," I said as I turned away from that outfit, not really liking it that much, but I would wear it to satisfy Alex.

"Don't forget...honesty, princess. If you don't like it, tell me. I promise I won't get mad."

"I like it. Too much booty being out, but I like it." I smiled as we looked at all the other outfits. I really didn't want him going to every single one, telling me what it was. I had a good idea, since I surfed the internet for a long time looking. He had some good stuff, but I knew where I could find some better stuff.

After we looked at outfits, Alex and I went out to get me a pedicure and manicure. That was a must-do. Then we went over to the Brazilian wax place. I had read that the shit hurt real bad. My pussy was already bald so I didn't know what else hair they could get out of that. As I lay there and they waxed me, I could have fucking died; I didn't like it. If people only knew the unbelievable pain you felt. This wasn't as easy as everybody said it would be. I ended up getting my legs waxed too. Everything had to be right for tonight. The last stop was getting my hair done. Since I already had long hair, Alex wanted me in Shirley Temple curls. That was good too. I didn't want any extra hair in my head anyway.

As it got closer to the time for our company to come over, I had to soak in a tub of strawberry, honey and milk water for about an hour. It felt good to be pampered. I really needed that.

ALEX'S THOUGHTS

As Siam soaked in the tub, I was wondering if I'm putting this girl through too much. The way she talks; it's like she is ready for whatever I ask, but something tells me that she might choke. What would I do if she denied me in front of the other Master's or their submissives? Of course, she knows better than to do that. Then again, maybe she will be a good girl and do as she is told.

I saw how she looked at my toys. Maybe I should deny her my toys if she is bad. That girl wanted to be dominated badly. My father was right that I was an extremist, but I didn't want to do her like that. It seemed like that's what her body craved though. My fear is of her wanting to leave because I was too violent or too rough. Maybe next time we talk, I will ask her and make sure of what she wants. I knew that I wanted to be extreme with our dominant/submissive relationship. I wanted to choke her and slap her across the face lightly, or take it to the next level but I'm scared. Or maybe I should just do it and fuck what she wants.

CHAPTER 7

Master Charles and his submissive, Linda, had to cancel so Alex replaced them with mistress A.J. and submissive Ashley. As we heard them pull in the driveway, he said, "Kneel down princess, and bow your head. When I let them in and close the door, then you can look up and greet them. Don't talk, don't say a word, just smile and nod."

"Yes, master, as you wish," I replied as I kneeled down and bowed my head.

"Good evening, master Alex," a female voice spoke. I tried to peep as this young white male got down on all fours in front of me. He was probably trying to take a peep at me too. I smiled to myself and then stood as Alex closed the door. It hit me that I was to wait until the door was completely shut, but I was anxious.

"Good evening mistress A. J.," Alex greeted the female. I thought mistress A.J. was a man, but it turned out to be a female and her submissive was a man. I thought, *why in the hell would he have a girl's name, Ashley*? I guess she renamed him or something. Never would have thought Ashley was a man.

"I see you have a nice looking black girl this time. She is very pretty and well built," mistress A. J. remarked as I bowed my head to her. She grabbed a handful of my hair and pulled me close to her. She kissed me passionately and to my surprise, I kissed her back, wanting more of her.

"Thank you, mistress A. J., glad to have you back in my home again. Let's proceed to the Pillars Dungeon," Alex said as mistress A. J. stopped kissing me and forced me to the floor. I kneeled down as Alex put his leash on me. Submissive Ashley and I crawled on the floor like dogs as they led us to the toy room. I didn't know it was called the Pillars Dungeon. Alex never told me the name.

As we entered the room, submissive Ashley stood up and so did I. I just watched him and followed his lead. Mistress A. J. took off his collar as Alex did mine. She grabbed my hair again roughly and led me over to the black bondage chair. I had worn the plain, red and white plaid schoolgirl outfit. Submissive Ashley took off my panties and sniffed them. He then tossed them to the side as mistress A. J. carefully pushed me down into the chair. Sitting in the chair, submissive Ashley took both of my ankles and tied them in the ankle cuffs, then tied my wrists into the wrist cuffs. My pussy was exposed.

Mistress A.J. began immediately tasting my bald pussy first, then submissive Ashley. I squirmed and moved all around in the chair as the two made me cum over and over, for about an hour. I felt so weak. Alex had stepped out of the room until they finished pleasuring me.

After he returned, submissive Ashley untied me and we crawled over to a bed that was towards the back of the room; I never noticed it before. As we got over there, submissive Ashley laid on the bed. Alex put both feet on the bed, straddling submissive Ashley. Submissive Ashley immediately began sucking his dick. Mistress A. J. had put on a strap-on and lubricated it. She gently entered it in Alex's ass. Alex moaned out with pleasure as I was directed to ride submissive Ashley. He was a nice-sized man. Alex reached over him and handed me a condom. I placed it on submissive Ashley's dick and rode him like no tomorrow. My eyes stayed glued to Mistress A. J., fucking Alex in his ass. After a few minutes, Alex laid flat on his back on the bed.

I continued to ride submissive Ashley as Alex lifted his legs and Mistress A.J. stuck her strap-on back into his ass.

She was a rough mutherfucker, ramming that dick hard in his ass. She grabbed his dick and started to jack him off as she fucked him.

After a few minutes of that, I got off submissive Ashley and Mistress A. J. directed me to back up to her. I got on the edge of the bed as she forced her strap-on into my soaking wet pussy. She just started fucking me out of control. The strap-on was flopping everywhere, causing me to explode as she hit me gently on my back with a flogger. Alex and submissive Ashley had gotten into the 69 position, sucking each other. I had never seen two men pleasing each other like that before. Submissive Ashley was deep throating that dick, something I hadn't mastered yet. Probably because Alex was much larger than an average sized man. There was nothing I could do with that, but submissive Ashley did. He was a pro.

Mistress A. J. pushed me onto the bed, took off the strap-on, and turned me over, lying me flat on my back. She straddled my face and we had a 69 position going on. Her pussy tasted good. For my first time, I liked it. I just began sucking on her clit and licking her. Putting my tongue in and out of her pussy made her moan more. I tried to stick my tongue deep like Alex did mine. Just slobbing on her pussy was awesome. Now I knew how men felt, kissing and sucking on that clit.

Alex put lubrication on his dick as he laid on the bed while submissive Ashley mounted him. Submissive Ashley began riding him. Mistress A. J. got up, pulling my hair as she pulled me in front of the two men. She forced my head down on submissive Ashley's dick. I began sucking his dick as she put the strap-on back on, placing it into my juicy wet pussy, fucking me again. This went on for a while until submissive Ashley began to explode. I just let him cum, hitting me in the face and mouth. I began sucking him again, trying to drain him.

Finally, Alex exploded and submissive Ashley swallowed every bit of his cum. He sucked and sucked until his dick was limp as a noodle. Alex got up and exit the room. Mistress A. J. then laid down on the bed over submissive Ashley's face. He began licking her pussy, trying to get her off as I began licking her ass. I stuck my finger in her ass as I kissed her on her cheeks. A few minutes later, she exploded her load. Submissive Ashley continued to suck her pussy as she screamed out. I stood up and noticed he was playing with his dick. I went around and began sucking him, then crawling on top to ride him. Mistress A. J. got down and submissive Ashley tossed me on the bed. He flipped me over, getting another condom, and putting me in the doggy style. My head was on the bed as my ass was in the air. He pounded me for what seemed like hours. My legs were getting tired and my pussy was getting dry. He finally exploded again.

They put on their clothes and bounced. Just like that, they were gone. I lay on the bed for a few minutes before I went looking for Alex. Staring at the wall, I couldn't believe what had just happened. I placed my hands on my pussy and smiled. This will be a night I will never forget.

Finally, I gathered myself and then went to find Alex. He was sitting at the kitchen table fully dressed. As he turned around and looked at me, I got on my knees and bowed my head. "What's wrong with you, master?" I asked as he continued to look at me.

"Get up, Princess, and come join me."

"Yes master."

Sitting on the cool stool gave my pussy a nice sensation. "So, what did you think about tonight between Mistress A. J.

and submissive Ashley?"

"Well, I had a wonderful time. I really thought they would be slapping me around and forcing themselves on me, trying to hurt me or something painful. I was looking for something painful to happen to me," I responded as I slid over my stool next to Alex and placing my head on his shoulder.

"You really need to stop reading those books. A lot of that stuff they say in those magazines and articles are what they make of it. If you haven't experienced it before, you wouldn't know. Every experience is different. Some people are harsh with punishments and others are soft with safe words," he explained as he placed a kiss on my forehead.

"You haven't given me a safe word yet."

"What do you want the safe word to be? It can't be anything we say every day. It has to be unique. Something different."

"I have been thinking about the safe word; Vatican. That's is a word we never use."

Alex looked at me and spoke, "Why Vatican?"

"It's a word that we don't use every day."

"You're right, I never use that word every day." He laughed. "Girl, you seem to amaze me at times. I just wish you stop looking at that *Fifty Shades of Grey*; that's not how things really are. It shows a piece of it, but not all of us are twisted or have something wrong with us."

"I know, I know. I just wanted to make sure that I knew stuff, because once I found my master, then I wouldn't be naïve to the situation. I would at least know what to expect. And once I found you, I really went searching through the internet for answers." I sat up straight and smiled.

"What do you expect from this dominant/submissive relationship? I mean, you said before that the only guy you slept with didn't do what you wanted and you didn't like it. I want you to love everything we do and worship it willingly."

I wasn't sure what Alex was trying to ask me, but I kind of had an idea. "That guy just wanted to get on top and fuck me. He didn't want to choke me. I wanted him to cut off my circulation, but not kill me. I wanted him to slap me across the face, giving me pain," I explained as I tried not to go deep into details. He would probably think I needed psychological help.

"You mean you like masochism. How far are you willing to go with pain? That's what my father meant when he said I was an extremist. I am a sadist. I want it to feel good, but I want it to hurt. Especially when you disobey me; I get to inflict harsh pain. I didn't want to tell you because I didn't want you to think I was sick," Alex stated as he looked down at the granite countertop.

"Me too. I thought you would say the same about me. That's exactly what I want. I love pain. Yes, it does hurt, but I want to feel it. It gets my heart pumping and my body just has a mind of its own. When you flogged my breasts, I wanted to feel more pain. That lustful, sexual, pain I crave for. Like now, my pussy is very sore, but I…"

Before I could finish my sentence, Alex grabbed me by the hand and took me to *Pillars Dungeon*. He tossed me on the floor and went over to the blue and black flogger.

"Open your fucking legs," he scolded harshly as I laid back and opened my legs.

"Like this, master?" I softly spoke.

"Yes. You've been a bad girl and you must be punished." Alex flogged me right across my already swollen pussy. Lick after lick, he struck me, making my pussy lips swell. I squirmed on the floor. My body was already exhausted, but I wanted more.

"Master, punish me. I didn't mean to be bad. I can't help but to be bad sometimes. I deserve to be punished. Punish me," I begged. Alex grabbed me off the floor by my neck softly and stared me in the face. He squeezed my neck like I wanted. His strong arms felt big around my neck. His other hand grabbed the back of my neck and squeezed.

"Take out my cock right now. You need Master to punish you for your crime."

I unbuttoned his pants and unzipped it. He let go of my neck and pulled off his clothes, tossing his shirt on the floor and kicking his pants across the room. Grabbing my neck again, he pulled me over to this *black thwacker paddle.*

BLACK THWACKER PADDLE

It was a soft black leather paddle that was perfect for punishment; it had a loop for hanging it on a belt.

Grabbing a handful of hair, Alex pushed me towards the brownish gold bondage chair.

"Bend over and spread your legs. I know you know exactly what I'm talking about. Do it now," Alex said as I placed both of my hands on the arm of the chair and spread my legs.

He hit me softly the first time. Then he hit me a little bit harder. *He's testing how much pain I could take.* Hitting me harder, I let out a cry. I could hear him tighten the paddle and swing hard with a little more force.

"Is that how you want it, bad girl?" he called out to me as he walked up to me and pulled my hair. My head jerked back softly as he whispered in my ear, "I see you are a very bad little girl. You can handle pain. Well, master has plenty more where that came from."

"I've been bad, master. Punish me again."

"Your wish is my command," Alex spoke as he continued to hit me over and over with the thwacker. Finally, I couldn't take it anymore, so I fell to my knees. I didn't want to use the safe word, because I wasn't ready for him to stop. He picked me up by grabbing my neck softly with both hands and led me out to the living room. Tossing me in front of the couch, Alex pushed me over onto the pillows and rammed my pussy, dripping wet from him spanking me.

"You think you're a tough girl. Let's see how tough you really are. You can't handle this pain," Alex boasted as he tried to enter my ass with his big ass dick. I tried to move so he wouldn't enter me; fucking me in the ass with no gel or lubrication would really hurt badly. I squirmed until he got tired of trying to hold me down. He entered my already sore and wet pussy and fucked me long and hard. He didn't make love to me this time; he just fucked me until we collapsed out on the floor.

I looked up at the window and it looked like the sun was coming out. I was having so much fun that I completely lost track of time. Alex held me right there on the floor. We slept for a very long time and when we did wake up, it was 2 p.m.

ALEX'S THOUGHTS

That Night: As I walked out of the bedroom, I didn't know what Siam was going to think of me. This is her first time seeing me with a man. Maybe it was too soon. "Damn it, Alex," I said to myself as I sat down at the kitchen table. This girl is going to think I'm gay. I wonder what is going through her mind right now. They are going to fuck her until her pussy is dry.

What will be my first words to this women? What will she say to me? Damn, my thoughts were all over the place. I didn't know what to think. Maybe I should just tell her to bathe and take her ass to bed. She didn't need to know why I fuck other men or why other men fucked me. At least she was getting the dick too. I fucked other women too. Well, it will probably really blow her mind when we go to the parties.

BDSM BLACK LEATHER COLLAR

CHAPTER 8

A couple of months later, Alex decided it was time for me to meet his mother. We were so busy wrapped up into each other that we disappeared from everyone we loved. My days were consistent of exercising to keep my body in shape, learning the rules he put in place and learning each other. We hadn't fucked anyone else since the last visit, because Alex was trying to prove to me about his manhood. He wanted me to know that he wasn't gay, but the truth be told, he was bi-sexual. I didn't understand why he was trying to prove that to me, if he liked fucking men or men fucking him then that was him. I didn't care about that because he had already told me how it was going to be with other people.

Interrupting my thoughts, my phone started buzzing inside my purse. Taking it out, I saw there was a text message from my mother.

Mother:

Hello Siam. We haven't heard from you in a while. Let us know that you are okay. Please.

I looked up to see if Alex was coming, then replied quickly:

Me:

Hey mother. I apologize for not contacting you. Please forgive me. I am well.

Mother:

We love you so much and you are so far away. Please keep in touch. Your father would kill me if something happens to you.

Me:

Everything is great here. I'm loving it and Alex is so very sweet to me. We are about to head out to meet with his parents. Please don't worry. Love you First Lady.

Mother:

I love you too, Ms. Siam.

That was the end of that conversation. I erased my messages and put the phone back in my purse. I called my mother, First Lady, because that was our secret way of saying, "yes, it's me texting," and nobody else. My mother would always be worried about little stuff. She was always very protective. After I became a police officer, she was even worse. I'm surprised that she didn't put up a gigantic fight about me moving to Canada. Maybe I should text her every day. Don't want her to worry herself to death about me. My brothers and father would kill me if I were the cause of her death due to worrying about me. I'll just definitely do better by my mother.

Interrupting my thoughts once again, Alex walked through the door wearing black jeans, and a white dress shirt, with white Nike tennis shoes. I kind of felt like I was overdressed, wearing a peach lace collar around my neck, with a peach neon dress just above my knees with straps across my back. My pink shoes were from Christian Louboutin. Alex also bought me a matching peach Christian Louboutin Sweet Charity Mini Chain purse. I was looking like a Georgia peach from head to toe. I didn't care much about the peach lace collar though, but Alex insisted I wear it.

"You're looking like a Georgia peach," he remarked as he looked at me with softness in his eyes. My heart rate started beating slowly as he entered the room. I thought he was going to have that dark, stone-faced look but he had a natural, relaxed face.

"Thank you, master. I was just thinking the same thing about being a Georgia peach. There is so much peach and I love it," I replied, hoping that he didn't get mad at me about the comment of too much peach. I almost messed up with that compliment.

"Are you ready to meet my mother and sister, Codie?"

"Yes master, I am ready to meet your family."

"They are strange but fun. My father is the crazy one, but you have already met him," Alex said as he walked over to me and planted a kiss on my lips. I put my hands behind my back as he grabbed me by the hair and pulled me closer to him, pushing his tongue deeper into my mouth.

After a passionate kiss, he continued, "You look so beautiful and it makes me want to fuck you right now."

"Take me, master. You own me, do as you please," I replied softly. That line was easy. I'd mastered saying that so many times in the mirror.

"I will take you later on tonight when we get back. I just needed you to learn the basics before me moved forward. And yes, I know I have told you over and over, but I wanted to make sure this is the lifestyle that you want to live with me."

"Yes master. This is exactly what I want to do. You have known this the first time you ever started talking to me. This is what I desire and more," I mumbled as I stared into his blue eyes.

"I know, Princess. I just want to be careful with you. You know what I have told you about my situation and the things that happened before you. I could have been in prison if it wasn't for my parents. Those girls were really after me. They wanted me locked up for life because of the stuff I had done to them. I don't want to make the same mistake with you." Alex's long-winded voice droned on as he put both of his hands on my face, caressing me.

"I remember you telling me those stories. I love pain and I want you to give it to me every chance you get," I explained as he moved his face closer to mine, staring at me.

"Princess, that's not what you want from me. I might take it overboard and can't come back from this. You don't want this," he harshly spoke with a little bass in his voice. He pulled my hair tighter in his hands, trying to excite my pussy. Even though, the passionate kiss already had me a little moist.

"Yes, it is, master. I keep telling you this over and over. Hurt me, make me feel the pain like you did to those other women. Why do you keep defying me?" I begged as I released my hands from behind me, and wrapped my hands around his back, pulling him into me. I then took his hands and placed them kind of roughly on my butt.

"This can't be what you want from me. When I go too far, don't say I told you so," Alex spoke out, then suddenly, he turned me around quickly with my back facing his front. He moved me quickly to the chair I was sitting in and bent me over. I put my hands on the back of the chair as he lifted my dress and pulled down my thongs. He hit me very hard across my buttocks. I moaned out, "Hit me again, master."

"Is this what you want?" He motioned as he pulled his arm all the way back and hit me again. This time, he kept hitting me over and over until my knees buckled. My body fell to the seat of the chair. My cheeks were on fire from the licks, but I loved it. Alex slowly bent down and began kissing my ass. He then found his way to my wet pussy. He licked and licked me until I was almost ready to cum and he stopped, right in the middle of giving me pleasure.

"Don't stop, master, please. I'm ready to explode," I explained as I turned around just a little, trying to push his head back into my pussy.

"We will finish this later. I want you to obey everything I tell you. If you want to cum later on, then I expect you to do everything I want you to do. I mean everything. If not, then you will be left like this for days," Alex threatened as he pulled up my thongs.

"Master, pleasure me right now. I promise to do whatever you want me to do," I begged, hoping that I could obey everything he says. Sometimes that police mode comes out and I forget everything.

"No, princess, I know you. Until you start doing everything I tell you, I'm going to leave you like this with no pain, no anything."

"I understand, master. I will do everything you want me to do."

"Sure, you will. You say that you want to feel pain, then so be it. When I start, don't try to stop me. You're trying to take me down a road I have tried to avoid for the past three years." He turned me back around to face him.

I straightened my dress and then stated, "If you give me that pain I want to feel, I want to endure, then I will do absolutely every single thing you want me to. No

112

disobedience, anything. Just give it to me, master. Please, I'm begging you."

"Princess, your wish is my command. Even if I don't give you pain, you will do what I want anyway," he stated as he stared at me with that dark, stone face. That stare was enough to make me do anything he wanted. His eyes seemed dark blue and evil.

"Yes, master," I replied as I grabbed my purse and we headed out the door to his parents' house.

As we rode in the car, my phone began buzzing again. I had it on vibrate so that it wouldn't disturb Alex. Looking out the window, I tried to ignore it, but it kept going off. Alex looked at me and spoke, "Give me your phone. Who's calling you?"

I reached in my purse and handed him my phone without even looking at it. As he looked at the screen, I tried to peep over without giving myself away.

"Your father called you. And now, he's left a text message. Message him back before we make it to my parents' house. See what he wants."

113

Alex handed me the phone back and I read my father's message:

Siam, you need to call me back. I can't believe you haven't reached out to us. Your mother is here sick over you. Girl, don't make me come to Canada and beat your ass.

Me:

Father, everything is good. I talked to mom earlier. I told her that I would try to contact you both every day. Please don't be mad at me.

I could tell he was angry with me.

Father:

Siam, you better stay in contact with us. We don't know what that boy is doing to you up there. Is he stopping you from talking to us? You know I don't like texting.

Looking at Alex, I smiled and texted back:

Father, he isn't doing anything to me but taking care of me. I told you and mother that we love each other and that's the truth. Please believe me. I was going to call you back.

"What is your father talking about, Princess? We both know that he doesn't like me." Alex asked, as he continued to look down the highway, not even looking my way.

"He's just upset because I haven't been texting or calling

them. He says that mother is sick because I am so far away from her," I explained, as I texted my father back.

Me:

Stop worrying, father. I am well and happy. I will be coming home soon to visit. We can Skype tonight when I come back home tonight from meeting Alex's parents. Love you.

Father:

We will be looking forward to seeing you over the internet, LOL

Love you too, Siam.

I let out a little giggle as I read my father's last text message. He would always say something to make me laugh.

"Did you hear what I said, Princess? Don't ignore me. See, that's the stuff I am talking about. You completely ignored me," Alex spoke harshly as he snatched my phone out of my hand and tossed it in the back seat.

"Yes, Master, I heard every single word that you said."

"Repeat it."

"You said that my father doesn't like you and I disagree. He just doesn't know anything about you, except for what I have told him and mother. You two haven't had a decent

115

conversation at all. He is very protective of me. I'm surprised he and mother didn't put up a big fight with me coming here," I answered, hoping that would satisfy him. Looking at him as he drove with that stone-faced look, his nose spread a little. I had never noticed that before. He must be frustrated with me.

"You were coming back with me, regardless of what they had to say. I didn't spend a year training you to be with me for nothing. You lucky I didn't come and get you the second week we started talking," he barked as he continued to drive and we arrived at this house.

"Don't be so angry with me, master. Why are you so angry?" I asked, hoping he would respond.

"I'm fucking angry, Siam, because you're trying to push me overboard with your father and all this other bullshit. You don't want me angry. You really don't want that," he angrily stated as he pulled up to the house and parked.

"I'm not trying to make you angry at all. Why do you think I'm here? If you had asked me to leave and come with you the second week we talked, I would have come. You're who I want and all I need. Please, don't be angry with me.

I'm here. I'm here in the flesh loving you, being with you," I responded, hoping he would accept that before someone in his family thought we were arguing.

"I know you're here, Princess, and I won't let you go. Never. There is no such thing as leaving me. Either we make this work or you die," Alex threatened as he smiled at me and exit the car. I swallowed and looked at him as he crossed the back of the car and opened my door.

Looking up at the front door of the house, an older woman came out on a red cane. She shouted, "Alex is here. Alex is here."

"Mother, I'm so happy to see you," Alex replied as he took my hand and we ran up to meet her. He almost pulled me to the ground running to her. Letting go of my hand, Alex gave his mother a huge hug and then turned to me. The way she looked, I would have mistaken her for his grandmother. She looked much older, like father Jason.

"You must be Siam?" she asked with a sweet voice.

"Yes, ma'am, I am Siam," I replied. I didn't know if I was supposed to say yes ma'am or what. Alex has things being so complicated at times and other times, it's normal. I was confused a lot of the times about what to do or don't do.

"You're so much more beautiful in person. Your pictures do you no justice. And your smile is so inviting," she added as she gave me a huge hug and I hugged her back with open arms.

"Come on in and meet Codie. She is a little nuts, but we love her," she joked. Then she added, "I apologize. I forgot to give you my name, it's Della."

"That's a lovely name," I stated as she held my hand, leaving Alex to walk behind us. I was kind of nervous and scared all at the same time. He was going to be mad because I completely left him behind. He liked to be in front or beside me, never behind me. Trying to look back at Alex, she rushed me on in the house, while trying to get around on her red cane.

"Codie, Alex and Siam are here," mother Della yelled through the house as she continued to hold my hand and walking through the house. I tried to look back at Alex, but he wasn't there. I stopped immediately.

"Where did Alex go?" I asked as I let go of her hand and walked back to the front door. Alex was standing at the car gathering my purse. I had walked off and left my purse, my cell phone.

"Damn it," I whispered to myself as I walked back out to him.

"Master, I'm sorry for leaving you. Please forgive me," I stated as I looked back at the door and mother Della was standing there looking at us. Can you say I felt embarrassed?

"Don't worry, Siam, you will be punished later. Just go and have fun with my family."

"You're going to punish me, why?" I asked as I stepped in front of him, looking into his eyes.

"You ran off without seeing to me. We're here to take care of each other. Your selfish ass walked off with my mother and left me here looking stupid," Alex cursed as he locked the car door and walked off from me. I didn't want to look dumb just standing there, so I rushed to his side. His mother looked at me funny. I bet any amount of money that she knows how he is. She knows.

"Is everything alright, son?" she asked as she looked at me.

"Everything is great, mother. I just had to lock up the car and retrieve my Princess purse and phone that she walked off and forgot," he sarcastically stated as he kissed her on the cheek again and walked off. I smiled at her and continued behind Alex with my head down. I didn't want her to see the embarrassment on my face.

"Alex," a kind of deep voice called out. I looked up and it was his father. He was in blue overalls, with a blue shirt and tennis shoes. Unlike mother Della, who was dressed like she was ready for a ball. She had on a purple ball dress with some type of white beads holding up her hair. Her shoes where stunning, looked like Chanel.

"Father," Alex called out as the two hugged each other like they haven't seen each other in years. He continued, "Where's Codie?"

"Here I am, Alex." This skinny little blonde-headed girl yelled out as she appeared from the back of the house. She had on blue jeans with holes in them and a light, peach colored shirt with flowers. Her hair was so long, it was all the way down to her butt.

"Codie." Alex hugged her tightly as he swung her around.

She was smiling from ear to ear, like a little school kid.

"Put me down, Alex, I want to meet Siam," she giggled as he stopped and put her down. She added, "I've heard so much about you, Siam. So happy to finally meet the lady who has stolen my brother's heart."

"Nice to meet you as well," I admitted as I gave her a hug and she hugged me back tightly.

"This guy right here means the world to me, so please be nice to him," she stated.

"I will always be nice to him, it's the other way around," I joked as she hugged me again and Alex gave me a strange look.

"Glad you're here," father Jason stated as he gave me a hug as well, taking away the tension.

"Thank you all for inviting me here, such a lovely home," I remarked as I looked around.

"Well come on and let's sit down," Codie interrupted as she pulled me by the hand into the living room. It was kind of elegant with high ceilings and drapes. The furniture even looked elegant. Everything was so clean.

Sitting down on the couch next to Codie, she asked, "So how do you like Canada?"

"It's nice. I really haven't gotten out to sightsee yet, but I bet it's nice here," I responded back, looking at her.

"What? Alex hasn't taken you out of the house? Girl, you are missing out on so much. There is always something to do here, especially the pubs."

"The pubs."

"Yes, the bars." She giggled as she put her hand up to her mouth.

"She's not allowed to go to pubs or any type of bars, Codie. So, don't be a bad influence," Alex jumped in and said as he took a seat across from us, crossing his legs.

"What do you mean she's not allowed?" she asked as her voice changed. I looked at her and then to Alex. This family seemed to have bipolar traits.

"Just like I said, she is not allowed to go to bars or pubs or clubs," he added. I was so embarrassed. Heat covered my face and I began to sweat a little.

"Don't say you're going to do her like you did the rest of them," she sadly spoke as she looked at him with sad puppy dog eyes. I wanted to ask what he did to the rest of them but something told me that I would be out of line, so I just shut up and listened.

"Codie, stay out of Alex's business. That has nothing to do with you," father Jason added as he held out his hand to me and I grabbed it. He continued, "Come Siam, it's time for dinner."

Father Jason and I took off into the kitchen. I looked back, Alex and Codie were just staring at each other. They looked as if they were ready to fight each other.

"Them too are always fighting," father Jason said as he looked at the expression on my face. He seated me at the table. Mother Della had already seated herself at the table. Father Jason took a seat. We were waiting on Codie and Alex to come to the table.

"Codie, Alex, it's time for dinner. Stop fussing with Codie and come on," mother Della called out at the two and then suddenly, you could hear them fussing louder.

"Don't run her off like you did the rest. She is nice,"

Codie yelled.

"Stay out of my business. Listen to what father tells you. This is none of your business," he yelled back.

"You better not hurt her. I don't want to lose you again," she stated.

Things got quiet as I looked around at the table at mother Della and father Jason. Everyone keeps saying that he ran those girls off. He must have been very bad to them. Codie acts like he killed somebody. Then the thought crossed my mind. Did he kill someone or not?

Entering the room, Codie looked like she had tears coming down her face. "Clean your face before you sit at my table," father Jason ordered as he pushed her chair to the table, not letting her sit down.

Codie just turned away and Alex took a seat next to me. He had this sour look on his face instead of the usual stone face.

"Are you okay?" I whispered to him. He continued to look down at the dinner table, not even acknowledging me.

"Calm down, Alex. We are all just concerned about you

and don't want things that happened in the past, to happen now," mother Della stated.

"Stay out of the man's business, Della. Don't piss me off, because you know what will happen. I think Alex has everything under control," father Jason assured as he looked at Alex shaking his head. Alex nodded back.

Codie returned to the table and sat down. Father Jason said grace and we began eating.

"Try this, Princess," Alex stated as he put some Tourtière, which was a meat pie made of pork and lard, on a fork.

"No thanks, sir, I'm stuffed," I replied as I rubbed my stomach. Looked like my dress was about to bust.

"It's really delicious. Mother makes the best Tourtière in Canada." He smiled as he looked at his mother and shoved the fork towards me again.

"Sir, my dress it about to bust if I keep eating," I spoke again, but this time noticing the look on his face. Codie looked at her mother and then to me. She took a long breath and put her fork down on her plate.

"Either you taste it or I'll shove it down your throat. I

125

won't ask you again," he demanded as I took his hand with the food and guided it to my mouth to taste. It tasted kind of salty, but I continued to chew. I didn't let him know that I didn't like it.

"Tastes delicious mother Della," I spoke as I swallowed the food.

"Glad you like it; Jason seems to think that it's a little salty," she replied as she hit father Jason on the hand.

"It is salty, Siam just doesn't want to hurt your feelings," he snapped back and smiled at me.

I grabbed the glass of wine that was on the table and began to drink. My throat had become a little dry. Alex had the stone face again. I really didn't know what I was doing. He told me to be myself, so that's what I was doing. He was going to punish me anyway later.

"Here, princess, take another bite," Alex said as he held up another piece of Tourtière.

"Do I have to, sir?" I asked and Alex just snapped out. He pushed his chair back from the table and grabbed me by the hair.

Codie yelled out, "Alex no. Just leave her alone. Mother."

"Alex please," mother Della begged as Alex dragged me by the hair into the back of the house. He was really pulling me very hard. I thought he was going to pull the roots out of my hair. I had grabbed his hand, holding him in place as he pulled me. We entered into the big room in the back. Alex tossed me on the floor. He locked the door and walked inside this closet, coming out with a leather black belt.

"You won't ever embarrass me again in front of my family," he snapped as he lifted the belt and began hitting me across my back.

"Master, please. Don't hit me," I yelled out and he stopped.

"Don't ever talk back to me when you're getting punished. I will do whatever I want to do. You said that you like pain and now, I'm about to give you pain. Shut the fuck up and take it," Alex screamed as he hit me over and over with the belt across my back. I had gotten up on my knees and hands in a doggy style. He kept hitting me like he did that night at my apartment. It felt like my father was punishing me for doing wrong.

After he finished punishing me like a dog, I continued to stay in one spot as the tears fell down my face. Alex got on the floor and pulled my thongs down to my bent knees. He rammed his dick deep in my pussy, gripping my sore ass as I moaned out loud. He was fucking me like he was a mad scientist. He rammed and rammed as I crawled forward, trying to stop the hard thrusts. As my head bumped the bed in front of me, I lifted my head up into the air. Alex held onto my hips and pounded me some more. I lifted myself up on top of the bed. Alex grabbed me by the neck and continued to pound until he exploded. He pulled out in time and pushed me to the floor. That meant I needed to lick and suck all the cum out his dick. As tears fell down my face, I sucked and sucked until he was bone dry.

"See, Princess, this is not what you want. This is not the pain you want to feel. I told you that I didn't want to do you like that, but you forced me. You gave me no choice," Alex stated as he pulled up his pants and lifted me off the floor.

"I was talking about sexual pain. This is just wrong what you did to me."

"Say it again. Say that comment again and I'm going to give you more. I keep telling you that this is not what you want. Once I go there, I don't know how to stop."

"Yes, master, I understand," I said as I straightened my dress and Alex guided me to the en suite bathroom.

"Clean yourself up and then come out. I don't want my family to see you like this. You're a mess," he stated as he tossed me a small hand towel and walked out. I waited for him to close the door and then, smiled to myself in the mirror.

"That's exactly what I wanted you to do, master," I giggled to myself in the mirror. Those licks he gave me were nothing. I was more embarrassed than hurt. The tears weren't of hurt, they were tears of happiness.

I ran water on the towel wiping my face. After I cleaned up, I went back to the dinner table. Everyone had gotten up, but Codie. She was still there waiting on me to get back.

"Where is sir?" I asked Codie as I sat down at the table and continued to eat the Tourtière. I didn't think about how full I was, I just sat there and finished the plate Alex had.

"He walked outside with mother and father. Are you okay, Siam?"

"Yes, Codie, I'm great. We just had a little disagreement. Things will be alright," I assured myself as I finished the food, then drank the wine. She poured me a glass of wine and I drank all of that too.

Placing the glass on the table, she asked, "Are you really okay? I know that my brother can be a pompous sometimes, but he really is a good man."

"Codie, I am really okay. He didn't hurt me that bad. It probably sounded like it from in here. But honestly, I'm really okay. So, what is a pompous?"

She giggled, "My bad. I was calling him a pompous jackass."

I laughed as I looked around to see if he was near. She laughed too. She drank her wine down then poured us more. We both drank the glasses quickly. Then she poured one more. Before we could drink it, Alex walks in, so I just took a sip from the wine glass.

"Are you okay, princess?" Alex asked as he sat next to me and drank his wine in one gulp.

"Yes sir, I'm wonderful. I finished the Tourtière. It was

delicious," I replied as I smiled at him. He looked at me with a face of a sad child. He knew he had hurt me. I really liked the pain he placed upon me. Now, if only I could get him to do it all the time.

After we sat there for a few more minutes, it was time for us to go. Mother Della and Codie walked us to the car. Codie walked behind me. She grabbed her mother's hand and they both looked at my back. It was real red but no blood. You could see whelps through my dress. If they only knew, that was nothing to me. I wanted to feel more.

SIAM'S THOUGHTS

The ride home was silent. Alex didn't look at me not once. He must have been feeling some type of way. I hope he's not feeling guilty about what he did. If so, he wouldn't give me the pain for my sexual pleasure that I need. It's time to turn up the heat. Alex knows what I want and he better give it to me. I loved him, but I will look further for a man to pleasure my desires. The pain fueled my sexual drive. I had to have it.

Sitting in the bathtub soaking, as Alex was in the shower. Seemed like he was crying, but I couldn't tell. He had the water running over his head. As he moved, I turned my head finishing my bath.

Damn it, I forgot to Skype my parents.... AGAIN!

CHAPTER 9

After a couple of days had gone by, Alex decided to take me back to Pillar's Dungeon. After my milk and honey soak, I patted myself dry and put on this sexy police officer costume that Alex likes. It had a police cap with a big silver badge in the front. The shirt was short-sleeved with the breasts half hanging out at the time and a tie coming down on top of the breasts. The slutty skirt was very short with fish net stockings and a silver badge as the belt. There were no panties with this outfit. I had on six-inch stilettos. The entire outfit was black. I put on a little deodorant and some perfume by Rhianna called, Reb'l Fleur. I had fallen in love with the fragrances.

Finally dressed, I walked down to Pillar's Dungeon and knocked on the door three times as ordered. It took a few minutes, but Alex opened the door and invited me in.

"Come on to my house of pain, Pillar's Dungeon."

"Yes, master," I softly spoke as he handed me a bottle of Moscato.

"Drink," he ordered. I turned up the bottle and drank as much as I could. Taking the bottle down from my mouth, he ordered me again, "Drink, I need you relaxed and inviting."

Alex hit the bottle with one of the floggers I had seen before. It had kind of a bitter taste, so I tried to take my time. I almost got lockjaw trying to drink. My mind was thinking, *I hope he didn't make me drink the whole bottle, I would be drunk. I wanted to enjoy my pain, not be a dead drunk, not feeling the pain.*

Handing him the half-full bottle, he ordered again, "Drink, I'm not going to keep telling you," he added as he tapped me on the leg with the flogger. "Drink the entire bottle."

"Yes, master," I replied as I started to feel a little tipsy. I added as I took the bottle down from my mouth, "I really don't want to be drunk when you do this to me. I want to be in my right mind."

"Are you talking back to your master, Siam?" he spoke, and right then, I knew he was very serious, because he called me by my first name.

"No sir," I softly whispered as I realized my mistake. Putting my head down like a kid that just got into trouble, Alex hit me with the flogger harder on my thigh. I jumped

133

from the sound of the hit.

"Don't fucking move. If you move again, I will hit you harder, Siam," Alex threatened as he raised the flogger to strike me.

I put the bottle to my mouth and drank again. The taste was becoming so bitter. Taking the bottle down from my mouth for a break, Alex hit me harder with the flogger on the other side of my thigh. He hit me again and again until I put the bottle back to my mouth and finished the entire bottle. By this time, my thighs were on fire.

"This is my dungeon and you will do whatever I tell you to do from this point on. The more you defy me, the harder your pain will be. You want it, you got it," he stated as he grabbed me by the neck and forced his tongue down my throat.

"Give it to me, I deserve it," I whispered again as I forced my tongue back down his throat.

"First, I want to introduce you to a few more toys of mine. Feel free to ask me anything you wish," Alex ordered as he took me by my hand, but still was holding the flogger in the other hand. He added as he pointed into the room, "Go to any

134

toy and I'll tell you what you want to know."

Letting go of his hand, I began walking around the room like a fat kid in a candy store. Looking at familiar toys I had seen on the internet, I questioned, "What is this here?"

Alex cleared his throat and responded, "This is called a *Lektor Zipper Mouth Muzzle.*

LEKTOR ZIPPER MOUTH MUZZLE

This is designed to cover your mouth, limiting your talk. It has the vinyl exterior and holes for your nose for breathing. The zipper goes over the mouth for closure. These here elastic bands secure the muzzle around your head." He smiled and promised, "You will be in this soon. That pain you want to experience, you might change your mind about wearing this muzzle."

"I don't know, master. I would love for you to muzzle my mouth," I suggested as I smiled back at him. He is probably thinking that I'm crazy. I'm not crazy, I just know what I want. Rubbing my fingers over the Lektor Zipper Mouth Muzzle, I continued on to something else that caught my eye. Asking, "I know this is a spreader bar but how does it work?"

"Yes Siam, this is a *Black Steel Spreader Bar*.

BLACK STEEL SPREADER BAR

This item here keeps you nice and wide for me when I really want to fuck you hard and deep. There are eyebolts here to each end, so I can attach your wrist and ankle cuffs. This will help keep you in place with not much movement."

"That is something I want to experience one day soon. I think I will enjoy the shit out of that." I smirked as Alex lifted the flogger and smacked me across the butt. He bit down on his lip and grabbed me by the nape of my neck gently. He pushed my neck down towards the floor. Touching my ankles like a good submissive, he went behind me and hit me softly with the flogger. I was expecting him to hit me hard. Luckily, I wasn't sore anymore from when we were over at his parents' house. Alex hit me again harder and I moaned out as I lifted my head, but continuing to hold my ankles.

"Is this what you want, Siam? Do you want me to continue flogging you? All this sex talk and me explaining these toys make my cock very hard. I'm ready to fuck. I will let you go through three more toys then the fun will begin." He smirked as he licked his lips.

Putting down the Black Steel Spreader Bar, I moved across the room looking at an odd toy. "And this?"

"This here is an Ostrich Tickler," he announced as he picked it up and held it at a distance. Continuing the conversation, he slowly mumbled, "Put your hands behind your back and close your eyes. No peeping out." I did as he demanded me to.

"I feel a little tipsy with my eyes closed," I laughed like a school-girl.

"Good. This *Ostrich Feather Tickler* is going to be fun with you right now," he advised as he put the tickler to my neck and moved around. I giggled so loudly.

OSTRICH FEATHER TICKLER

"That tickles," I hollered out as I laughed some more.

"I know it does. This here tickler will make you squirm as you're being blindfolded. You'll have no control and of course, you will try to figure out my next move. I will definitely have to tie you down because you will not be still," he instructed as he continued to tickle me a couple of more times.

"You will definitely have me squirming for sure," I confided as I opened my eyes, trying to balance myself. Alex caught me before I fell over.

"I can tell that you're feeling real good right now. The expression on your face, how your eyes look like they're about to close: little Chinese eyes. And, your giggle is even different."

"I am feeling great like Tony the Tiger," I remarked as I walked on to pick out another toy, with Alex trying to hold me up now. I am feeling more than tipsy at this moment.

"I guess this here strap-on is for me to wear," I burst out as I felt the head of it.

"Yes, you will be wearing this. I call it the Big Daddy Hollow Strap-On."

"Will I be fucking you in the ass?" I surprised myself by asking such a question.

Responding quickly, he said, "Yes, if I want to be fucked. Or maybe it will be for you to fuck other women. Whichever way you want to do it."

"Do you like getting fucked in the ass?" I remarked.

"I see you are getting bolder and bolder with the questions you are asking, but I will answer it honestly. Sometimes, I like getting fucked in the ass. It makes me nut fast," he revealed as we both looked down at the strap-on.

"Can I fuck you now?" I uttered as I rubbed my entire hand up and down the strap-on.

Ignoring my question, Alex continued to explain, "Also, if my cock goes down, I can rest it comfortably inside the hollow part of the dildo. That way if I'm limp, I can continue to satisfy you if your pussy is still hot and inviting."

BIG DADDY HOLLOW STRAP - ON

"Sounds good to me, but I don't think you ever go down," I mentioned as I looked down as his hard cock pointing out in attention. Alex had no clothes on when entered Pillar's Dungeon and now, he is in a full-blown hardness.

"One more, Siam, and make sure you pick carefully. I'm at full attention," Alex informed as he began rubbing his hard cock and licking his lips.

"We don't have to go on, Master. Do whatever you want to me now."

"No, Siam, one more toy."

Reaching over, I picked up a set of anal beads. "I know

these here are anal beads."

"Yes, they are. I call them the *Ondula Silicone Anal Beads*, which offers six inches of beaded pleasure in your pussy or your ass.

ONDULA SILICONE ANAL BEADS

The more I put in you, the bigger the balls gets. This flange at the base allows me to pull it out safe and not rip you," Alex described as he put this silly looking grin on his face.

"Oh okay, I don't know about that. I've never been fucked in my ass before." I motioned as I put the anal beads down and grabbed my ass.

"You're in luck, because tonight is the night for that virgin ass to be fucked. And don't fight against me about it, because if you do, I will take your ass. I will ravish your ass over and over until you like my cock up in it," he warned, as my eyes got big. My ass will be busted open tonight. I'm looking at his eleven-inch dick and immediately became

141

nervous, but excited.

"Yes, master, please fuck my ass. I want you to ravish me. Take control of every part of my body," I begged as I turned around towards him, purring like a cat.

"You'll get it in due time, Siam."

"What happened to you calling me, princess?"

"Princess is your name outside of Pillar's Dungeon. When I call you by your name, I mean serious business," he explained as he grabbed me and walked me over to the bed. Pushing me down, I fell slowly. Laughing out loud, Alex walked back over to the spreader bar and attached both the wrist and ankle cuffs.

Moving slowly towards me, I continue to purr like a cat and clawing into the air, until he stands directly in front of me.

"Turn that sweet ass over and get into position," Alex snickered as he continued to stroke his cock a few more times.

"Yes, master, anything for you," I teased as I winked my eye at him and turned over. Alex quickly attaches the spreader bar. He sassed, "I got your ass exactly where I want you. You just don't know how long I have been dreaming to get you in this position."

"I know, master. I've dreamed of this position as well for many nights," I admitted to him as my pussy began getting very wet from being tied up like that. It did something to me that I couldn't explain.

"I don't want you to say a word, just take this pain I'm about to dish out," Alex taunted as he walked over and picked up this red and black flogger. Picking up the Lektor Zipper Mouth Muzzle, he placed it gently over my face. I am trapped with no words to express myself.

Alex revealed, "I'm going to hurt you badly. This is one ass whipping you will never forget; then I will fuck you to sleep. You have been bad, Siam. All this talking back, embarrassing me at my parents' house, not defending me at your parent's house and the list goes on. You can scream all you want, nobody will hear you."

I felt so drunk that I just laughed at the words coming from his mouth. Alex pulled me to the end of the bed and taunted me with his dick. He flogged me across my back quickly. He stepped a little closer, unzipping the muzzle and putting his cock into my mouth. Grabbing my head, he pushed his cock deep into my mouth, trying to choke me. Trying to move my head backwards, he shoves more dick in my mouth while gently hitting me with the flogger.

After about five minutes, Alex pulled his cock out of my mouth and began to flog my pussy kind of hard. As he hit me, I became wetter and wetter. Alex hit me across the ass a couple of times gently. I'm thinking to myself, *he said he was going to punish me.* I lay my head down on the bed with disappointment, hoping it wasn't the kind of pain I hated, and suddenly, he smashed that flogger very hard against my back. That shit really got my attention.

"I knew you were going to get bored. I was waiting for you to put your head down," Alex whispered as he zipped the mouth muzzle back up over my mouth.

Walking off, Alex walked out of the room. He left me sitting there like a dumb ass, tied up. Waiting for a few minutes for him to come back, but no Alex. It seemed like I couldn't keep my eyes open. I knew as soon as I fall asleep he was going to come in and hit me with that damn flogger. Before I could look up, he was standing there with a bottle of

Moscato in his hands. He was drinking it so fast, almost emptying the bottle.

Alex leaned over me and began biting me on my back softly. I moaned out loudly. He began to bite me more and more across my back, as he placed his hand on my pussy. He didn't enter me at all, but placed his hands there. I began to move around as much as I could try to get him to drop his finger in my pussy. He stood up and drank down some more Moscato. Walking to the back of me placing himself between my legs, Alex leaned over and began kissing me all over my ass and even putting his tongue on the lips of my pussy. I wanted to call out to him and let him know to fuck me, but I couldn't say a word.

Alex took the flogger and began hitting me on my legs softly, then to my thighs and on my back again. Hitting my pussy a couple of times, he stuck his fingers between my pussy lips. "Damn Siam, you're so fucking wet right now. I love the way you get that pussy ready for me," Alex admitted as he took off the mouth muzzle, allowing me to talk again.

"Please fuck me, master. I'm so hot right now. "

"I'm not fucking you tonight, Siam. I should just leave

145

you here like this but I'm not going to tonight. I need to teach you a lesson." Alex chuckled as he helps me get on my knees as I continued to be tied in the spreader bar. My ass was up in the air as my head was lying flat down on the bed. Alex poured Moscato on me from head to toe. He just threw it on me like I was nothing. The stone look he had in his face was even harder. His jaws were clenched together as he spoke out, "How many men have you really fucked? You can tell me because I don't believe you have been with just one man."

"Master, I promise I have been with only one man. You're the second man I have ever fucked," I slurred as I tried to make my words clear.

"Don't fucking lie to me," he shouted as he hit me with the flogger across my back. I moaned out loud. He hit me two more times and asked again, "How many men, Siam?"

"Master, I'm telling you the truth, you're the second man I have ever been with sexually. Please, believe me," I informed him as he poured more Moscato on my ass.

"Don't lie," he yelled as he continued to hit me repeatedly with the flogger so softly, my body began to shake and he fucking made me cum. My pussy exploded right there without him even touching me. I squirted everywhere. Alex had to stop and take a look.

"You fucking came, Siam? You fucking came without me? You fucking bitch," Alex hollered as he went behind me and placed himself between my legs.

"Master, I'm sorry. I'm sorry, please forgive me," I interrupted him as he got down on his knees and pushed his head into my pussy lips. He was licking and lapping my pussy like a dog drinking his water. He was hungry for my nasty cum. Alex ate my pussy so good that I cum again, right into his mutherfucking mouth.

"You're busting nuts back to back, Siam. Damn, you've gotten me so hard right now," Alex announced as he entered my pussy from the back. I was so sloppy and wet. Alex pushed deeper and deeper into my pussy as I could barely hold myself up. He fucked me like he'd just gotten out of jail. He held me by my hips some kind of way and fucked harder. I could feel he was deep in my stomach. Seemed like he was pushing my intestines to the side. Suddenly, pulling his cock out of my pussy, he stood up on the floor by the bed. Alex got some baby oil off the small table in the middle

147

of the room and retrieved a pair of red anal beads, with a small string attached to each ball.

"What's wrong, Master? Did I hold my pussy high enough for you to fuck me?" I whispered. I felt drunk as a mutherfucker.

"You are doing well, Siam. I'm ready to see how much you can really take," he stated as he poured the baby oil all over my ass, getting me all slippery. He eased his index finger into my ass. I tensed my body up and then it released on its own. I had no control over my body. My mind was like, *take your ass to sleep*, but I couldn't with this man's finger up my ass. Alex moved his finger in and out of my ass. He poured more baby oil on my asshole and chuckled, "You're handling this like a champion. Then again, it could just be that you're drunk," he commented as he took that finger out and put his long finger in my ass. Moving in and out, he grabbed the anal beads and began gently inserting the smallest one. I clenched again as he poured more baby oil on me.

"Just relax, Siam. This won't hurt as much if you let your body relax."

"I'm relaxed, master. I think it's the thought of you pushing beads up my ass," I giggled as he pushed more and more. It was five anal beads and he was at four.

"Just one more bead, Siam, and then that's it."

"That seems like a lot," I laughed as he eased the last bead into my ass.

"How does that feel?"

"It's not as bad as I thought it was going to be," I answered. Alex lay flat underneath me and began licking my pussy passionately. He pulled one anal bead out of my ass gently as he continued to lick my delicate pussy. The intense sensation was so fucking amazing that I was ready to cum. He pulled the second and third anal bead out and I damn near lost my mind. The sensation was rushing to my pussy as he pulled the rest of the anal beads out of my ass and I came all in his mouth.

"Fuck. Fuck," I yelled as I exploded. I tried to get off his face and he clamped down on my hips and pulled his mouth deeper on my clit. I screamed out so loud.

Alex laughed as he blurted out, "I knew you would love

those anal beads and now it's time for the real deal."

Alex poured more baby oil on me quickly as I tried to recover from the explosion of my pussy. He sat his dick up to my ass and I clenched up so tight.

"Don't, Siam, just relax. It's going to hurt," Alex said as he tried to convince me to stop clenching up.

"I'm scared, master," I whispered, just before he pushed his big dick inside my ass slowly. I tried to move up, but the spreader bar had me trapped. My heart began racing like a car with no speed limits. I began sweating and seemed like I was going into a panic.

"Relax, Siam, relax. I can feel you tensing up," Alex informed me as he hit me on my ass cheek and continued to move in and out of my ass. He started playing with my pussy as he fucked me in the ass and I almost died right there. That shit was so powerful. My pussy was so wet and sloppy with his fingers moving all over the place around my clit that I forgot he was fucking my ass. Alex picked up speed as I cried out louder and louder. He began to ram harder and harder and I squirted all over his hands.

Alex body slowed down and he began to shake violently.

150

"Fucckkkkkkk," he called out as he took out his cock and emptied his load onto my wet ass. He stroked his cock, making sure all the cum was on me. Slapping his cock against me, he chuckled. "Damn that ass was nice and tight."

"You almost gave me a heart attack." I laughed as he took me out of the spreader bar. My body collapsed on the bed. I was more tired than a mutherfucker. Alex fell down on the bed next to me and he drifted off to sleep.

SIAM'S THOUGHTS

As I lay next to Alex, almost falling asleep, I take another look at Pillar's Dungeon. There were so many toys that I wanted to know about. I started to get up and look, but my body was tired. I was feeling drunk and there was no way that I could stand up on my own right now.

I turned over, facing Alex as he had fallen asleep facing me. Peeping down at him, I took a long hard look at his dick. It had cum oozing out of it as it lay glued against his leg. I looked over at this handsome man who I had wanted to spend the rest of my life with. He was the man I had been craving for, the one I just can't live without.

Then a thought came to me about what just happened. I moved slowly to feel my ass. It felt sloppy, and wet back there as I inserted a finger into my sore ass. I smiled at the thought; I just got fucked in the ass. Alex just pushed eleven inches of cock in me. And those anal beads, damn, I wanted to feel that sensation every single day. I smiled and looked over at Alex. His beautiful face was so pretty when he slept. His blonde hair lay across his face as I slowly moved it back. I wanted to see his full face. Placing a kiss on his forehead, I closed my eyes and went to sleep.

CHAPTER 10

Hearing a buzzing sound, I gradually lifted my head and noticed my cell phone laying on the bed next to me. My head was hurting so bad from drinking all that Moscato last night. Sitting up in the bed, I looked at my cell phone and it was my mother blowing up my phone. I read all her text messages:

Siam, are you there?

Next Message:

You forgot about your Father and I again!

Again:

I can't believe you're treating your parents' like this! Are you crazy?

Again:

You need to call us now.

Again:

Siam!

I'm looking at these messages like what in the world is going on with mother this time of morning. I looked at the time and it read 7 a.m. This was the second time that I forgot to exercise. Master was going to be very upset with me. I looked on the bed and noticed he was gone, but the door to

Pillar's Dungeon was wide open. I get up off the bed and two more messages come in quickly back-to-back:

Again:

We're coming to Canada!

Again:

Call me now!

I immediately reply:

Mother, do you know what time it is here? I will call you in a few minutes. Let me gather myself.

Her reply:

Call me now!

I go to details in my phone and call her. What could be so important this time of morning? "Hello mother," I softly spoke, trying to wake up and get my head together.

"What's wrong with you, young lady? Your father and I sat up most of the night waiting on you to video chat with us. Is this how they teach you to treat your parents?" she angrily yelled through the phone, almost busting my eardrum.

"Mother, you don't have to shout at me. I apologize for not video chatting with you. I had been drinking over dinner and didn't feel well when I got home," I lied, hoping she

154

would calm down.

"That's not an excuse to dismiss your parents. You could have texted us and told us that you didn't feel well."

"If I could do that, I would have. Please don't be angry at me, First Lady. I apologize for not video chatting with you," I expressed as I rubbed my head. My shit was pounding hard.

"Well, I will forgive you this time, but you have got to keep in touch with us. You're all the way in Canada and we really don't know who this man is. Is he treating you well? Please don't lie to me," she stated, as the phone was silent for a second or two. "Siam," she yelled out.

"Mother, I can hear you. Why do you keep yelling? My head is hurting real bad."

"I apologize, but I need to know that this man is not hurting you up there. God knows what he's doing to you." she expressed as I saw Alex appear through the door with what looked like a glass of orange juice.

"Mother, if he was treating me bad, I know how to come home. Alex is great. He is a kind and loving man," I replied as Alex walked over to me and gave me the glass of juice and two pills.

"What's this?" I asked him as I laid the phone down on the bed next to me.

He replied as he put my phone on speaker, "It's Tylenol Extra Strength for your headache."

"Siam, maybe you should come home," my mother's voice interrupted us as he placed a warm kiss on my forehead.

"Hey, Mrs. Wilson," Alex shouted through the phone sending my head into a tailspin. Grabbing my head, I took the pill and drank all the orange juice.

"Hello Alex," Mother replied, but it sounded kind of dry.

Alex continued to say, "I promise you and your husband that I'm taking very good care of your daughter. I won't harm her at all. Just trust me, I won't hurt her. I love her too much."

"I need you to take care of my little girl. She's just so far away and we can't take care of her way up there. Promise me again that you will take care of Siam," mother asked as Alex picked up my phone and replied.

"I promise to love and cherish her. I will take care of her," he stated again. Seems like she was assured, but you never know about my mother.

"Well, why doesn't she call home and let us know that she is okay? We are having problems with her texting and calling us. Are you trying to keep her from her family?" she asked. Alex looked at me and pushed my head lightly.

"Mrs. Wilson, I promise from this day forward, she will keep in contact with you and your husband every single day. I don't know why she doesn't, she has her cell phone on her to call or text whenever," he explained to mother as he looked at me.

"Mother, it has nothing to do with him. I will keep in contact with you. Can I please call you back?" I asked as I sat up on the edge of the bed.

"Sure, Siam. Just keep in touch and I hope you feel better. I love you," she softly spoke.

"I love you more, mother," I replied right there in front of Alex.

Hanging up the phone, I fell backwards on the bed. The

room was spinning a little as Alex placed his hands on my stomach. "How are you feeling?"

"I have the biggest headache I have ever had. My head is pounding right now," I answered I continued to lay back on the bed. Alex eased off the bed and moved down toward my nakedness. He began rubbing his nose gently across my pussy, immediately arousing me. I pulled my legs apart and he began tasting my salty pussy. Placing my legs up on the bed, he tongue fucked me until I exploded in his mouth. It didn't take long to make me cum, even after a long night of fun.

After I exploded my juices, Alex grabbed me by the arm, pulling me up. I was trying to concentrate on the spinning room, then he asked, "Are you okay?"

"I feel like I'm going to be sick," I whispered as I held my stomach. It growled and I looked at Alex. We both began laughing out loud.

"Sounds like you're hungry. You did have a long night last night," he snickered.

"Yes, I did and I loved it. Thank you for showing me a good time. Something different," I added.

"You're welcome. Come on, let's get you in the tub while I cook us breakfast. Today is going to be our safe day. Would you like that?" he suggested.

"I would love that, master." I smiled as I stood up and Alex grabbed me. We headed out of Pillar's Dungeon and into the master bedroom downstairs. I ran my bath water and stepped in the tub. The water was so hot and inviting. Stepping in, I didn't realize that I had run so much hot water. Sitting down, my ass had a little sting to it. That was because of the anal sex. *He busted my ass open with his big ass dick,* I thought as I smiled.

After I finished my bath, I walked into the kitchen and breakfast was served. Alex had cooked grits, bacon, eggs, and blueberry pancakes. He had two different syrups on the table; maple and blueberry.

"Everything looks so delicious," I complimented him as I walked over and gave him a nice passionate kiss on the lips.

"Thank you, princess. I wanted everything to be perfect for you. And of course, you know I heard your stomach growling like a bear," he joked as I gently placed my hands on his chest and laughed.

"You're right. I don't think we ate anything last night after we left your parents' house. Maybe I had gotten hungry through the night," I replied as we both sat down and Alex said grace.

After eating breakfast, I washed up the dishes. Alex went into his office to do a little work. That gave me the opportunity to clean up the house. I hadn't cleaned, well, since I had gotten there. I retrieved my iPod and began my cleaning. All the supplies were in the laundry room. So, I gathered them and cleaned the kitchen first. Afterwards, I cleaned the bathroom and bedrooms. And last, I went into Pillar's Dungeon and cleaned the items that we had used. Taking my time, I studied each one as I cleaned them up. I remember Alex giving me a pamphlet on how to clean the toys. *It read that one of the common ways to get a bacterial infection is to not clean your sex toys well. You could get exposed to harmful bacteria. Therefore, the sex toys should be cleaned with mild soap and warm water. I was never to submerge the part of a sex toy that had batteries. The silicone toys could be boiled on the stove for about 3 to 5 minutes to be sterilized. If the sex toys we were using weren't 100 percent silicone, then I would have to use the sex toy cleaner to make sure that I didn't damage the toy. When I do get a chance to use the Big Daddy Hollow Strap-On, I would have to clean it up with mild soap and water or just sex toy cleaner. All the plastic toys had to be wiped down with sex toy cleaner or rubbing alcohol. The metal toys were nonporous, so clean up was very easy. I had to use about 10*

160

percent bleach solution, boil them and use a mild soap and
water. I had to make sure it was thoroughly cleaned and
dried carefully because I didn't want to rush them. There
was so much to do when it came to cleaning up the sex toys.

After I finished cleaning up Pillar's Dungeon, I took a quick shower and sat down in the living room. Alex was tucked away, still in his office. At first, I was beginning to think he didn't have a business or then again, he was probably trying to make sure he had me right where he wanted me to be.

A few minutes later, he appeared with a devilish grin on his face. "Did you enjoy cleaning Pillar's Dungeon? I went searching for you and saw you cleaning. You looked so beautiful."

"I did enjoy cleaning it. I didn't realize it was a lot of work cleaning up the toys. I thought you just clean them and keep it moving, but you have to be careful and clean them a certain way. I remember the pamphlet you gave me to read over on how to clean them." I giggled as embarrassment came across my face. Don't know why I felt like that.

Sitting down on the couch, Alex turned to me and communicated, "You know today is safe day. We can talk

161

about anything you want. Ask me anything and I will do the same."

I kind of looked away and then blurted out, "What happened at your parents' house that you had to beat me like that? Your parents and your sister knows. I felt so ashamed and embarrassed. And your father, he didn't say a word about any of it."

"Don't be ashamed or embarrassed. My parents and my sister have seen worse. Princess, I had a terrible attitude and whenever my submissive don't obey my commands, I would flip out and just go belligerent. Whenever I demand you to do something, I expect it to be done. Don't defy me, especially in front of my family. You had already pissed me off and it just took me over the edge," he explained as he looked at me very seriously.

"When I said pain, I wasn't talking about beating the crap out of me. I mean, I love pain but not like that," I confessed as I put my head down.

"Stop putting your head down when you confess something to me. Whenever we have a safe day, I promise I won't take it out on you. This is a day to open up and learn the do's and don'ts of our relationship. This is my chance to know you."

"I try not to look down, but I feel like such a school girl explaining myself to you like this." I shrugged as I pulled my hair back behind my ears.

"Well, the best way to resolve the issue with you getting your ass beat, is to do what I demand of you. Stop trying to be the boss. I know that you had to do it in your professional life, but now, that life is gone. You must learn to be submissive to me."

"I understand, master. This has been on my mind for a long time and I wanted to ask but didn't know how."

"Ask me, Princess."

"When you found out that I was a police officer, what was your first thought?" I yawned, hoping to cover up the question.

"At first, I wanted to stop talking to you and just let you be, because someone in your profession doesn't know how to be submissive. Well, until after you learn. I felt like it would be too hard to train you and a waste of my time if it didn't work out. That's why it took me a year to actually come and see you. I had plenty of chances to come, but I just couldn't do it."

"Why master? You knew that I would have done anything to be with you."

"Yes, but I wanted you to be in this relationship for me, not because of this dominant/submissive relationship. You just kept expressing to me how happy you were you found someone like me. I had to make sure that your feelings were sincere."

"My feelings are sincere about you. I love you so much and now that I'm with you, I don't ever want to be out of your sight. I crave to be near you all the time," I responded as tears formed in my eyes.

"Don't cry, Princess. We are finally here together and I feel the same way about you. That's why I express myself in anger whenever you defy me."

"But you don't have to be so violent with it."

"Remember, you like pain. So, I give you what you want. I told you that I didn't want to go down that road. That's the only way I can give you pain. Either you deal with it or you don't. I'm there on your level as you want me to be. There is no going back for me," Alex fretted.

I gasped as I said, "I see."

"Don't shy away from me now. You asked for this shit and I'm definitely going to give it to you. So remember that whenever you decide you don't want to do what I command you to do. Learn to listen and be submissive. Stop being so hard-headed."

At that moment, I felt like the conversation was going south, so I decided to change the subject. "I really enjoyed the anal beads last night and how you made me feel."

"I can tell that you enjoyed it. You came many times, especially when I started licking on that pussy and pulling those beads out of your ass. Your body was shaking so bad; I loved seeing you move like that. You pushed that pussy down on my mouth and worked that thang," Alex joked as he laughed out loud.

"You had me horny as ever. I didn't think those anal beads would have that effect on me like that. I want to keep trying it."

"What about when I rammed my dick in your wet ass? Did you like that or not?"

"Of course, I loved it. When you started playing with my pussy, did you notice how my ass just opened up? You excited me like that. If you want to fuck me anally, play with my pussy. It will help me," I explained as I clenched my legs together thinking about last night.

"I noticed that, Princess. Your pussy got so wet and your ass, wow. I couldn't stay in it long without busting a nut. That shit felt good," Alex acknowledged as he sat back on the couch and his dick was rock hard.

"I see you're ready for me again."

"Yes, princess, come suck your master off. Pleasure me."

"Yes master, anything for you," I offered as I crawled to him. He began taking his pants off without me helping. His cock stood so tall. Licking up and down his shaft, I massaged his cock with my mouth. I spit on the head, rubbing him gently, then placing my mouth on him. It was hard at times trying to suck him because of his size, but I did it. It didn't matter when he forced it in my mouth. I only hoped that my teeth weren't scraping him.

166

After about ten minutes of sucking and slobbing on his cock, he exploded in my mouth. I pulled and pulled on his cock, getting every bit of cum. I didn't want to waste any.

"Damn, that felt good, Princess. See, it's not hard to satisfy me," he sighed.

"No, it's not, master."

"Did you enjoy when Mistress A. J. and submissive Ashley came over to Pillar's Dungeon?" I asked before he could gather himself.

"Of course, I did; I loved it. Did you enjoy it, princess? I should have asked you before I did it, but I figured you wanted to."

"Yes, I loved it too. It was different seeing you with another man..." I trailed off, hoping he wouldn't get mad at me again.

"I know it was different for you, princess, but get used to it. I mean, I don't do it all the time, but when I do, it's nothing but raw fucking. I want you to be a part of that. I don't want to do anything without you, except for when I'm mad; then you can just watch," he advised as he rubbed me on top of my head. I had taken a seat in between his legs. Alex pulled up his pants and continued, "Well, I'm happy that you loved it because we will be seeing another couple soon."

"Sounds good to me, master. It's whatever you want me to do."

"There you go again with that statement. Don't think I haven't noticed you saying that."

"Saying what?"

"Whatever I want to do, you will do? What about you? This is what you want too, right?"

"Yes, Master. I'm sorry if I keep saying it like that. I just want to satisfy you and love you. I've fallen so deeply in love with you that I don't know what to do."

"The feeling is mutual, princess. If only you knew that I would kill for you. Anybody ever try to hurt you deliberately, I would kill them," he ranted. Alex was dead serious. He didn't blink once as he made that statement.

"I hope no one tries to hurt me. I don't want to lose you," I added as I thought about something else. "What happened that you almost went to jail? I noticed you have mentioned it and your family too."

Alex looked away for a few seconds, then he turned to me and smiled. "There were several times that I almost went to jail, but I will tell you about one incident only."

"Yes, sir," I spoke eagerly, ready to hear what he had to say. "It just kept scaring me when everybody kept saying it."

"There was this girl named Emily. She was from here and I loved her so much. One day, we were at my parents' house and she got into a fist fight with Codie. I lost it and began beating her with my fist, until she stopped moving. My father and mother were trying to get me off of her, but I didn't realize that I was beating her. It seemed like it wasn't real. Afterwards, Mother took her to the hospital. My parents threatened to kill her and her family if she told on me. My parents sent me to my grandparent's house in Los Angeles that summer. When I returned that winter, her family had moved away after she died. They couldn't prove that I did it. When they told me that she had head trauma, I knew it was from me beating her," Alex explained as he searched the expression on my face. I tried not to show any fear at that time.

169

I gulped down my spit and said, "Oh."

"Don't be afraid of me, princess. I promise I won't hurt you. You have to believe me," Alex begged as he grabbed my face turning me to him. He gave me a passionate kiss.

"I'm not afraid, master," I lied to him, hoping that made him feel better.

"Don't lie to me, princess. You will be severely punished if you do. I have to be able to trust you."

"I'm not afraid; scared, but not afraid."

"I promise I won't hurt you, my love."

"I love you so much," I whispered as I placed my head on his knees.

"You have no idea how much I love you."

Getting over the fact about Alex confessing to me about being involved in a murder, I continued to ask, "What about the rules? When we first met, you were throwing them out like nothing. But yet, since I have been here, I haven't heard you say them."

"That's because you're here with me and I don't see a

need for me to tell you the rules. If you forget the rules, then you will be punished. Don't get it twisted, all the rules still stand. Like I said, it's only twenty-five rules. You really don't want to be punished anymore, do you?" Alex snapped as he softly gripped a handful of my hair and pulled it tight.

"No, master, I don't want to be severely punished anymore."

"I didn't think so," he uttered as he let go of my hair. Then, he added, "Do we need to go over the rules right now, or what?"

"No, Sir, I know what they are."

"Are you sure?"

"Yes sir, I had to go over and over them for a year. I am pretty sure that I remember them like the back of my hand."

"Good, because I don't want this to come up again about my rules. You must have a problem with following my rules?"

"No sir, I don't have a problem. My problem is loving you," I smiled shamelessly at him. Alex stood up and lifted me off the floor.

171

"I love you more than anything. Just promise me that you will never leave me. Promise me."

I stared into his blue eyes and replied, "I promise to never leave you."

SIAM'S THOUGHTS

As Alex took me sightseeing around Calgary, all I could think about was that this man just confessed to me that he murdered someone. A submissive who fought his sister. What if he attacks me and accidentally kills me? What if I tried to leave and he kills me? My mind was running in full speed. He probably told me that lie just to keep me in line. Well, he got my attention. I won't do a damn thing for him to hurt me, fuck that. I love my life. All I came to Canada to do was to be loved and fuck like rabbits. It was definitely a bonus, fucking other men and women. My thoughts were to be dominated by my man, not be scared. But deep down, I wanted to feel that fear. That's what I had been wanting. Someone that wasn't afraid to take my life at any time. Someone who was capable of taking me out without a second guess. I knew if I told Zoey this kind of shit about me, she would recommend a psych doctor. My parents would lock me up and throw away the key. I really didn't know what to feel. A part of me wanted to fear him. It did something to me sexually just to know he would kill me at any moment with his bare hands. I liked to be suffocated every once in a while. The thrill of asphyxiation was exciting to me, but I didn't want to die. Deprive me of a little air, I would be okay. I smiled to myself,

172

knowing I had to be fucking crazy.

ALEX'S THOUGHTS

Fuckkkkk. I shouldn't have told her the story about Emily. It was altered anyway. I didn't lie, but I didn't give her all the facts. Sooner or later, she will try to leave me like the rest. I wanted to cry because I messed up but I didn't want her to know. Later on, before we went out that day, I took a shower and cried. I cried and cried until I couldn't cry anymore. The fear of Siam leaving me had me crazy. I wanted this woman to love me and not judge me. I wonder, did she judge me? I noticed that during the day she would smile, but then it faded quickly. I tried my best to keep her happy and it looks like I failed. I could only pray that she didn't leave me. I don't know why I told her that story. What in the hell would make me tell her? Maybe it was the fact that she would fear me and never leave. I knew she was already a little scared of me, because whenever I raised my voice, her eyes get big and glossy. I wanted her to fear me in a sexual way, not see me as a monster. But damn, it's too late now. I couldn't turn back now; the story is out. That's just one submissive. I won't dare tell her about the others. Emily was the only one who died, everybody else just suffered minor bruises. Siam doesn't know what she has asked me to do. If she wants pain, then I will give her that. Deep; I didn't want to go there but she had given me no choice.

THIGH & ANKLE CUFFS

CHAPTER 11

Arriving at the airport months later, I see my father awaiting my arrival. Alex had to go to South Africa for business, so I decided go home. Well, he more like demanded that I go home to my parents until he comes back home. I didn't object to that. It gave me some time to relax and see family.

"Siam, my baby. I didn't think we were ever going to see you again," my father joked as he gave me a big hug and kissed my forehead.

"Father, I'm so happy to see you. Where's mother?" I asked, looking around for her.

"She is at the house preparing dinner for you. Girl, I'm so excited you are finally home. I don't know about you going back to Canada," father objected as he grabbed my luggage from the terminal.

"Father, you're talking nonsense. I'm going back to Canada. My future husband is there," I responded as I grabbed a smaller bag with my personal hygiene items.

"So, you're disobeying your parents now?"

"I'm not disobeying you or mother. Don't forget, I am grown now. I have to live my life, just like you two have to live your own lives. You don't have time to run behind me," I joked as I tapped father on his shoulder.

"We both have retired, so we have time," he chuckled. I laughed at the thought of those two trying to keep up with my every move. Well, in a way it wasn't hard, because Alex never really let me go anywhere. I was always home or going to his parents' house. He had taken me sightseeing once and that's it in all of those months. Shaking my head, I hurried to father's car and jumped in.

"Have you heard from Zoey?" I asked.

"She was over at the house helping your mother, but had to run off for a minute. She said that she would be back to welcome you home," he replied as he started the car and we headed home.

Pulling out my cell phone, I had to text Alex and let him know that I arrived safely. It would be hell on me if he worried.

Hello, Master. I have arrived safely. My father picked me up from the airport. Headed home now. Love you.

Alex:

I'm happy that you have arrived. Please let me know when you make it to the house. I want to make sure you get there and not detour anywhere with Zoey.

Me:

You don't have to worry about that. I'm doing exactly what you told me. You said to stay home and wait until you return, so you can fly me back to Canada. And that's what I plan to do, Master. No detours.

Alex:

I did tell you to stay home with your parents but that doesn't mean that you will do just that. There is no telling what you will do, not being in my presence. Don't disappoint me, Princess.

Me:

I will do nothing. You're my man and I love you dearly. I won't do anything to hurt you. Remember, you told me to trust you. LOL

Alex:

Don't try to use my words against me. Just do what you're told and everything will be fine. Have to go. Chat later.

Me:

Okay, Love you.

Alex:

I love you more, Princess.

I smiled to myself as I put my phone back in my purse. My father had this weird look on his face. "I hope you're not going to be on the phone talking to him the whole time you are here. We want some alone time without him."

"Father, why don't you like Alex? He hasn't done anything to you. Please lose the attitude, because we are going to get married one day and have children. He's going to be in my life for a very long time. And, it would make me so happy if you and mother like him. Please father?" I declared.

"I don't see how you could be in love with a man you found over the internet. Georgia has plenty of men here. I just don't understand you young kids these days. Y'all have to go on the internet and find a man. It needs to be like the old days where you find someone in your own city."

"Just give him a chance, father. It took us at least a year to get to know each other. I didn't run off the first week with him. Even though, I wanted to. You make it seem like I went online out of desperation." I laughed, but father didn't find my joke funny.

"Girl, I would have beaten you black and blue if you had run off with that man in a week. You would have killed your mother with that stupidity. You're my only daughter and I'm not losing you to a man that you found on the internet."

"Stop blowing things out of proportion. You two are back in the old days. There are plenty of women on dating sites finding their husbands. I just wanted to see how the website worked and the first day, I started talking to Alex. I was cautious at first about it. It took me a month to decide if I wanted to join the dating site or not. It took me one day to find my true love."

"It's sad too, and desperate. If you wanted a husband that bad, I would have found you somebody here in Atlanta. And now, you're telling me that you ran up on this man in one day. He must be desperate too."

"Well, if you want to call me that, then so be it, but I'm going to marry Alex and have your grandchildren. I wish you would let it go that I found him on a dating site. As long as I am happy, it really shouldn't matter how I found him."

"You mentioned having children twice. Are you

pregnant?" he asked with such a serious look on his face.

"No, father. We don't want to have kids right now. We are too busy having fun."

"Well, don't go into details because I don't want to know what kind of fun y'all doing up there." He gawked.

"Stop it, father."

"So, how was it up there? Is it anything like down here?"

"It's a very elegant place. The air is crisper and fresh. And his parents' house was gorgeous. His father reminds me of you. Just mad all the time about nothing."

"I don't be mad all the time. Y'all just think I'm mad; I just be expressing myself. If you can't handle the truth, then you don't need to talk to me. You know I have always been this way," he stated as he glanced over at me.

"True, and very strict," I mumbled.

"I was strict. Look at you, you turned out to be a nice young lady. I think the police job you had done something to your brain, because you have fell in love with a man over the internet."

"Father, here you go again about finding a man on the internet. I will pray that you get over that part. You and mother didn't believe he was real. You kept telling me that he was after money or that he was probably a killer. That all this fairy tale was a scam…" I trailed off as I thought about what Alex told me about Emily.

"I still think something is wrong with him, and you. How can you find love on the internet? Impossible."

"Father, it's not impossible, because I succeeded in finding love. Stop being such a Grinch and complaining all the time. Just let me be happy," I insisted as he pulled up in the driveway.

Mother was standing outside waiting on me to arrive. Their house was maybe twenty minutes from the airport, but father insisted that he come and get me. Shit, Alex demanded that only my parents could pick me up.

"Baby, you're home," mother yelled as she grabbed me and pulled me in her arms. I hugged her back softly. She still smelled like roses from working in her rose garden all the time. I missed smelling her.

"I'm happy to see you. You look so beautiful," I stated as

we continued to hug each other tight.

"My baby's home," mother happily yelled at Father.

He grunted, "Yep."

"Don't start your complaining now. Our baby is home," mother blurted out to father as he walked on in the house with my bags.

Stopping at the front door, he turned around and smiled, "I'm not complaining. Siam, you know I'm happy you're home. I just wish you wouldn't go back up there."

Shaking my head, I looked at mother and spoke, "Father did enough of that in the car. He complained from the airport all the way here. He keeps going on and on that I found Alex on the internet, on a dating site. I told father that he needs to get used to the idea of me being with Alex, because we are going to get married one day and have children."

"Are you pregnant?" she instantly asked as she looked at my stomach.

"No mother, I'm not pregnant. I'm just eating well. His family believes in eating well," I stated as I took her by the hand and we walked into the house.

182

"I was wondering because you look like your hips are spreading," she mocked as she rubbed my stomach.

"Eating good, mother, no babies right now. We don't want children right now. That is the last thing on our minds." I wanted to tell her, eating and fucking, but I didn't think she wanted to hear about that. I laughed to myself as we entered the house. She had pink and white balloons everywhere.

"Wow, mother, you did all this for me? It's beautiful," I whispered as tears began to form in my eyes. It felt so good to finally be back home visiting my parents.

"Yes baby, I wanted to make sure that you knew you were missed. I missed seeing your pretty face and everything. Whenever a patrol car comes around that corner, I start looking for you," she whimpered as tears rolled down her face.

"Oh mother, don't cry. I missed you and father so much. I know that I didn't text or call every day, but you two were on my mind all the time."

"Well, I couldn't tell you missed us. You didn't call home, or text me or your mother," Father interrupted as he came over and gave me another hug.

"I apologized over and over for that. Alex is making sure I don't forget to call home," I stated.

"Why does this man have to remind you to call home or check on your parents? He shouldn't have to remind you of your parents. We're losing her," he smirked to my mother as she frowned her face.

"I didn't mean it like that. It just that we be so wrapped up into each other and sightseeing that I mean to call home, but lose track of time. I don't mean to not text or call. Seem like the days go by so fast," I explained as my parents walked into the living room and I kept walking to my old bedroom. I really didn't want to hear any more of their bullshit. I came home to enjoy myself and not be interrogated.

I didn't think they were going to scold me about not communicating with them. I'm surprised that my mother is ganging up with my father to convince me to stay in Georgia. I wanted to tell her, *fuck Georgia*. But, I had too much respect to come at her like that. Hearing my phone go off, I reached in my phone and it was a text message from Zoey

I hope you have your happy black ass back here in Georgia. I missed you.

Me:

I just touched down and at my parents' house. Seems like

they are trying to gang up on me about staying in Georgia. You need to come rescue me from this mess. This seems like more of an interrogation than a welcome home.

Zoey:

Shit I would beg you to stay too, but I know you love you some Alex. Your parents are used to you coming by their house every day. I miss seeing you every day too, but I want you to be happy. You seem so happy since he has come here.

Me:

I am very happy we are finally together. My parents don't believe we are in love. Father keeps going on and on about the fact that I found him on the internet. He complained all the way from the airport to here. Hurry up and come over here. I miss you.

Zoey:

I will be over there soon. Have to run some errands for my mama. You know that's an all-day thang. I don't know why she didn't ask my sister to do this shit. She knew you were coming home today.

Me:

Well, I will be here waiting. Rescue me!

Zoey:

You're funny, but coming. I will see you soon. Love you.

Me:

Love you, Zoe.

Throwing the phone on the bed, I remembered that Alex wanted me to text him when I got home. I will text him later, right now I'm about to take a bath and enjoy my family.

Getting in the tub to relax, I heard my phone going off. It was Alex. I had set his ring tone to Nicki Minaj's song "*Grand Piano*". I loved that song. It kept going off, I couldn't enjoy myself. I decided to get out of the tub and go answer my phone, before his mind is all over the place, thinking I hooked up with Zoey or I'm out fucking some man.

Picking up my phone, a text message came through:

You're really pissing me off, Siam. I told you to text me when you arrived at your parents' house. Don't piss me off.

Me:

Master, don't be pissed at me. I apologize for not sending you a message that I'd arrived home. I just had a conversation with my parents, trying to convince me to stay in Georgia. They are getting on my nerves.

Alex:

Don't say that about your parents. You should always be respectful and well-mannered towards them. Same thing when you are away from me.

Me:

I know, master. I came here to relax though.

There was silence for a few minutes. I waited until he responded, but there was nothing. The first thought came through my mind was that he was coming to Georgia to beat my ass. Suddenly, the phone rang and it was Alex.

"Did I make a mistake by sending you to your parents' house? I don't want them putting any ideas in your head about not coming back." Alex sighed.

"Master, you didn't make a mistake. It was time for me to see my parents anyway. I already told my mother and father that we will be married one day. So, they better get used to the idea of that," I explained before he started in on me.

"You know that I love you and I will give you the world, but you have to come back to Canada. Do I have to come get you, Siam?"

"No, Alex, you don't have to come get me. I assure you that I'm coming back to be with you. I promise that I am

187

coming back. Why are you so worried about that? That has never been a discussion of this."

"I guess just insecurity. I love you so much and if I have to come to Atlanta to get you, then I will."

"I love you too and I give you my word that I'm coming back to you," I assured him as I giggled.

"Why are you laughing?"

"Because you should know that I am coming back. We have spent a year just planning to be together and now, this."

"I'm just making sure that you come back. I don't want them putting negative things in your head about me and you're not coming back home. You mean the world to me and I won't let anyone get in the way of that."

"I know, master."

"You do realize that you called me by my first name."

"Yes, I did and I realized it, but it was too late."

"That's a spanking for you," he warned.

"Spank me hard, master. You know how I like to be spanked."

"Yes, I do. Don't get me started. My dick's already trying to rise now, just thinking about smacking you on that fat ass of yours."

"Oh yes, spank me, master," I whispered just before my father bust through the door.

"Are you going to be on the phone the whole time you are here? Come in here and be with us. Your mother worked hard putting everything together," he angrily spoke.

"I will be there in a minute, father. I'm on the phone right now," I answered him, hoping he would go away but he stood in the door, waiting on me to move.

"I guess my father is going to stand here in the door until I get up and join them," I gasped to Alex, hoping he would catch the hint and not be mean about it.

"That's right, let him know that you're trying to enjoy your family," father mocked.

"Father, you don't have to be mean. I said I was coming."

Alex interrupted and stated, "Don't talk to your father like that. Apologize now.

189

"I'm sorry, father. I am coming now." I apologized.

"Sir, can I call you back?" I asked Alex, hoping my father missed the fact I called him "Sir".

"Yes, princess. Tell everyone hello and enjoy your family. Text me when you get settled in bed."

"Of course, I will. I love you."

"I love you too, princess," he whispered as he hung up the phone. I looked up at my father, who was still standing there with this dumbfounded look on his face.

"So, he got you calling him, sir? What the hell is really going on?"

"I choose to call him sir, so don't start no crap. What is wrong with you, being so rude and nasty? I don't appreciate your attitude," I roared as I rushed past him and headed to the living room to talk to mother.

She was in the kitchen, so I headed there. "Mother, what has gotten into father? I was on the phone, trying to talk to Alex and he came in, being all rude. Have you two realized that I am grown now? If you don't want me here, I will go over to Zoey's and stay."

"He just misses you so much and is afraid that he will lose you. I'm afraid too, Siam. And no, you don't need to go to Zoey's house. We are your parents and you should stay here with us," mother added.

"The conversation is really getting on my nerves. I haven't been here an hour and I'm ready to go. It shouldn't be like that."

"Don't feel like that, Siam! We don't mean any harm. It's just that we love you so much and we're trying to get used to the fact that you live in Canada. That's so far away from here, if you hadn't noticed," she replied.

"I know it's far away, but please stop trying to convince me to stay here in Georgia. I don't want to be here anymore. I want to be in Canada with Alex."

"I understand," she slowly replied.

"Everything looks so nice here, mother," I said, changing the subject.

"Zoey and I did it. I wonder where is she anyway? She was supposed to be back by now. She assured me that she would be back before you arrived," mother stated, sounding concerned.

"I texted her earlier and she said that her mother has her running all over town. Why didn't you invite anyone else?" I asked.

"Because we are the only important one, plus Alex texted me and said that he didn't want you around anyone else but us," she replied.

"Alex texted you?"

"Yes, he did. Is that a surprise to you?"

"Yes, it is surprising to me. Why would he text you to keep people away from me? I'm grown," I stated.

"Well, I agreed with him that it would be just the four of us. He didn't want Zoey to be here, but I knew you wanted to see her. She is your best friend."

"Wow. I didn't know that. He has never mentioned anything to me like that, but oh well. I will discuss that with him later." I replied, still surprised. But there is no telling with Alex.

"Don't tell him that I told you."

"Why not, mother?"

"Because I promised him that I wouldn't tell you, that's why."

"Mother."

"Siam."

We both giggled at each other. She cooked so much food for just her, father, and me because Zoey still hadn't showed up yet. I wanted to text her, but my father would probably go crazy, thinking I'm texting Alex again.

After we ate and cleaned up, I decided to go to bed. Zoey still hadn't showed up yet, so I sent her a text.

Where are you, big girl?

Zoey:

Where are you?

Me:

I'm in the bed because you didn't fucking show up to welcome me home. What's up with that? I said to come and rescue me, not neglect me.

Zoey:

I'm outside. You know how my mama does stuff. She wanted me to run her big ass all over town after I finished running her errands. Get dressed and come on.

Me:

I can't go anywhere. I promise Alex that I would stay home. Come in the house.

Zoey didn't respond back. I jumped up and ran to the front door. My parents were fast asleep. Opening the front door, Zoey came through the door.

"Girl, I missed you so much," Zoey spoke as she hugged me tightly.

"I missed you too. It's seems like years since I have last saw you."

"I know. Feel like I don't know your ass," she remarked.

"Girl, boo," I shot back and continued to say, "Come on in. I missed you so much."

"Same here, Zoey. What have you been up to?"

"First, I want to say that I'm so sorry for fucking Alex like that in your apartment. I know you love him and..." she trailed off.

194

"Don't tell my parents," I whispered as I pushed her back out the door.

"I didn't mean to say it out loud, but I needed to get it off my chest. I'm so sorry for hurting you. I know how you feel about that man. Especially now that you have moved to Canada with him. Please forgive me, Siam. Please," Zoey openheartedly spoke.

"Girl, I'm not stressing that. I've forgotten about that. I just want to be happy with you and him. I'm just glad that you two got along," I stated as I hugged her. Truth be told, I really didn't care about it. Alex was going to fuck other women, whether it was Zoey or another woman. I realized that now and accept the fact it will happen.

"Don't lie to me, Siam. You know I love you."

"I love you too and I'm not lying. I'm being sincere right now."

"Well, come on and let's ride." She grabbed me and pulled me off the porch.

"Where are we going? Look at how I'm dressed; I have on jeans and a shirt."

"Girl, boo, I have on the same thing. You're acting like we're going to the club."

"I know you, Zoey. You will trick me into some shit and I don't want to get in any trouble by Alex."

"Stop worrying so much and come on," she ordered as we jumped in her car and took off.

Zoey had me everywhere. We did indeed go to a hole in the wall club that night. Sundays were always jumping off. We drank a couple of beers. Zoey and I talked for hours. The sun was coming up and she took me home. I was scared that Alex would be pissed off at me. My phone had died at the club. As soon as I plugged it up, the text messages started coming in back to back.

Alex:

Where in the fuck are you? Don't make me wake your mother up and ask her if you're at home. Stop fucking around, Siam. Answer me!

Alex:

Fuck Siam. Pick up your phone. You must be out fucking. You better not be with that damn Zoey.

Alex:

Has something gone wrong. Are you hurt? Don't piss me off again. I'm worried about you. Fuck it, I'm calling your mother.

Alex:

Siam, pick up the fucking phone. I'm coming to Georgia right now. You have lost your fucking mind, I see. When I get my hands on you, it will be hell to pay. Answer the phone!

Alex:

You have really proved yourself to be not trustworthy. I put my heart into you and this is how you do me.

Alex:

Siam!

My heart sank to my panties. I was hoping that he didn't make up his mind to leave me. Damn, I have really fucked up. I called and called him, but no answer. I called him ten more times, but still no answer. I have really fucked up. So, I decided to text him:

Master, please talk to me?

Me:

Please talk to me. I'm so sorry. I fell asleep and my phone died.

Me:

Master, please, please talk to me. I'm so sorry. I will give anything just for you to text me back. Please sir.

Me:

I know I am in the wrong for not texting you last night, but I ask for your forgiveness. You mean the world to me and I truly apologize.

I waited for a response, but he didn't answer my texts or call me back. I was so tired and exhausted from drinking, I just took a quick shower, put on my pajamas and went to sleep. Hopefully, when I wake up, Alex will have called or texted back. I checked my phone to see if the ringer was up, then went to sleep.

"Siam, baby, wake up. You've been asleep all day," I heard a soft voice call out as I felt someone place their hand on my thigh. Turning over, I see my mother's beautiful face and inhale her sweet rose fragrance.

"What time is it?" I asked as I gathered myself and sat up to face her.

"It's four o'clock in the evening. You have been sleeping all day," mother stated as she pulled my hair back.

"I can't believe that I have slept all day. Why didn't you

198

come and wake me up earlier?" I replied as I jumped up and rushed over to my phone that was on the charger. Looking at my messages, there was one from Zoey:

Get your ass up because I'm coming around six to get you. Love you.

Zoey:

Answer me girl. Are you rolling with me or what?

Showing the disappointment on my face, mother asked, "Are you alright? You don't look good."

"I'm fine mother, I can't believe that Alex has not texted or called me. He must be really pissed off at me for not answering the phone last night."

"I talked to Alex and told him that you were sleep. He asked me about last night and I told him that you went to bed early, but that was it. He seemed like he didn't believe me, but I assured him that you were in bed last night."

"Mother, I wasn't in bed last night. After you and father went to sleep, Zoey came by and picked me up. We went to this hole in the wall club and drank beers," I confessed as I looked at the disappointment in her face.

199

"Siam, you didn't," she blurted out.

"I'm sorry, Mother, I just wanted to have fun and not be stuck in the house all day and all night," I pleaded as I sat on the bed next to her.

"You don't have to sit in the house all day and all night. We are going to get out and do a little shopping today."

"I mean in Canada. That's all I do is sit in the house, all day and all night."

"Why are you sitting in the house all day and all night?" she asked being a concerned parent.

"Because Alex works all the time and I'm stuck because I don't know anybody. I don't have no friends or family up there to visit. Alex doesn't want me going out by myself, because he doesn't want me to get lost trying to find my way back home."

"Well, that's all the more reason you should stay here in Georgia where your friends and family are. I really don't ever want you to leave me."

"Why would you think I'm going to leave you forever? Mother, if you can't understand that I have found love, then you never will. I have finally found someone that loves me and I love him back. He doesn't want me for my body, but for my love and affection. It's hard to find true love like his. You will probably never understand," I expressed as I looked at her with tears forming in my eyes.

"I understand that you love him and he loves you back. I just wished he loved you here," she joked.

I laughed at her and replied, "I know."

"Get up and come eat this dinner I cooked for you, hours ago," she laughed.

"I'm so hungry. I hate that I slept so long and Alex hasn't texted me or called. He is very upset and I don't know how to fix it. This is unlike him, not to respond to my call or text."

"Baby, he is just mad. Give him time to calm down. I am sure he wants to talk to you, just as much as you want to talk to him. Then again, he is out of the country working. He probably doesn't have any service right now," she explained trying to make me feel better.

"Alex is pissed off at me. I am hoping that he doesn't

leave me here in Georgia."

"There's nothing wrong with Georgia."

"No, it's not, but my man isn't here."

"Girl, your man. Bring your butt in here and eat," she giggled.

"I'm coming, mother. Just let me freshen up. I don't want my breath to be stinking when I'm talking."

"You're right." She fanned at her nose as she rushed out of the room, pretending that she could smell me at long distance.

As soon as she closed the door, I immediately texted Alex:

Alex, please baby, text me back. I'm missing you so much. I apologize for losing my mind. I love you. Please, talk to me. Please, forgive me.

Alex:

What do you want?

Me:

Please forgive me for not texting you or getting on Skype like you told me to do. I won't do it again. Please forgive me.

Alex:

Do you really think I'm supposed to forgive you for this kind of behavior? I asked you to do one thing and you didn't do it. You did what you wanted to do. I am beginning to think you going to Georgia was a mistake.

Me:

I apologize. I hung out with Zoey and lost track of time. And my phone went dead and I couldn't text or call.

Alex:

Really!

Me:

Really. Please call me. I want to hear your voice.

Alex:

You're full of shit. I won't put up with that kind of behavior. You can just stay in Georgia with your family, if that's how it's going to be.

Me:

Please don't do that. I promise it won't happen again.

Alex:

Good-bye.

Me:

Master, please forgive me.

I sat there on the bed waiting for him to respond, but he didn't reply back. There were so many thoughts and emotions going through my mind. I wanted to cry for hurting him like that. I said I wouldn't hurt him and I did it. I wanted to beat my own ass for going out with Zoey. But it's not her fault, I have a mind of my own. I wanted to go and I did. It was only one night. Alex should be happy. At least I didn't fuck anybody, well, I didn't have anyone to fuck anyway, but that wasn't the point.

"Come on out that room," I heard Zoey's big mouth yelling through the house.

"I'm coming," I said as I texted Alex:

I love you.

I didn't wait on a response, I just walked into the living room, holding the phone in my hand hoping it would buzz back.

"It took you long enough to come out here and join us," Zoey joked as she grabbed me by the hand and led me into the kitchen with mother.

204

"Baby, the food is ready," mother stated as she looked at me with my sad face. I felt so bad about going out and doing what I wanted to do. I promised Alex that I would do right and I basically lied to him.

"What's wrong?" Zoey jumped in as she sat down at the island.

"Alex won't talk to me. Well, he did for a few minutes, until I told him that I went out with you. He stopped responding. I feel so stupid right now," I explained.

"Don't feel stupid. You deserve to have fun and be around people that you know. What do you do up there besides sit in the house?" Zoey stated as she cut herself a piece of the chocolate cake that was on the island countertop.

"Cut me a piece too," I slid in there as she gave me a "get your own piece" kind of look. I continued, "I don't do anything besides sit in the house for now or visit his parents. Alex hasn't planned anything else. I am so in love with him that I really don't want anything to go wrong between us. And Zoey, this is all your fault."

"How is this my fault? I just asked you and you jumped your happy blankety-blank, in the car," she replied, trying

205

not to curse in front of mother.

"I told you that I couldn't go anywhere, but you kept on. You shouldn't have influenced me," I giggled.

"Girl, boo, you have your own mind. I didn't force you to get in the car. All I said was let's go and you jumped in the car," she responded, while trying to stuff the cake in her big mouth.

"Well, you should have told me to go back in the house."

"Siam, I told you that he has to calm down. Just stop bugging him and enjoy yourself. He will call you when he is ready to talk," mother blurted, trying to assure me that Alex was going to call.

"All men are a little jealous," Zoey added, as if she really knew that.

"How do you know? You don't have a man," I sarcastically spoke as I cut my own cake and placed it on the plate.

"Girl, I've had plenty of boyfriends. I know."

"Mother, why is she giving me advice?"

"Like she said, she has had plenty of boyfriends." We all laughed and mother took out a stool and sat down. We talked and talked until it was time for Zoey to run off again.

Mother and I began watching this movie, *The Notebook* as we lay up on the couch. She was on one end and I was on the other. I kept looking at my phone, hoping Alex would text me back but he didn't. The phone was silent.

After the movie was over with, I went to bed. I wanted to cry myself to sleep but I couldn't. Just like mother said, he will call me when he is not mad anymore. I picked up my phone for the last time that night and texted Alex:

Good night. Love you!

I watched the phone laying in the dark room until I fell asleep, hoping the phone would light up.

The next morning, I felt like a train had run over me. I'd stayed up late looking at my phone. It lit up once but that was because it was telling me the phone was charged. Checking my phone and still, I had no messages, not even from Zoey.

Tuesday and Wednesday flew by so fast that I didn't

realize the days had gone by. I stayed in the house both days, not even going out to eat with my parents. I talked to Zoey over the phone or texted her, but I didn't leave again with her ass. I had texted Alex repeatedly, but there was no reply. I texted him my every move, because that's exactly the way he wanted me to do the first time. I should have done what I was told, instead of what I wanted to do. We were in this relationship together, not just me.

Thursday rolled around and I decided that I was tired of doing the right thing with Alex. All the no-calls and no texts just drove me insane. He knew that was a way of hurting me, taking himself out of my life. I called Zoey.

"What's up, girlie?"

"Not shit. Just chilling right now. I might go out to the club later on. What's up with you, besides being in the house depressed because of Alex? Have you heard from him?" she asked while she smacked on some gum.

"No, I haven't heard from him. I have apologized over and over and over but he still won't respond. I'm so tired of trying. I love him, but I'm tired." I sighed as I looked at the last text message he'd sent me.

"Well, what's up? What do you want to do tonight?"

"Let's go somewhere and do something. I'm tired of sitting in this damn house. Mother and father act like I'm twelve years old."

"Girl, I'm on my way. Put on some clothes, because we're going back to the hole in the wall."

"Not that old ass club again," I chuckled.

"Girl, you know you like them old ass men gawking at you."

"Hell, no I don't. I don't want any men older than my father looking at me, lusting," I screamed.

"Bye, Siam. I'm coming."

"Bye, Zoey." I said as I hung up the phone.

Suddenly, a message comes through. Looking at my phone, it was Codie:

Alex is back from South Africa. Be careful. He seemed a little pissed off when he stopped by here to talk to Mother.

My heart dropped and I changed my mind about going anywhere with Zoey.

209

Me:

I am at my parents' house right now. We had a small disagreement. Thank you for warning me. And yes, he is pissed off at me. I messed up and went out to the club. He won't respond to my calls or texts. He even threatened to leave me here in Georgia. I hope he doesn't leave me.

Codie:

Girl, you deserve to have a little fun, as long as you didn't do the nasty with anyone. Did you?

Me:

Of course not. I would never sleep with anyone, besides Alex. We just drank a few beers and talked, trying to catch up. I wouldn't do anything to hurt Alex. He is taking things too far. I'm not understanding him right now.

Codie:

Alex is a very jealous person. When he falls in love, he falls deep. Just be careful, because he can be a handful. If he threatens to leave you there, then he might leave you there. Alex is a control freak, but I know you know this by now. He wants it done his way or no way.

Me:

I know he likes to be in control and I have no problem with that. I did know he would probably be mad at me for going out with Zoey. He told me not to and I did it anyway. I hope he forgives me.

Codie:

Alex likes to hold grudges, so be prepared for anything. If he doesn't come and get you, I will come down there and pick you up.

Me:

Trust me, I know he holds a grudge. Thank you for the suggestion. I hope he was just playing about leaving me here. I would die without him.

Codie:

I doubt you will die, but just be prepared for anything concerning Alex. I have to go. Love you.

Me:

Love you too. I will be prepared, I hope.

I began calling Zoey, but she didn't answer her phone. I knew that she was probably on her way and I couldn't go. Suppose Alex showed up here and I was out at the club? He didn't even tell me that he was coming back on Thursday. I thought he would return on Saturday. Then it crossed my mind; I hope he doesn't come and get me early. I wasn't ready to go back yet. I wanted to spend more time visiting other family members and friends.

Interrupting my thoughts, Zoey bust through my bedroom

door. "Don't tell me that you ain't going because you're going."

"How did you know that's what I was going to say?" I asked.

"I've been knowing you since second grade. I knew you were calling to cancel. You have me out of the house now, so get your ass up and let's go," she demanded as she pulled me by the arm.

"I'm not going. Seriously Zoe, I just got a text from Alex's sister, saying that he has come back from South Africa."

"Let me see the messages, because you might be lying so you can't go," she stated as I gave her the phone and she read Codie's text messages.

"What does she mean by be careful? He must be beating on you or something," Zoey asked, going in defense mode.

"No, he's not beating on me. Just a little jealous, that's all," I said as I stood off the bed and motioned my arms in a downward motion over my body.

"Girl, boo. Come on. I promise to have you home by

twelve."

"You will have me home earlier than that," I laughed.

"What time?"

"Ten."

"It's seven now. We won't have enough time to have fun. Shit, it will take fifteen of those minutes just to get to the club," she laughed.

"Ten, Zoey, or I'm not going," I demanded as I sat back down on my bed, acting like I wasn't going.

"Damn, Siam, ten."

"Great."

We both headed out the door. Mother looked at me with that, "you better not take your ass out the door" look. "I will be back by ten," I yelled out at her as I ran up to her and placed a kiss on her cheek.

"Sure."

"I will be home, mother."

"Sure."

"Zoey, promise my mother that you will have me home by ten." I motioned for her to promise. I knew she couldn't lie to my mother.

"Do I have to?" she asked, with a mean look on her face.

"If you don't promise her, then I'm not going."

"Fine, I promise to have Siam home by ten," Zoey promised as she stumbled out the door like a little kid.

"You better keep your promise," mother said as she waved her fist at Zoey.

"Yes, ma'am, I promise." Zoey smiled back and then gave me a mad look.

We ran off like girls skipping class for the first time. We drove to the hole in the wall in about fifteen minutes like she said it would be. I texted Alex again, saying I was leaving with Zoey, but he didn't respond.

Getting to the club, we partied even harder than the first time. This time, I got on the dance floor with a couple of different men, just having fun. Zoey just stood back and watched. A few guys approached her, but she didn't like to dance. She just wanted to drink.

Looking at my phone, it had 9:45. I ran over to Zoey and flashed my phone. She jumped up and said, "Bring your ass on. I promised your mother."

"I can just text her if you want to stay longer."

"Girl, boo, let's go," Zoey said as she pulled me by the arm and we rushed out the door. I think she was on two wheels taking me home. We arrived at 10:10.

"Don't tell your mother what time you arrived home. Sit your ass on the porch and get some fresh air first."

"Girl, you're acting like we are still in high school. I'm grown. I said I would stay if you wanted me to," I responded as I checked my phone again and saw a text message from mother. It read: *It's ten.*

Well, Zoey, you can forget that idea I said as I showed her Mother's text message.

"Fuck, Siam, you should have told me sooner what time it was. You did this shit on purpose," she whined as she put her head in her hand.

"I didn't do it on purpose. I forgot, just like you did. I thought we were grown."

215

"We are grown, but I promised your mother. Hurry up and tell her your ass is here."

I texted her:

I'm home, Mother. We're outside in the car.

Mother:

I see. Tell Zoey she didn't keep her promise.

Me:

Yes, ma'am. We are sorry.

I looked at the window for any movement in the curtains. "What did she say?" Zoey asked as she tried to look at my cell phone.

"She said that she sees I'm home."

"Damn it, Siam. You have gotten me into trouble. Get your ass out of my car," Zoey barked as she tried to reach for the door handle.

"Girl, stop trying to throw me out. I know how to get out. My mother isn't going to whip your fat ass."

"She might try. I wouldn't dare hit her back. She would just have to chase me." She laughed and I opened the car door.

"Bye Zoe," I smirked as I closed the door and she let down the window.

"Bye, Siam, you fucking early bird." Then she drove off.

I walked into the house and mother was on the couch. I walked into the living room and sat down on the floor by her feet. She began to rub my hair as I looked at television with her. We never said a word to each other. After a few minutes, I looked at my phone then went to bed.

Friday flew by so fast. I called to confirm my flight for Saturday morning, but it was cancelled.

"My flight has been cancelled," I spoke crestfallen, as I couldn't catch my breath.

"What happened?" Mother asked as she walked over to me as I held the cell phone to my ear. The customer service representative at the airport had hung the phone up in my face.

"Alex cancelled my flight. Mother, he is more than pissed off at me. I have to call him," I called out as I dialed his cell phone. There was no answer, so I called continuously, but still nothing.

"Maybe it's for the best," mother said, adding her two cents in where it wasn't needed.

"Mother, this is the man I'm supposed to marry one day." This can't be happening to me. I kept calling and calling then finally, I texted him with a nasty message:

You fucking bastard, I can't believe you cancelled my flight. You can't possibly be that mad at me for going to a club. You know I love you and you're doing this to me.

Alex:

Don't text my phone again with your bullshit. If this is the game you want to play, then okay. I understand that you want to do what you want to do. I gave you an order and you disobeyed me. I don't have to put up with you and this nonsense that you think you're going to put me through. Bye.

Me:

You didn't have to cancel my flight. But if you don't want me anymore, okay. I understand I'm not the one for you. But at least you could have been a man about it and tell me in my face. I understand that you are mad at me, but this is a little extreme. I feel used and insulted by this. I made one mistake and you act like a child. I could have come back home and we talk about things. Not you getting rid of me.

218

Alex:

Glad you understand that you are not the one for me. Don't text or call my phone ever again. Goodbye.

I looked at his message and broke down in tears. My mother came over and placed her arm around me. I fell to the ground, crying my ass off. The man of my dreams has slipped through my fingers. He was gone, just like that.

I cried and cried for weeks about losing Alex. I had started counting the days and a month had gone by. I was texting and calling him all day, every day. I told him everything. If I got up and went somewhere with my parents, he knew. I didn't go anywhere else with Zoey. She tried, but I wasn't hearing that shit. I had already fucked up. I didn't know how I would win Alex back, but I was ready to do anything. I should just take up Codie's offer to come get me. But if I went to Alex, he would probably disown me for sure. I had to suffer for my consequences.

After a month had gone by, Alex responded:

Do I have your ATTENTION?

Me:

Yes, master, you have my attention.

Alex:

Get your shit together I will be there tomorrow to pick you up. And that "do what you want" attitude better stay in Georgia. I won't tolerate it.

Me:

Yes, master. I won't disobey again.

He didn't respond anymore after that. I began running like a chicken with my head cut off. I was finally going back to Canada with my man. LESSON LEARNED!

SIAM'S THOUGHTS

I laid in bed that night smiling to myself, until tears flowed down my face. It was traumatic for me to lose him suddenly like that. There I had no thoughts but to rest. He must have forgot Rule number16:

I am free to leave my Master at any time, without the fear of permanently losing him.

There should be a rule for him never to drop his submissive permanently at any time he felt like it.

CHAPTER 12

Alex didn't say a word to me on our flight home. He had this disappointed look on his face. Words couldn't describe how I was feeling at that time. My heart felt heavy, knowing that I had let him down. In the back of my mind, I was thinking he wasn't supposed to punish me like this. I read on the internet that this was a hard limit. A dominant was never to stop talking or touching his submissive. I guess Alex didn't play by the rules on the internet; he had his own set of rules.

After pulling up in the driveway, tears fell down my face because I thought I would never see this place again. I saw Alex peeping at me out the corner of his eyes. I was so happy to be back at his home that I wanted to jump up and down, and shout even. I won't be going out with Zoey anytime soon. I would blame her, but I have my own mind. I should have stayed my black ass at home with mother and father.

Walking through the door with my luggage, I noticed that my collar had been switched out to something else. It was a harness that looked like a dog bone. Looking at it, Alex spoke for the first time. "That is a restrictive Bone Gag Head Harness. You will wear it until I say take it off. I don't want to hear shit you have to say. You have disappointed me and I haven't gotten over that. I felt like you deliberately disobeyed what I told you to do. That's a sign of disrespect and apparently, you don't have respect for me, but you will have a few days of punishment. It won't be the kind of punishment you like either."

"Master, can I please explain," I managed to get out, before he snatched the bone gag head harness out of my hand and immediately put it on my head. He didn't say a word. I was happy to be home but damn, I wanted to talk about things. I felt like him leaving me at my parents' house for a month was punishment enough. He made me suffer. I cried every single night being away from him, and I almost fell into a deep depression. That was harsh punishment, but I guess he didn't think it was enough.

"See how you just deliberately disobeyed me again? I told you that I didn't want you to talk and you continued to do it anyway. Once I finish with you, you will obey your master. I love you so much, but I can't have you disrespecting me either."

I shook my head and picked up my luggage, bypassing a huge ass *bdsm sex cage* sitting in the middle of the floor.

BDSM SEX CAGE

I'm looking at Alex like, *what in the fuck is that? I hope you don't expect me to be in the cage like an animal. I'm not doing this shit, you can send me back to Georgia*, I thought. But I changed my mind quickly, fuck going back there.

"Yes, that cage is for you. Since you want to act like an animal and not do what I tell you, you will be in a cage for a couple of days. There are soft cushions in the bedroom you can put in there to sleep on. You won't be sleeping in my bed, acting like you're crazy. I need you to do exactly what I say."

I shook my head and I continued to the bedroom. I put our luggage away and then proceeded to the bathroom. Alex wanted me to take a bubble bath. He said it would wash away my sins that I committed in Georgia against him. I thought, *he was full of shit. What sins*?

After soaking in the bathtub for about an hour, he walked

223

in and dried me off. Not a word was spoken as I stared at him. I wanted him to at least tell me that he loved me, but he just kept silent.

Putting on my clothes, I heard females' voices coming from beyond the bathroom. I looked out the door and stared.

"You don't need to worry about them. They are here to pleasure me. See, Princess, since you have been gone, I have been fucking other women. You gave me no choice. I wanted you, but you had to be taught a lesson," he boasted as he grabbed me by the arm and led me to the living room.

Entering the living room, there were two Asian looking females standing there with lingerie on. As soon as we walked into the room, they both got on their knees and bowed their heads. Alex opened the cage and motioned for me to get in. Somebody had already put pillows in there. I hesitated at first, until he gave me a nudge. Looking up at him, I turned around and got into the cage. He closed and locked it. I motioned to see if it was really locked and it was. He was really leaving me this cage for going out to the club. I could only imagine if I had fucked someone; he would have probably given me away to another dominant.

After Alex put me in the cage, he left the room. The two girls got up and began moving the furniture out of the way. Everything that was in the middle of the floor was now against the wall. They laid out huge, thick blankets.

They began pulling off each other's clothes. The skinnier girl had on black underwear with two white handprints on the back of them. The thicker girl had on purple lace thongs. The skinny girl took off the other girl's panties as I sat on the pillows and stared at them both. They looked at me with silly grins on their face. The thick girl got into the doggy style as the other one placed herself behind her and began eating her pussy from the back. The skinny girl moaned and cried out with pleasure. I was beginning to get moist down below. I could hear her licking the other girl's pussy. She was making all kinds of noises, turning me on. After a few minutes, they both got into the sixty-nine position and began sucking pussy and screaming out like wild animals.

I got my hand and began rubbing my pussy, until Alex came back in with two fur looking handcuffs. "Give me your hands. You won't be playing in that pussy tonight."

Giving him my hands, he cuffed them, one on each side of the cage. And I was spread out like an eagle. It was plain

225

as day that he had a hard on. The two girls continued to play with each other as he sat down on the blanket next to them. The skinny girl got up and positioned herself on top of the other girl, placing her pussy against the thick girl's pussy. They began bumping and rubbing against each other passionately. I didn't think females could actually get off like that. They kissed and fondled each other's breasts as they breathed hard and Alex watched me. He was trying to get a reaction out of me. I was sitting there looking crazy. I wanted him to come play with me. Or just fuck me.

After a few minutes, the girls lay flat on their backs. Alex moved in, sticking his fingers in each one's pussy then tasting it. My heart fell down in my panties. I wanted him to taste my pussy, not these random girls I know nothing about. The rules were that we played together, not me watching him eat and fuck other bitches. I wanted to cry, but I was too hot and horny. I was on my knees and moved one of my feet to position it right by my pussy.

"Don't do it or I will be forced to tie you down, and you won't be able to move at all," he barked out as he looked at me. The two girls looked at me and laughed.

"You should always obey your master," the skinny girl

said as all three of them continued to look at me. I felt kind of embarrassed because of how they continued to look at me.

Continuing what they were doing, he started back eating the skinny girl's pussy, while his finger was in the thicker girl's pussy. Then he switched up. The skinny girl went behind Alex and began licking his ass and placing kisses all over him. My pussy was dripping wet by now. I was ready to explode, but I needed Alex to take me there.

After that, Alex laid on the blanket and the thicker girl mounted him backwards. She jumped down on his big ass dick and began rocking back and forward. He moaned out as he looked back at me. I just put my head down until he turned away. I thought, *Damn, I need to be fucking with you all too*. I regretted what I did, because now he may never fuck me again. I would probably have to watch him fuck all these girls. *Damn it, Siam*.

Looking up at the three, the thicker girl was riding him wildly and the skinny girl sat on his face. He was meeting the thicker girl's every thrust. Pushing the thicker girl off of him, she lay flat on her stomach. He mounted her and began digging deep into her pussy. She elevated her ass so he could pound her harder. He got on his knees and all you could see was him pushing his cock against her roughly. Her moans and cries was inviting as the other skinny girl got in front of her with her legs wide open. Alex stopped fucking her. The thicker girl got on her knees as Alex moved over and entered her pussy. He was up high in that pussy. She was so wet that you could hear the juices sloshing in her pussy. The skinny girl got up and walked back to Alex. She placed her hand on his shoulder as he removed his cock. He leaned back on his feet as she got on top of him and inserted his cock. He pulled her next to him and they rocked with each other, fucking. It was like he was making love to her. Choking her, she called out, "Fuck me, master."

Alex immediately stopped. He angrily stated, "Who told you to talk? Get the fuck out, bitch."

"I apologize," she called out.

"Fuck your apology, I told you not to talk."

He jumped up, grabbing her by her hair and tossing her out the front door. She didn't get any clothes or nothing. She was out there naked. In a way, I felt bad for her.

He rushed back over and takes this other girl in the missionary style. They grinded against each other for a long time, fucking and kissing. I moaned out and he looked back at me. "See princess, this is what you're supposed to be getting. Do you like me fucking other women like this?" He turned the thick girl over and began fucking her from the back again. He was looking from me to his cock going in and out of this girl's pussy. Slapping her on the ass pretty hard, while she moaned out with pleasure. He fucked and fucked until he got tired, then she got on top of him and rode his cock. This shit happened almost all night. I was so caught up in them fucking each other that I forgot about my own pussy. I wanted to cum. *Damn you, Alex.*

I was so happy that the night had ended. Alex let me out of the handcuffs, but I continued to stay in the cage. He slept on the couch as the thick girl slept on the floor. I decided to go to sleep because all that fucking left me so horny.

Waking up later on, I saw the thick girl fully dressed and walking out the door. Alex was still on the couch asleep. Before she walked out the door, she turned to me and blew a kiss. I thought, *Bitch.*

Waking up to a rattling of the cage, I opened my eyes to see Alex standing there. He opened the cage and helped me out. I stood in front of him. He took off the Bone Gag Head

Harness and stated, "Your breakfast is ready. And please, don't talk to me. Just don't say a word to me."

I'm thinking, *we need to talk about you fucking these two girls. You issuing out cock and I haven't fucked since the last time you fucked me. I'm horny as hell.* My mind was about to explode from withdrawals.

Taking a quick shower as he watched me, we sat at the table and ate a healthy breakfast. He let me eat as much as I wanted. There was no limit today. He must have felt guilty about what he did last night.

Grabbing my hand and leading me into Pillar's Dungeon, there was a gray-looking air mattress on the floor, with an orange-looking bowl next to it with some type of clear liquid in it. Alex pulled off his clothes, then motioned for me to pull off my clothes. We both stood naked as he lay flat on the air mattress.

"You will give me a full body massage with this massage oil. Don't try to fuck me or suck my cock. If you do, you will be on the other side of my door as well. I need to make sure that you can follow the rules." He added, "Get the massage oil and rub your body from head to toe. Make it quick."

I did as I was told, then began placing the oil all over his body. I rubbed his body slowly as I took in all of his muscles and hardness of his thick cock. My mouth was watery, ready to fuck. Alex placed his hands between my legs and rubbed my clit. "Damn, you're very wet. Must be from last night."

I didn't say a word, but smiled. I figured he wanted to see if I would say anything. He pulled me on top of him and ordered, "Massage my cock with your pussy without me going in."

I laid on top of him as I moved my pussy up and down against his dick. There were many times that I was tempted to fuck, but didn't want to disobey. I rubbed my slippery breasts against his chest. I took the opportunity to move my pussy up and down against his dick, then getting off of him. I massaged his cock with my fingers until he exploded and I continued until his cock went limp. He reached over and stuck a finger in my pussy. "You're wide open. That pussy is ready."

Smiling, I wanted him to take me right there. *Fuck me hard and show me whose boss*, I wanted to say. After, I cleaned up the mess as he watched me. He took a shower as I sat on the toilet with my hands handcuffed behind my back.

231

He was making sure that I didn't get myself off.

Soon after, I ended back up in the cage with my arms handcuffed to each side. He moved around the house working. I didn't know what I was supposed to do then. I wondered how long was he going to keep punishing me by not fucking me. I read on the internet that it wasn't supposed to be like that. The dominant wasn't supposed to withhold sex from his submissive. Seems like I read a lot of shit on the internet. It seems like the dominant makes up their own rules as they go and nobody could stop them. As long as I accepted it, he would continue to treat me like that. But, I couldn't let him go, I wanted him so badly. His love was so addicted or perhaps, the shit we were involved in was so addictive.

Dinner came around; he took off the handcuffs and I ate in the cage this time. Supper came around and the same thing; I ate in the cage. There was no action that night. He just turned the light off on me and went to bed. I knew it was a set-up. He wanted me to get myself off so he could punish me. I'm not falling for that shit. I want his love and attention again like before.

The next morning rolled around and he had me up at

5:30am. "It's time for you to start back exercising again. You need to continue this even if I'm not around you. Staying in shape is a good thing. If I stay in shape, you will stay in shape. Be prepared for a workout," he warned as we took off running to the gym.

Getting to the gym was at least 3 miles from the house. I had given out of breath, falling behind. He ran off and left me one time, but circled back to get me. "Keep up or you'll be lost without me. I can't keep stopping for you."

Shaking my head in a yes motion, I continued on with the run. After getting to the gym, he and the trainer worked me until I could barely move. With such an intense workout, we finally finished and walked those three miles back. Alex was still full of energy. As we walked up the driveway, there were about six cars parked there. I looked at Alex and then looked at the cars. He just walked past me and opened the door.

Walking into the door, there stood about eight men standing there naked. Alex put on my Bone Gag Head Harness and motioned for me to strip off my clothes. I did as I was told.

Walking over to this table with Alex, he ordered, "Bend over this table and stretch your arms out."

I did as I was told. He put handcuffs on my arms and then shackled them to the table. Alex sat out a container with gold packets of condoms in them. He pulled my hair as one of the guys wrapped up with a condom and entered me quickly. I felt relieved as he began stroking. I wanted to throw it back, but I couldn't move as much with my arms stretched out like that.

He fucked and fucked, until I thought he was never going to finish. As he came, he slapped the head of his dick on my ass cheek. Another guy mounted me; he was kind of soft. It was like he was making love to me, then he began throwing his hips from side to side, pushing against my walls. It hurt in a way, but was feeling good all at the same time.

Hours passed and my pussy was feeling dry. I was already tired from exercising. One of the men poured baby oil on my ass and he used his fingers to rub it on my pussy. He rammed me quickly and fucked me even harder, pushing me and the table forward. I moaned out beyond the harness. I moaned loudly as he punished me with no mercy. The next guy did the same and the next. When they finished fucking me stupid, it was around three o'clock in the afternoon. Alex yelled out, "Fellows, it's three p.m., come back around seven and there will be a round two. She will be ready by then. I'm giving her a break to eat, piss and shit or whatever the fuck she needs to do to keep that pussy wet."

The men didn't say a word but left out. Alex walked away from the table, leaving me there. A few minutes later, he returned with the handcuff key to unlock me. As soon as he did, I fell to my knees with exhaustion. He grabbed me by the hair softly and dragged me to the kitchen. I screamed out beyond the harness. Sitting on the floor in the kitchen, Alex took off the Bone Gag Head Harness and he sat my plate down on the floor next to me. I began eating and eating like a hungry dog.

"Slow down before you make yourself sick. Those men are coming back to fuck you again. You will get what you deserve. You want to be fucked then I will give you that, but you won't be fucking me. When you start obeying, I will fuck you, touch you, and do whatever you desire."

I didn't say a word but slowed down eating as he had demanded me and finished my food. He gave me bottles of water to drink. After I sat there with a full stomach for a few minutes, Alex returned back to the kitchen and pulled me up. He walked me to the bathroom where the tub was filled with water. "Get in and soak. You're going to need it for later on."

Nodding, I did as told. Sitting down, I felt so good. He walked out of the bathroom as I laid back and closed my eyes. I was tired and sleepy. I thought, *when am I going to sleep? I need rest. He has punished me and this is still not enough? What else is there? I had to prepare to be fucked again for hours mentally and physically.*

Seven o'clock came and only four men showed up, but they began fucking me immediately. Alex didn't tie or handcuff me, but he did put back on the Bone Gag Head Harness. One of the men fucked me in the missionary style for a while, until another man was ready. He pushed my head towards the other guy for him to fuck my mouth. Alex had left the room. They would fuck me and then toss me around to another guy. They tossed and fucked me until they were tired. By this time, five more guys had showed up. Alex let them run a train on me. He handcuffed me again and this time, tied my wrists with a rope, and then tied me up on the table. My pussy was sitting at the edge for them to fuck. I was in a very odd position. I had a man on each breast, sucking my nipples hard and biting me all over, while another fucked me. Some were biting harder than others. I began to cry as they punished my body. Pouring baby oil on my pussy to help me stay wet, the last guy that came in began fucking me. He didn't raw dog me, but took his time and pleasured me. I didn't think I had any cum left in my body, but he brought it out of me. He stroked and stroked me while massaging my clit. My body began shaking and I came on his cock. He was moving in and out very slowly, as he watched his cock turn whiter with cum. After he came, a few more guys were still hard, and they fucked until they got off.

Clearing out the house, Alex untied me and walked off. I eased off the table with a sore pussy, now standing on the floor. I took off the Bone Gag Head Harness myself and placed it on the table. Getting on my knees, I crawled to the cage and got in laying myself down. I was so exhausted that I quickly went to sleep. Damn I was tired.

I couldn't remember what day it was. I wanted to ask, but that would go against everything. After exercising, nobody was there when I got home. That was a relief. I was hoping that he would take a nap so that I could too, but he didn't. *That didn't surprise me though*, I thought as I smiled to

237

myself.

Alex didn't let me shower, but strapped on the Bone Gag Head Harness, and he put me across one of the bondage tables in Pillar's Dungeon and tied me. My back was exposed. Alex grabbed one of the Tomcat Tail Whips, and walked slowly over to me. I tried to follow him as he stood behind me.

"This is going to hurt me as much as it hurts you," he said as he cracked the whip across my back. He didn't hit me hard, but it wasn't soft either. My pussy was so dry that I didn't get wet. My body was like going into shock from all this he was putting me through. Alex raised the whip and hit me over and over until I cried, begging through the harness. If I remember correctly, this Tomcat Tail Whip is supposed to offer a nice stinging sensation when struck against the skin, not this. He whipped me as if I were a child. He hit me across my ass, my back, and my legs. After the intense ass whipping, he began biting me all over my body. He didn't actually hurt me, he was just barely pulling the skin. I was already hurting from those men biting down on me. They didn't take it slowly.

After a few minutes passed by, Alex walked in front of

me with this butt plug. It had a long, blonde silky tail that swayed from the base of the plug. I read about that, it was designed to stay in place. The anal butt plug will keep you stuffed, while you walk around for your dominant as the tail brushes gently against your legs. Grabbing some water-based lubricant, he walked to the back of me and spread it on my ass. It stung a little, but I guess that was from the whelps he placed on me. Alex stuck his finger in my ass, moving in and out. I clenched as he did that. "If you don't relax, it will hurt worse. See, you don't listen."

I moved my head in and up and down motion, saying that I do listen. Trying to relax myself, I felt him pushing the butt plug in my ass. He didn't care that I moaned out, he just pushed until it was in place. I relaxed after it was all done, but going in was a mutherfucker. My heart rate had speeded up and my palms were sweaty. Damn, I'm glad that's over with.

After whipping me some more while this anal butt plug was still in my ass, Alex untied me. I stood up and he took off the Bone Gag Head Harness. We went to the kitchen to eat. I had to stand as he sat down to eat. He continued to let me eat everything I wanted that was there. Soon after eating,

I continued to walk around and clean up. I was happy that damn harness was not around my mouth. It made my mouth dry and I was so thirsty. At the end of the day, Alex eased the butt plug out of my ass. He helped me move the steel puppy cage into the garage. I cleaned the house from top to bottom and sanitized the sex toys. I was tired.

Later on that night around ten, Alex took me by the hand and sat me down on our bed. Seemed like months since I slept in my own bed.

"Starting now, you can talk to me again, princess. I need to know; do I really have your attention?

"Yes, master, you have my attention," I replied.

"I am serious. Do I really have your attention?"

"Yes master, you have my attention."

"I hope you don't ever forget this punishment. If you disobey me again, I won't ever come back to get you. Do you understand that?"

"Yes, master, I understand," I replied. I wanted to ask him why he didn't think leaving me a month in Georgia was harsh enough, but I didn't. I just wanted to rest. I felt too tired and exhausted.

We went to bed and he held me for the first time in a long time. He held me so tight that I thought I was going to suffocate. His body language told me that he missed me as much as I missed him.

SIAM'S THOUGHTS

I really don't know what to think but I am happy that it's over with. My punishment is finally over. Hopefully, he return to the man I fell in love with. When I said that I wanted a dominant/submissive relationship, I had no idea it would be like that. He had already warned me that we would fuck other people, but we both would participate. I must have gone to the wrong websites reading up on this shit. It's totally different once you actually get into the lifestyle. I guess the ones wrote those articles, experiences were different, some good, some bad.

As I continued to lay in Alex's arms, I began rubbing his arm and kissing it. I wanted him to know that I didn't hold him countable for anything that happened to me, I deserved it all. Keeping his love and affection from me for so long made me realize that I didn't want to lose this man. He was put in my life for a reason. I shouldn't be pushing him to inflict pain on me. He gave just that but the pain of not living him isn't what I was talking about. The experience I went through taught me a lesson: If I don't do as I am told, then I couldn't have him.

Planting a few more kisses on his arm, I thought I was going to fall asleep, but Alex stuck his hands between my legs and rubbed my clit. Then moving to my breasts, he caressed them gently. I still ached from the bite marks, but his touch was inviting. A few moments into all the teasing, Alex entered my pussy gently. After all that fucking, I could have waited days from now. But, I opened my juicy wet pussy and let him make love to me. He didn't get carried away and pound me like a mad man, he made love to me. We stroked and stroked, meeting each other's thrust. Alex continued to caress my body and massage my breasts. My back began to hurt, but him going deeper took my mind away, as he grabbed my neck and choked me lightly. That made me bust right on his cock. He exploded right behind me. We laid there and fell asleep with his cock still in me until it went limp, easing out of me,.

CHAPTER 13

Alex woke me up with a boner. He just slid back in and worked me. We fucked like rabbits this time. Pussy pounding, cock ramming, just straight raw fucking. The house was cool and my nipples stood tall as I welcomed my master into me. He tossed me over, putting me in the missionary position as he slapped cock in and out of me. I held my legs back so he could give me more, until my insides started hurting. Wrapping my legs around his hips, I slowed him down. Flipping me back over on my stomach, he slid in my wet pussy and dug deep. I slightly lifted my hips, like that thick girl did that night as he pounded away. I lifted my head backwards as he planted kisses on my forehead. He began breathing loudly and I moaned out with pleasure, as he busted his nut then collapsed next to me. I smiled at him and he smiled back.

We took a shower together and got dressed. "Can I talk?" I whispered, hoping I didn't violate the rules again.

"Yes, princess. Today will be a safe day for us, but the rules still stand," he blurted out before I interrupted.

"Thank you, because I need a safe day. I want to talk

about everything that has gone on between us."

"I know you do, princess. That's why I suggested it."

"I do have a question right before we eat breakfast and go on about our day," I added as I turned to face him.

"Ask me anything."

"Do you really love me? Or am I here just for the dominant/submissive relationship you crave for?"

"You do know that's two questions in one?" he laughed out loud.

"Yes, I know."

"Yes, I love you so much that it drove me crazy when you were away from here. I cried some nights because I felt stupid for punishing you like that. But you had to learn to obey me. I don't care if I am in the next room—obey," Alex explained, as he walked away from me.

"That's it? You don't have anything else to say?"

"I mean, my love for you has become obsessive and as far as the dominant/submissive relationship; I love it, but that's not why you are here. The question is: are *you* here just for the dominant/submissive relationship?"

"The feeling is mutual. I've craved the dominant/submissive relationship for so long, that's all I seem to want." I tried to explain as best as I could, without him feeling some type of way.

"So, you don't love me? You're just here because of what I can give you?" he harshly spoke.

"I do love you. Don't ever say that I don't. Do you know how long I cried and felt depressed when you magically disappeared out of my life? Promise me that you won't ever do that again."

"Princess, I really can't promise you that, because if you disobey me again, I will be forced to leave you again. It's up to you if you want to do the right thing, because you know what it takes to keep me and what it takes to get rid of me."

"I read an article, that punishment is a hard limit and a submissive shouldn't have to go through that."

"Princess, I really wish you'd stop reading all these fucking articles. It is only on the internet. Some of that shit is not real. Only the people that have experienced it knows exactly what they are talking about, and those who have written articles and have experienced a relationship like ours, is totally different from anyone else. You can't say that the person who wrote one of the articles you read has a relationship like ours. Our shit is totally different. So, stop throwing it in my face about all of these articles you have read," Alex snapped as he fixed a bowl of cereal and fruit.

"I didn't know that it would offend you, about the articles that I read, but I wanted to be prepared for our relationship once we met in person. But I see it's a problem and that I should have never read anything," I talked back.

"That smart mouth of yours will never get you anywhere and just because this is a safe day, does not necessarily mean you are safe. I just want you to open up and talk to me, without all of that smartness," he remarked.

"I don't mean to be smart with you. I just want you to know exactly how I feel and those thirty days that you left me unattended was very harsh and painful for me to go through. I don't want to experience that again. And now, you're telling me that it might happen again if I don't obey you? What if I want to be bad?"

"You can be bad when you want in the bedroom, but outside of the bedroom, you need to obey the rules. Do we need to go back over the rules so that you understand what I am talking about?" he asked as I fixed myself a bowl of cereal and we sat down to eat.

"I don't want to go over the rules again, because I know them like the back of my hand, I say and rattle them off.

Rule #1 – Do not engage in any conversation with another man, unless it's business.

Rule #2 – Never be disobedient or I will be punished severely and not the way that I like.

Rule #3 – Bar and Clubs are prohibited, unless accompanied by my master.

Rule #4 – I shall incorporate a sexual attitude and hunger in everything I do.

Rule #5 – I shall offer parts of my body to those selected by my master.

Rule #6 – Lying is prohibited.

Rule #7 – I don't own my Master, he owns me.

Rule #8 – When sitting, I shall sit up straight with my legs together and my palms down on my thighs.

Rule #9 – I am Master's girl. He will protect and nurture me.

I freely give myself to him.

Rule #10 – I worship my master's cock. I will beg to suck it and pleasure it. I live to serve all of my master in any way.

Rule #11 – Whenever master walks into a room I am in, I shall kneel on both knees. If not able to do so, physical contact is a must or direct eye contact.

Rule #12 – The home is to be kept clean at all times. Neatness, cleanness, and being organized is a must.

Rule #13 – I must ask for permission to do any activity not involving my master.

Rule #14 – Write a one-page letter on pain and how I truly feel.

Rule #15 – If I am sent to another dominant, I will serve him and his submissive. No questions asked.

Rule #16 – I am free to leave my master at any time, without the fear of permanently losing him.

Rule #17 – When standing, I shall keep my legs and feet together. Both hands behind my back and my head bowed, unless otherwise ordered by master.

Rule #18 – My body shall be kept clean at all times. No body hair. Manicure my nails. Pedicure my feet. This routine will happen every week, including exercise. When my period is on, I get to relax those days unless otherwise ordered.

Rule #19 – I must never tighten my body when whipped,

slapped, belted, spanked, bullwhipped, caned, or paddled. No tightening during anal or vaginal sex.

Rule #20 – I will not display any anger or fighting behavior towards master. There are safe days to express that, but no hitting because if I do, he will hit me back.

Rule #21 – Never show disrespect towards Master, no matter if I am in his presence or not.

Rule #22 – My limits do not have to be respected. My master's intensity is all that matters, except when he feels like a need for my intensity.

Rule #23 – Master is allowed to own more than one slave. I will accept that and live with it.

Rule #24 – There is one safe word. Otherwise, safe talks are allowed on master's term. I am just his slave.

Rule #25 – Realize that I am a slave. I am my master's greatest treasure.

"I see that you do know the rules. That means you will not disobey me again. Once I tell you to do something, that's exactly what I mean do it and shut the fuck up."

"Yes, Master, I will obey the rules. I will do anything you command me to do inside and outside of the bedroom, but you do know that most of those rules aren't enforced. Seems like once I moved here, you became different in a way," I angrily spoke as I got quiet and ate my cereal in peace.

Alex looked at me and laughed. "So, you wanted a safe day so that you could be angry at me all day and we not have fun? As far as the rules, they are enforced. I just don't have you saying them out loud, but I can start."

"How are we supposed to have fun if we are stuck in this house all day, every day just fucking, sucking, licking each other's ass and that's it?" I snapped back as I held my head down. I didn't want to look up and see that stone face.

"So, that's all you seem to think we do around here? If you are miserable with me, then leave. I don't want you here if you don't want to be here," he stated as he got up and attempted to walk out.

"So, you're going to walk away from the conversation just like that? It's like you don't care about me, only yourself. Leaving me by myself is not what I want. I didn't spend a year or so on this relationship to be back at square one," I blurted out as I ran out into the living room behind him. Alex was high on my trail as I jumped down on the couch and began crying like a baby. He stood there for a few minutes and watched me, then sat down next to me, placing his hand in my back.

"I care for you and your feelings. Our love for each other will never die. It's like we are obsessed with each other. It's like an addiction to me. I just can't get enough of you." He looked at me then added, "Stop crying, princess. Please." Alex begged.

"I don't know how to feel. One moment we are in love and the next moment, you are punishing me. If you're talking about the club Zoey and I went to, it was nothing," I explained as I sat up and wiped my eyes.

"But I told you not to go nowhere."

"All I do is stay in the house all the time. These walls are closing in on me."

"I know how you feel. That's why today I wanted a safe day for us, so we can go out and have fun. I don't want you to be stuck in the house being depressed and mad at me. Right now, you are showing me just how angry you really are."

"I'm not angry. I didn't know that I would be spending all my time with you in the house. Are you ashamed of me?"

"I'm not ashamed of you, princess. Don't ever think that."

"God forbid if I fucked another man without your consent. I would really be out the door," I snapped out of nowhere. Alex stopped talking for a few seconds.

"Let's be real, princess. If you had fucked another man without my consent, you both would be laid up in the hospital by now, with all kinds of broken bones or perhaps dead somewhere." Alex threatened as he looked at me seriously. He added, "When I said you were mine, that's what I meant. You are mine. I own you."

"Yes, master, you own me. I agreed to it and I have to accept that."

"Truth be told, you don't have to accept it."

"Yes, I do have to accept it. I agreed and that's what I want to do. I want you to own me," I agreed as I stopped my tears.

"Face it, princess, we love each other deeply and neither one of us want to be apart from each other."

"I agree, master."

"Is there anything else, princess, you want to get off your chest?"

"Yes."

"Well of course it is," he agreed with a big smile on his face.

"Why did you let them men have their way with me like that? We said we would do stuff together like that. You let them fuck me like savages while you were in another room.

They hurt me, Alex. They hurt me," I softly spoke.

"I thought you wanted other men, like I want other women. We agreed, princess, before you moved here. You were excited about that."

"I'm still happy about that. What happened the other day was me, all alone..." I trailed off.

"That's what you saw, me walking off. I was in the other room getting serviced by men too."

"Serviced how?"

"Do I really need to spell it out for you? Men were sucking my cock and I fucked them in the ass."

"I didn't know that. Why didn't you just do it in the room with me? I wanted you there to feel safe and protected. But you left me unprotected with those savages," I replied as I looked down at the floor.

"I never meant to make you feel unsafe. I guess it bothered me so much the first time I was with a man around you, that I didn't want you to feel uncomfortable and think I was unmanly."

"I rather you be in the room with me fucking another man or woman, than to leave me unprotected. I really thought they were going to hurt me when you walked out."

"Damn it, princess, you should have said something. I was just teaching you a lesson. I promise from this day forward, I will keep you safe. I am here to protect you from any harm," he promised as he pulled me to him and I placed my head on his shoulder.

"I won't ask about the whipping because I asked to feel that pain. I don't want permanent marks," I confessed.

"I should have taken care of you after all those events you went through, but I refused."

"It's called the aftercare," I interrupted.

"Let me guess, articles," he chuckled.

."Of course," I giggled.

We laughed at each other and then headed out on our day.

Our first stop was at this place called Devonian Gardens located on 317 7th Avenue, South West on the 4th floor in the CORE Shopping Centre. This urban oasis was on the only indoor park in Calgary. There were so many tropical plants and plenty of natural light, many walkways led the people past water fountains, and over tree-decked plaza to ponds teaming up with fish. There was an attraction they called a "living wall" within the Devonian Gardens. Alex and I took a lot of pictures with each other. It felt so good to finally have a relationship I craved.

After taking pictures, he gave me a pamphlet of Devonian Gardens. The park featured over 500 trees, 50 varieties of plants, and of course, the 900 sq. ft. living wall. We saw several families having birthday parties. Children were playing on the playground, not giving a care in the world. I really enjoyed myself, looking at all the trees and plants.

As the day proceeded, Alex took me to the Glenbow Museum on 130 9th Avenue, Southwest. It was located in the heart of downtown Calgary, between Stephen Avenue and the Olympic Plaza Cultural District. Alex explained that Glenbow Museum is never the same place twice. They were known for traveling exhibitions from around the world, as well as some intriguing displays curated from the Museum's collections. New tours are developed throughout the year for all rotating feature exhibitions, such as the Blackfoot Gallery Tours and the Mavericks Tours. During our visit, we went to see the JUNO Tour of Canadian Art. The Canadian Art projects pairs great Canadian music with great Canadian art. It was great. I had never been to a museum like this one before. Perhaps a dinosaur museum, but nothing like this.

After those two tours, we decided to get something to eat before we proceeded with our day. We walked back to the CORE Shopping Centre and ate at the Metropolitan Grill. This nice restaurant was a premium casual dining establishment, committed to giving their guests a well-deserved dining experience. Alex ordered the Creole chicken and prawns, which was chorizo-stuffed chicken supreme, ocean wise grilled spiced prawns, with seasonal vegetables, buttered mashed potatoes, and lemon butter sauce. I ordered the Crispy Salmon, which was seared, skin-on salmon with butternut squash, dried cranberries, goat cheese and quinoa salad including butter sauce. I just had to try the lobster mac and cheese too. It had butter-poached lobster, with white truffles, smoked bacon, wild mushrooms, and smoked gouda.

After we stuffed our faces, we got in the car and drove to the Calgary Zoo on Zoo Road.

"Sir, I see it's getting late, so can we go to the aquarium instead of the zoo? I want to see the sharks." I asked as he parked.

"Why you didn't tell me that before?" he laughed.

"I didn't know that we were coming here. You're keeping everything a secret."

"I'm not being secretive, princess, I just wanted to surprise you and make sure that you enjoy your day. I want to apologize to you for keeping you shut up in the house like that. I guess I wasn't thinking. I figured for the first few months, you would want to be with me and learn about each other. Explore each other sexual appetites and other stuff," he explained as he held my face in the palm of his hand.

"That's exactly what I want to do, but I want to get out too. Just seemed like those walls were coming together. I hadn't even spent any time outside without exercising. I just want to enjoy you and the life here."

"I know, princess, and I will do better by you."

"Same here, Alex. I want the same as you."

"What do you want?" he asked, trying to get me to say it.

"I wanted to do better by you. Pleasure you in every way and be the woman you will never let go," I replied as leaned over and gave me a kiss on the lips.

"Let's go to the aquarium; it's not that far from here. Well, maybe," he joked as he started the car. Then he added, "I just thought about it, if you want to see the sharks, then we would have to go to Toronto, to Ripley's Aquarium of Canada. We can go Franco's Aquarium. It has a lot of beautiful fish, but no sharks. The one in Toronto had everything you want to see."

"Well let's go to Toronto to that one."

"Well, you get ready for a long drive, because it's thirty-three hours from here," he laughed as he looked at the expression on my face.

"Thirty-three hours. Wow, I don't think I'm ready for that

trip." I laughed too as I grabbed onto the door handle.

"Where are you about to go without me?" Alex asked as he looked at my hand.

"If it's that far away, then we might as well go in here. I mean, you brought me here and I want to enjoy it. We can always visit the aquarium in Toronto."

"Princess, if you want to go to Franco's, we can go."

"That's okay. I rather see what type of animals they have here. The zoo in Georgia wasn't that much fun, but of course, I have been there all my life so the animals looks the same. No change in scenery or nothing," I joked.

"Let's go in and look around." He motioned as he turned the car back off and we got out walking inside.

"I'm so excited," I said, clapping my hands together like a little kid.

"You know, the Toronto Zoo in Ontario, Canada has one of the largest zoos up here. It has about five thousand animals from four hundred and sixty species from all around the world. You can go on camel rides and touch the stingrays there."

"Why is everything in Toronto? We can't go there. Do they have grizzly bears here? I would love to see one up close," I asked.

"Yes, they do. There are grizzly bears and black bears," he replied to my question as we stood in this long line, trying to get in.

"How do you know so much about Toronto? I thought you were originally from Calgary?" I asked, being nosey.

"I was born in Toronto. We moved here when I was ten. My parents used to take Codie, my brothers, John and Jack, and me everywhere. During the summers, it was all about vacations. What about you and your family?" he asked as he motioned for me to move forward.

"We went on summer vacations too, but mostly to visit family in Mississippi and Florida."

"Family everywhere I see."

"Just about; we have a big family. I don't visit everywhere or keep in touch with them like I should. Do you have cousins, aunts, uncles? You haven't mentioned any of them," I asked.

"My mother has four brothers and two sisters. Father has one brother, one sister. There are plenty of cousins, I just don't have time to be with them all."

"Why not?"

"Why don't you?" he chuckled.

"I don't know why I don't, but maybe I should. But honestly, after I got out of high school, I went straight to the police academy. So, I really didn't have much time."

"I am always working my butt off. It has taken me over ten years to get the life I want right now. It's complete, now that I have you in my life. I can't believe that I have found someone who truly loves me for me and not because of the dominant/submissive relationship," he spoke as he looked at the expression on my face. Deep down, that's exactly what I only wanted, but his love was addictive too. He could be a real charmer once he wasn't in dominant mode.

"I understand that," I replied without saying anything else. I felt like he wanted me to say more, but I couldn't. Reality was, that's exactly what I wanted from him.

Entering the zoo, we grabbed a brochure and began

looking through it. "Wow, they have tigers here. I'm so excited."

"They have Amur tigers, red pandas, the grizzly bear, the black bear, and you won't believe it."

"What?"

"They have a Western African dwarf crocodile."

"Really? Does that mean the crocodile is short?"

"Yes. It is the smallest extant of the crocodile species."

"I am ready to see. Let's go," I replied as I grabbed his hand and we ran off.

As we walked through the zoo, we walked up on the grizzly bears. They were laid out like the tigers. I could see that they were very large. One of them would probably swallow me whole. Continuing through the zoo, we looked at the gorillas and other animals. The last on the list was the African dwarf crocodile. He is much smaller than the crocodiles I've seen before. I stayed there gawking at him, until Alex motioned for me to keep it moving.

Finally ending our day, we made it back home. I was

feeling exhausted, but Alex seemed like he wanted to talk. Sitting down in the house, he looked to me and asked, "Do you want to continue our safe day?" We can do this for a week and then if you want to go back to our dominant/submissive relationship, we can do that."

"Sounds good to me. Will we continue to use the toys and stuff like that?"

"We can use them on each other. But no other parties will be involved, just us. I just want to see how things would be."

"I understand," was my remark as I looked down at the floor.

"You don't want to continue our safe day for a week's time?"

"I will do anything for you, sir."

"I want you to want to do it too. This works for the both of us, not just me. I'm not in this relationship alone."

"Yes, I want to try it."

"Great, let's do it."

****** *A Week Later* ******

I was really about to lose my fucking mind. Alex was acting like he was so in love that it made me kind of sick. He didn't try to dominate me at all. He just wanted to hold me and just make love. I wanted him to ram his cock in my pussy and make me scream. I wanted to feel the pain I knew he could give me. He made my pussy cum, but not like I wanted to do as the pain hit my body. I craved that pain and he wasn't giving it to me. Damn him for not satisfying me.

"We need to talk," I stated as Alex came home from his parents' house. I didn't want to go because I was so sexually frustrated. I had to get myself off most of the time. A lack of sex was killing me.

"What's wrong, princess?"

"It has been a week now and I want to go back to our original dominant/submissive relationship."

"I thought you were happy with us being like we are."

"Don't get me wrong, I am happy being like this, but I want that ownership over me. I want you to own me, to possess me, to tell me what to do. I crave it. Please don't take it away from me. I thought you said this is what you wanted too."

"It is what I want, but I don't want to share you anymore. I've fallen so deep in love with you that I'm going insane."

"You've had so many other submissives, besides me. What happened to them? Really? Did you fall in love and stopped the dominant/submissive relationship?"

"I told you the truth about them. I did go too far and hurt a couple of them. Emily is the only one who died," he expressed as he looked to the floor.

"When did she die?"

"She died a few months before I met you. I vowed that I wouldn't hurt another woman, but you bring it out of me and like I said before, I don't want to go too far with you. You're the only one that has captured my heart like this."

"If I had known she had died just months earlier, I wouldn't have talked to you."

"Why not?"

"Because you really haven't had time to heal."

"I'm over her. I am healed."

"No, you're not healed," I expressed.

"I'm in love with you and nobody can change that. I want us to be together forever and always. I can't help that I'm in love and don't want to share you."

"You mean you don't want me to fuck anyone else but you. I thought we agreed to this before I came up here."

"Is that all you want from me? Tell me," he harshly spoke.

"That's not all I want, but a good majority of me does. I don't know if I can continue to be with you, if you don't. I hate to say that to you, being that you told me that the other women wanted only the dominant/submissive relationship," I confirmed.

"I figured that's what you wanted too. You're basically just like them. You don't want to be loved. You want a mutherfucker to beat your ass and control you," he angrily fussed.

"Don't curse me. You said you wanted me to tell you the truth and I did. Why are you so angry with me right now?"

"Because I just told you that I wanted to be with you and no other woman, but you insist on fucking other men. You don't want to love only me. But if that's what you want, I will do it," he insisted as he got up to walk off.

"Don't walk off. Are you serious right now?" I expressed as I began to get mad at him. I came to Canada totally on the fact we would have this dominant/submissive relationship.

"I'm not serious, Siam. I just wanted to see what you would say," he implied as he walked out of the room with a smile on his face. Something told me that he really wanted to stop this dominant/submissive relationship. The conversation didn't set well with me. He was backing out without coming out to tell me.

SIAM'S THOUGHTS

As I soaked in the tub, the conversation with Alex kept playing over and over in my head. He was dead serious about ending this dominant/submissive relationship we had. I didn't understand him. When we first met, he was controlling and dominant, which turned me on. And now, he is ready to fall in love and forget it. Would I stay with him and continue being a couple, or would I go if I didn't get that dominant/submissive relationship? It was tearing me about which way to go. Why all of a sudden, did he want this? The way he fucked those girls that night, he was definitely into other pussy. And the experiences he has with other men? I just don't see how in the hell he would let that go, especially being with a woman who doesn't mind it. Something didn't seem right about that. I wondered if he was having a relapsed from that Emily girl. Maybe I should talk to his mother or sister and find out. Then it hit me; shit, I haven't texted or called my mother. She's probably pissed off with me. It was strange that I haven't heard from my father either. Alex gave me access to my phone twenty-four hours a day. I couldn't tell them before that I only had my phone at a certain time.

Getting out of the tub, I put on one of Alex's shirts and proceeded to bed. He was already in bed asleep. I cuddled up next to him and went to sleep.

ALEX'S THOUGHTS

What if Siam leaves me because I don't want the dominant/submissive relationship anymore? I threw it out there for her, but the look on her pretty face tell me that I might lose her if I didn't continue. The conversation replayed over in my head. Something told me not to stop the dominant/submissive relationship, because if I did she was going to leave me.

CHAPTER 14

After our daily routine of exercising, we had a doctor's appointment to get physicals. Alex was pushing for us to get checked out before we moved forward with our relationship. To me, he should have thought about that shit from the beginning of the relationship, when I moved to Canada with him. He claims that he wanted to see if I was okay. The truth be told, with all the people we had fucked, he must've had some concerns. I figured everything was good because he was the one who knew these people, not me. Seems like he wouldn't fuck someone he didn't trust, but in this day in time and having orgies, you never know what is going on with other people.

"Are you going to tell me the truth about why we are going to the doctor?" I asked Alex as we drove downtown to his doctor's office.

"The truth about what?"

"Why you are so determined to get me to the doctor's office? I haven't been irritated down there or having any type of discharge. Everybody used condoms we had sex with. I figured you knew those people," I stated with concern.

"No, that's not it. I just want to make sure that you and I are healthy, but the doctor is going to check for all of that. This isn't about you, it's about us. Do you trust me, princess?"

"Of course, I trust you, sir. I wouldn't have come all this way if I didn't trust you. I just wanted to make sure this was about us, and not me. You had me fucking all these people I have no clue about, so I figured you knew them," I responded.

"I do know all of them. I wouldn't invite people to my home that I didn't know. I have dealt with all of them at some point in my life. So, don't think I'm just letting you fuck random people," he stated, as we pulled up at the doctor's office and entered.

We went in and we went straight to the back. That was the first time I ever went in a doctor's office and immediately went to the back.

"Hello, Ms. Siam," a handsome young black man said as he walked in with muscles piercing through his coat.

"Hello, Sir."

270

"Call me Dr. Billards."

"Okay, Dr. Billards," I softly spoke, while getting all hot over this man. He had a low haircut and his skin was so smooth and beautiful.

"Now that we've introduced ourselves to each other, we can proceed with the doctor visit."

"Great, but I would like to let you know that I'm not from Canada. I'm from Atlanta, Georgia," I replied.

"That's cool. The nurse is going to come in and get some information from you. I just need to get your medical records before I proceed. You don't have to worry about insurance because Mr. Tremblay is paying in cash."

"I think he is," I replied hoping that he was, because I didn't have any type of medical, dental, or vision insurance. It didn't hit me until Dr. Billards mentioned it.

"Yes, he is. I will return in a few," Dr. Billards stated as he walked out of the office.

A few minutes later an older white woman came to me and took my information. She then left the office. She didn't seem friendly and I didn't push it. I wanted to tell her ass to smile because that is better than frowning, but I just kept my peace.

After she left, I decided to text my mother:

Hey First Lady. How are things with you? I'm at the doctor's office getting a check-up. Alex insisted we get physicals every month.

Mother:

Siam, why are you at the doctor's office? Is something wrong? Are you pregnant?

Me:

No, mother. Neither one. Alex and I are just getting check-ups. How is father? I wish you would stop with the pregnancy stuff... LOL

Mother:

He is well. Planning a trip to Los Angeles for our vacation. We are going to miss you traveling with us this trip. Your brother, Charles, is too busy and you know your father don't deal with your brother, Dean.

Me:

I wish I could visit Los Angeles again. I had so much fun.

Mother:

Please tell me if anything is wrong with you, Siam. You can always come home. I know you don't want to hear it, but I'm at home 24/7, I can take care of you if something is wrong. I just threw it out there about you being pregnant.

Me:

Mother, really. I just said that I was fine. This is just a regular check-up, nothing more. Got to go, the doctor is coming back in.

Mother:

Take care and I love you, Siam.

Me:

I love you more, First Lady.

Putting my phone back into my purse, the nurse had appeared again. This time she took blood and urine from me, then disappeared again. Picking up the phone, I started looking through things on my Facebook page. Nothing but mess and drama, but there were a few good pictures of mother and father on there.

After about an hour, the doctor returned. "Ms. Siam, we still haven't received your paperwork back yet. I don't know what's taking them so long, but I have checked your bloodwork and everything looks great."

"That's a good thing. So, I don't have a disease or

273

anything that could kill me?" I joked. He smiled so big with those pretty white teeth.

"No ma'am, you have no diseases."

"And me being pregnant?"

"You're not pregnant either. From the looks of your bloodwork, you're a very healthy young lady. Did you have any type of complications or anything you want to tell me about?"

"No, I don't, but are you going to check me down below?" I snickered.

"Our Ob/Gyn is going to do that. Her name is Dr. Lyles. She will be in shortly, since you don't have any questions or concerns for me," he said as he shook my hand. Soon as he disappeared, the nurse returned.

"I need you to put on this gown. Make sure it's open in the front," she mumbled and walked out.

"Of course," I said to myself and I got undressed. Stripping off my clothes and putting on the gown, I felt a little draft. Looking up, the cold air was blowing directly on me. I held myself as Dr. Lyles and the older nurse entered the room.

"Hello, Ms. Wilson, I'm Dr. Lyles," she introduced herself. She was a redhead, with freckles all over her face. She seemed to be nice.

"Hey, Dr. Lyles. How are you?"

"I'm wonderful and yourself?"

"I'm great, once I finish all this."

"I know what you mean. I need you to lay back and put your feet in these stirrups." I did as she instructed.

After the examination, which was quick, Dr. Lyles asked as she examined me, "What type of birth control are you taking?"

"I was on the pill, but I don't have any more. I took my last one about two weeks ago."

"Do you remember what kind?" she asked.

"No, I don't. I just took them," I laughed.

She laughed too and told me, "Okay, well you can get dressed. I will make sure that you get more. Start taking the pills when your period comes on."

275

"Yes, ma'am. I will do that."

Both women left the room. I got dressed and the only thing on my mind was, I hope my pussy didn't look old. I tried to look at my pussy lips, smiling to myself.

Sitting down, the nurse returned and told me that everything looked great. She gave me the birth control pills in a bag with condoms.

Leaving out, I followed her until I got to the waiting room. Alex was already finished and waiting on me.

"How did things go?" he asked as he grabbed my hand and we walked out the door.

"Things went well. Dr. Lyles said that my paperwork from Georgia has not come in yet. And that, my bloodwork looks good. They checked my pussy and it was good too. I threw that in, just in case you wanted to know," I smiled.

"That's wonderful, mine too. But of course, I already knew that. I try to get by here at least once a month. I like to stay healthy."

"Once a month is a little too much. Maybe every three months," I remarked.

"You're silly. What do you have in the bag?"

"I have more birth control pills and condoms."

"Condoms?"

"Yes, condoms."

"Condoms?" Alex repeated again as we drove back to the house.

"Why do you keep saying condoms?" I smiled as I punched him lightly in the arm.

"Because we don't need condoms."

"No, we don't, but what about with other people? We should be almost use them for our guests. That would be safer, I think," I said hoping I didn't offend him.

"You're right. I don't want either one of us catching anything, but the people I encounter with are kept clean. We all use this doctor's office. Most of them, I met here," he stated.

"Really, how is that?"

"Long story."

"I have plenty of time to hear this long story," I remarked.

"No, you don't, because tonight we are having company."

"Who?"

"His name is Marvin."

"Marvin."

"Yes, Marvin. He is coming over to entertain us."

"Yes, sir." I smiled. I was very happy. Finally, we are getting some action. I was wondering about Alex for a minute. I still couldn't get over our conversation about him wanting to get out of the dominant/submissive relationship. He was a strong dominant and I liked that.

Later on that night, Marvin showed up. Alex had given me my black collar with the spikes back. He dressed me in another schoolgirl suit. I put on a solid black wig with two ponytails, and some black hanging earrings with the fishnet stockings. The stockings had the crotch missing. Alex said it was easy access to my pussy.

"Hello Marvin, come on in," Alex invited as he came in the door, staring at me. I was kneeling on the floor with my head held high. As soon as he moved closer to me, I had to put my head down. They say it was showing some type of respect to the dominant.

"Hey Alex. What a lovely surprise you have for me tonight."

"I figured you would love my surprise," he spoke as Marvin looked from me to Alex. They gave each other a hug. I began trying to peep, because the two were still hugging. I saw that Marvin had grabbed Alex's dick, massaging it. I thought to myself, *Damn, this must be Alex's night. If Marvin is gay, then I won't be getting fucked down no time soon.*

"Come to Pillar's Dungeon," Alex invited as the two men held hands and walked away. That was my cue to follow behind them.

"Your home is very lovely. Just like I remembered before. It's been a long time since you have invited me over here," Marvin stated as Alex opened the door to Pillar's Dungeon.

"I had been going through a lot with the criminal cases and things going on."

"Yeah, I did hear of the little trouble you got into."

"Yes, but that's over with."

I continued to listen, hoping they'd go into more details and shit, but they became quiet as Alex closed the door.

Alex guided me to the bed and laid me down on my back. He slid me to the end of the bed and my head hung off. Good thing that I had the wig tight on my head. That would have been ugly. As I lay hanging off the bed, Marvin had stripped off his clothes. Alex pulled out what looked like nipple clamps. He walked over to me, pulling down my small schoolgirl top and began placing the nipple clamps on my nipples. I didn't think it would hurt like that my first time, but damn. Those nipple clamps hurt in a bad way. I began to hold my breasts and Alex adjusted the nipple clamps.

"Siam, it's going to hurt at first, but you will get used to the pain. You love pain. Remember?" Alex mocked as he put on the other nipple clamp and I almost fell out. As Marvin walked over and pulled my head back, he hit my mouth with his dick. Just patting a couple of times, until I opened my mouth and I invited him in. As he slid his cock in and out of my mouth, it went deeper and deeper into my throat. That's the reason why Alex put me in that position, so I could take more and not try to hold back. Accumulating spit all over my mouth, Marvin took his dick out of my mouth and rubbed it across my lips. I licked out my tongue, teasing the head. He slammed his cock deeper as he squeezed my breasts with the nipple clamps. I thought it would hurt worse, but it didn't. Alex crawled on the bed and began licking my pussy. He was biting and sucking that clit softly; I almost came in his mouth. Sticking his fingers in my pussy, Alex began moving in and out, caressing that pearl tongue with his thumb.

Marvin massaged my breasts gently and I put my hands on his hips and guided him deeper into my mouth. Taking his cock out of my mouth, I began to play with it as he moved it across my face, slapping me with it. I didn't know whether to focus on him or Alex. They both were pleasing me like I had never been pleased before. I caressed Marvin's dick with my tongue, moving up and down as I sucked.

Alex stopped licking my pussy and walked over to one of the floggers. He came back and began flogging me across my stomach and pussy. The more he hit my pussy, the wetter I became. I moaned as Marvin slowly entered my mouth again and again.

After a few minutes, Marvin said, "I'm ready to fuck."

Alex moved out of the way and Marvin crawled on top of me. Marvin stood back on his knees as Alex put a condom on him. Then, Alex stood watching above me with his big cock hanging close to my mouth. Marvin pulled me onto the bed and mounted me missionary. Entering me, he began fucking me slowly and soft. Marvin started kissing me softly on my neck and my pussy was reacting to his every stroke. I placed my hands around his neck and invited him more into my body. I had completely forgot that Alex was standing there. Marvin and I were acting like a couple deeply in love. We thrust against each other and I moaned louder. My body was feeling some kind of way.

"Fuck me, please fuck me," I whispered as I held his body tighter. I pushed my head into his neck and began to kiss him back there.

"Do you want this cock?"

"Yes, I want you so much."

"Tell me."

"I want your cock. Fuck me please. I want you so deeply in me," I moaned as I rocked my hips pushing him deeper.

"That's right, fuck me back."

We continue to stroke at each other for a long time. I came at least four times. Marvin got off me and instructed, "Sit on my face. I want to see how that cum tastes."

I did as he told me, not even acknowledging Alex standing there, stroking his cock to our lovemaking. Marvin lay on the bed and I sat on his face. His tongue was so long and fat. He sure knew how to eat pussy. I moved back and forward as he ate me out. Alex moved closer to us and I grabbed his cock, stroking him. Marvin pulled on my pussy lips, bringing me to an explosion. My body began to shake and I moved slowly over his mouth as cum escaped my body. I had taken Alex's cock into my mouth and he was pushing his cock within my throat. I couldn't do him like I did Marvin, because he was much bigger.

After my escaped cum leaked out of my body, Marvin gently moved me off his head. Letting go of Alex's cock, Alex motioned for me to lay down on the bed. I did as ordered and he began licking me. Marvin got down on the floor and started sucking Alex's cock. He was taking that big dick easily. How could he possible take so much down his throat without the teeth scraping against him? As Alex licked my wet pussy, I leaned up on my shoulders. I wanted to see what all Marvin would do to Alex. Marvin moved to Alex's ass and began eating him out. Alex moaned as he continued to pleasure me, then he stopped. He was caught up in his ass being eaten out. I stuck my fingers in my pussy and rubbed. It was damn near dry, so I had to spit in my hand and lubricate it.

Marvin got up and put spit on his hand, then rubbed his cock. He entered Alex from the behind, opening his ass. Alex cried out as I watched with excitement. I was enjoying seeing two men fuck. It made me even hornier. Alex moved closer to me and began rubbing my stomach. He motioned towards my pussy and stuck his tongue in as Marvin pounded away. Sticking his fingers in my pussy, I moaned and groaned until my body was about to explode but stopped. I couldn't let go of that cum. It was like it was stuck. Moving my hips so that Alex could finger fuck me, there still no cum.

Finally, Marvin pulled out his dick and came on Alex's ass. He stood back admiring what he had done. Alex crawled onto the bed over me and pulled me upwards. He entered me with his still hard dick. We fucked like rabbits for a few minutes. Looking around for Marvin, I noticed that he was gone. Alex got up and spoke, "He is gone. He never stays around to say goodbye. He hates goodbyes."

"Oh okay," I replied as I lay back on the bed and stared at the ceiling. Alex left Pillars Dungeon, then returned a few minutes later. His dick was still hard.

I asked, "Can I fuck you?"

"Yes you can fuck me."

"I mean put on the Big Daddy Hollow Strap-On and fuck you."

Alex looked surprised that I would ask him to do that, but he didn't object. He grabbed the strap-on and brought it over to me. He helped me put it on. Alex went over and got the water-based oil.

After putting oil on the strap-on, Alex got on the bed on his knees with his ass held high. I stood at the edge of the bed. Motioning him to bend down so I could reach him, I slowly entered his ass. It was amazing how easy it slid in. But then again, Marvin did just slam him in the ass. As I moved in and out, I wanted more. Alex began throwing that ass back, I tried my best to give it back to him. I pounded him for the first time as he stroked his cock to cum. It felt good. Now, I see why when he is fucking me in the doggy style, he wants to push it deeper within me. That shit felt awesome.

After we finally came together, I cleaned up while he took a shower. Once he was finished, I showered and got into bed. My fucking nipples were hurting badly, but that was the most awesome thing I had ever felt. Seeing two men fuck, had me horny all over again. The thought of him fucking another man set me on fire. I wanted more.

ALEX'S THOUGHTS

I wondered how Siam really felt about fucking me in the ass. I loved the fact she fell into place and pleasured me like that. At first, I didn't know how I was going to convince her. I am completely convinced that she enjoyed fucking me as much as I enjoy fucking her. There are so many other things I wanted to explore with her. I finally found a woman who was willing to fuck me in the ass because she wanted to, not because I am making her do it. No matter what we did sexually, she seemed to join right on in. Maybe this dominant/submissive relationship is for me after all. Emily's dying was just a mistake. Siam could take way more pain than she could. From now on, it's me being the dominant and she being the submissive. No more having second thoughts about this shit.

CHAPTER 15

Alex was sitting on the couch as I sat on the floor by his feet, when suddenly, the doorbell rang out. It made the weirdest sound I ever heard. It reminded me of the music on *Sleeping with the Enemy* whenever he made love to Julie Roberts.

"That must be Codie." Alex sounded excited as he jumped up. I was happier than a gay man with a bag of cocks. I don't know why I thought of that statement, but my grandpa used to say it all the time before he died.

Alex opened the door, and Codie stood there with two black bags. "Come on in, girlie," Alex said as he gave her a big hug and took her bags. I wanted to jump up, but waited for Alex give me the nod. As he did, I jumped up and ran to her.

"Hey Codie. I am so happy to see you," I stated as we exchanged hugs.

"I'm so happy to see you too. Alex has been keeping you all to himself," she replied as she gave him another hug.

"You know I am always greedy," he added as he kissed

her on the cheek and walked out of the room.

"What brings you here with overnight bags?" I said, being nosey. Since I had been here, she has never come over to visit.

"Alex asked me to come and stay the night. I was shocked when he invited me."

"Really? Why you didn't text me and let me know you were coming?" I asked.

"Because we wanted to surprise you. I am so happy to spend time with you, " she hugged me again. She grabbed my hand and sat on the couch, I sat on the floor until Alex said otherwise. We had talked about our dominant/submissive relationship and he is in it full force. I think I pissed him off when I told him that I wanted to continue it this way. He was definitely trying to get out of it. I didn't know why, because I thought he loved the fact of owning me.

"Why are you on the floor? Come sit with me up here."

"How about you come sit on the floor with me? I like it better," I lied. That floor was hard as fuck, but that's what I wanted.

"Is that what you want or Alex told you to do that?" she snapped.

"Codie, sit your ass on the floor," I laughed as I pulled at her pants leg. She laughed and slid down on the floor next to me.

"See, it's not that hard."

"If you say so."

She put her arm around me and smiled. Something didn't seem right. It was the sad look in her face that gave her away.

"Are you alright?" I had to ask.

"Yes, I am great. Why did you ask that?

"Because you seem different from the very first time I met you. You're not happy."

"How do you know all that?"

"Girlie, I can see it. I used to be a police officer back in Georgia and I profiled a lot of people, even though we weren't supposed to. You're not the same person. I can sense

289

a little sadness," I replied as I moved her hair back from her face.

"You were a cop?"

"Yes, I was."

"And you let Alex treat you like crap," she shot back.

"He doesn't act that way all the time. Alex is very sweet. I truly love him," I defended him.

"That day he..." she trailed off with tears in her eyes.

I quickly responded, "That's over with. We can move past that."

"I thought he had run you off and you would never come back."

"It was a little embarrassing," I whispered as I turned around to see if he was coming back in the room. I put my hands to my lips, hushing her.

"I know it was, but I am glad you decided to stay here. Alex really loves you. He texts mom about you all the time. She doesn't tell me about what they talk about though."

"I didn't know that. I hardly ever see him with his phone,

except for when he is in the office working."

"Well, he does," she giggled.

"Enough about Alex, what about you? Are you going to tell me why you are so sad?"

But before she could respond, Alex walked back through the door. "What are y'all whispering about?"

"You must've been ear hustling if you knew we were whispering," Codie snapped as Alex sat down on the couch.

"Smart ass. Why are you on the floor?" he asked her.

"Because Siam is on the floor. Why can't she sit on the couch?" she snapped again. I wanted to bop on her the head for saying that.

"Because I told her to sit on the floor," he said, not hiding it at all.

"You're still that same controlling Alex as before. I thought you were changing after Emily died," she spoke as she looked in his face.

Ignoring the question, he said, "I thought you wanted to spend time with Siam, not drill me about my life."

"I was just asking a question. You really shouldn't treat her like that," she said as she began a full-blown cry. I was shocked and Alex moved closer, putting his hand on her head. I reached out and grabbed her. She fell over into my arms and cried. Alex and I didn't say a word. We just listened to her cry, until he went and brought back some tissue from the kitchen.

After a few more minutes of crying, he asked, "Are you okay? What's going on with you?"

"I didn't come over here about my problems. I am happy that you invited me," she explained as she cleaned up her face.

"Codie, stop fucking playing. What's wrong? Tell me now," Alex demanded as he raised his voice.

"It's nothing I can't handle myself."

"Apparently, you can't handle it yourself if you're crying. Tell me, Codie."

I kept looking from Alex to Codie. They sounded like Zoey and me.

"It's Chance. We got into a fight and he beat me up," she

mumbled as he looked to the ground.

"How did he beat you up?" Alex demanded an answer.

"We argued. I slapped him across the face and he began hitting me with his fist, punching me everywhere. And when you called, I just packed some bags and took off," she explained as more tears escaped down her red cheeks.

"Punched you?" he yelled as he stood up and pulled up off the floor.

"Here," she replied as she pulled up her shirt and bruises were everywhere. I immediately jumped off the floor staring at her. Her bruises were black and red. Her back was the worst. Seemed like when Chance beat Codie, her back was exposed.

"Damn it, Codie. I am going to kill that mutherfucker," Alex expressed his anger as he walked to the small table in the foyer and grabbed his keys.

"Alex, no. You can't get in any trouble because of me. Just leave it be," she yelled as he opened the front door and walked out. She ran behind him and I ran behind her.

"Go back in the house, Codie. Siam get her ass back in the

house," he screamed like I have never heard before.

"Alex, please don't go. Please, I need you here with me. Don't go," she called out and he stopped.

"I love you, Codie, and vowed to take care of you. I will find him. So, go in the house with Siam until I come back," he spoke as he entered the car and left.

"Alex. Alex," Codie called out, but Alex kept driving. We stood there until the car disappeared.

"I hope Alex doesn't find him. He will kill him."

"In that case, I hope he doesn't find him either. Let's get you back in the house," I stated as I took her by the arm and led her in the house.

"I just need a hot bath and to relax. It's been so much drama going on the past few days," Codie mumbled as we entered the bathroom and I began running her bath water.

"Do you want it hot or lukewarm?" I asked.

"Lukewarm is good. Hot water might blister me up more. I don't need that right now," she giggled.

"No, we don't need that."

"The water is ready," I stated as Codie stripped off and entered the tub. She didn't care if I was standing there, she just undressed.

"Thank you, Siam. This water feels so good," she said as she stuck her head under the water and come back up. Foaming bubbles were all in her face. I grabbed a small towel and tossed it to her.

I sat on the edge of the big garden tub and asked, "Why did Chance hit you?"

"Because I told him that I was pregnant," she muttered.

"He doesn't want a baby?"

"No, he doesn't. We have been together a little over a year. He says it's my fault."

"How is it your fault?"

"Because I want a child and I purposefully got pregnant. Please don't tell Alex I planned this. Promise me, Siam. He will beat my ass." She asked me to promise as she looked at me with those big pretty blue eyes like Alex's.

"I promise not to tell him as long as when it comes out—

because it will come out—he doesn't know that I knew about it," I said.

"I won't throw you under the bus, Siam, if that's what you're saying." She laughed.

"That's exactly what I'm saying." I pointed at her with a big smile on my face as well.

"I feel comfortable talking to you. When I first saw you, I prayed that Alex didn't run you off. He really has changed after Emily died. He just doesn't seem like the same Alex, except for the other night when we all had dinner at Mama's house."

"Can you please tell me what really happened to Emily? Every time I turn around, her name comes up. Is she really deceased?"

"Yes, Emily is dead. When she died, she was pregnant with Alex's baby. He didn't know about the baby until she was admitted into the hospital. Emily and I had become very close. She was a pretty, redheaded girl with green eyes. She was very short and had a pretty big smile, with some big ears." Codie giggled as she went down memory lane, describing Emily.

"Sounds like she was a very pretty girl. I didn't know that she was pregnant. Alex never mentioned that part," I whispered as I looked at the floor.

"He hasn't mentioned it to anyone. She was about six weeks pregnant."

"How did she die?"

Codie took a deep breath and mumbled, "From Alex."

"How?"

"She and Alex had a fight one day. Emily jumped in the car and ran off. Alex tried to stop her, but she was so headstrong about leaving. Later on that night, her mother called and said she was hit by another driver and was killed instantly," Codie explained as she lay back in the tub.

"Okay, when you said from Alex, I was thinking that he killed her by putting his hands on her, possibly beating her to death or something of that sort. The way he talks, it's like he murdered her himself."

"That's what he thinks because when they did fight that day, he beat her real bad. When she jumped in the car and pulled off, Alex told me that she was black and blue. He said he didn't mean to beat her that bad, but he did. Mama and I came over to comfort him and his fists were bloody, so that led us to believe she was bleeding. He claimed that he just blanked out and when he finally realized what he had done, he stopped."

"Does he blank out like that all the time? I have never noticed it."

"That's the only time I ever heard of them blanking out like he said he did. We can only go by his word."

"True. Nobody really knows but him and God. I hope that he is alright," I said to her.

"I do too. Chance always carries a gun on him. Those two might kill each other."

"I hope not. I want Alex in my life forever. I don't want to lose him, not now, not ever."

"You must really love Alex?" she asked as she watched the expression on my face.

"I love him more than I love myself. He is the man I have been waiting for such a long time. He is a loving and caring person."

"Controlling too," she laughed.

"Yes, that too, but I don't mind the controlling. That's what I need in my life."

"Siam, really? Or did Alex brainwash you to think that's what you need?" she laughed again.

"I told him that's what I wanted."

"Girl, really?"

"Yes, really," I stated with a serious look on my face.

"You're dead serious."

"Yes, I'm dead serious. I don't mind the controlling and telling me what to do."

"I didn't think black girls would go for something like that," she laughed.

"I'm not like most black girls," I laughed too as I put my hand in her water and tossed it at her back.

We both began laughing and continued talking a little more, before she decided to get out. She wrapped herself in a towel and dried off. We walked to the guest bedroom and she got dressed. After about an hour of waiting on Alex to come home, we went to bed. I slept in the bed with Codie, since she didn't want to be alone.

"Do you ever miss your parents?" she asked as we lay in the bed, looking at the ceiling.

"I miss them all the time. My mother gets on to me for not calling or texting her every day."

"Girl, I can't go a day without talking to my mama. She would hunt me down and beat me if I didn't."

"My mother would too. She's just not close enough," I laughed.

"I know what you mean. I couldn't stay gone from my mama long periods of time. I would miss mama so much. She is always comforting me and showing me the world. I love traveling with her. She is a big spender when it comes to trips."

"I could tell from when I went over there for dinner."

"Summer camps were the worst for me. I would be so homesick that she would have to come and get me."

"Really, mama's baby," I joked as I pushed her on the

arm.

"That's me."

"I do miss my mother though. When I was at work on patrol, I would stop by her house and talk for a few minutes until I got a call. This is the first time that I have actually been this far away from her," I explained.

"Well, I hope you love it here. I wish that we could spend more time together, but Alex is greedy. He wants to keep you all to himself."

"Maybe he doesn't want us to be close like you and Emily were. He might be afraid of that. Did you distance yourself from him after she died?"

"Yes, I did. I didn't think about that."

"That most definitely could be it."

"Probably so, but I do know that I would love for you to be my sister-in-law one day."

"Me too, Codie. That is the plan."

"Great. I am happy to hear that."

"I don't plan on leaving Alex at all. He will be my

husband one day," I smiled as I looked at her. She smiled back and we fell asleep.

The next morning rolled around and there was no Alex. Codie was still asleep as I moved through the house, looking for Alex. I walked into the master bedroom and picked up my phone. The only text I had received was from my father:

Hey Baby. I would love to hear from you.

I wanted to text back, but it was too early. I will give him and Mother time to wake up. Looking at my missed calls, there was nothing from Alex. I decided to call his phone. No answer. I called and called three more times and still, no answer.

Texting:

Please, Alex, let me know that you're all right. You have me worried about you. Please, call me.

I waited for a few minutes, but he never responded. I laid my phone down and began getting my clothes out for today. Taking a quick shower, I dried off and put on my blue jeans and a red t-shirt with red socks. Suddenly, I hear my phone go off. I ran and saw it was Alex calling me back.

"Hello."

"Princess, I'm okay. I will be home in a few."

"You had me so worried. Are you alright?"

"I'm alright. I couldn't find that dirty bastard nowhere. He wasn't at any of the hiding places I thought he would be at. But when I do find him I am going to pound him badly. How is she doing?"

"She is doing great. After you left, she soaked in the tub and we went to bed. I slept in there with her," I replied, wanting to tell him that she was pregnant, but I'd promised her that I would not tell.

"Well, I will be there in a few. Love you, Siam."

"Love you too, Alex," I replied as he hung up the phone.

Putting the phone back on the nightstand, Codie startled me, "Why didn't you wake me?"

"You seemed like you were tired with all that snoring you were doing last night, so I decided to let you go ahead and rest."

"I was snoring?" she laughed.

303

"Yes, you were doing more than snoring," I giggled.

"I'm sorry about that. I guess I was tired. Where's Alex?"

"He hasn't made it home yet, but he says he will be here in a few minutes."

"He's been gone all night. Did he say if he found Chance? What happened?" she called out question after question.

"He didn't find Chance. He said he went to all of his hiding places and didn't find him."

"I'm so happy that he didn't."

"Me too."

"I have to go, but I will be back," Codie blurted out and ran to the guest room.

"Where are you going?" I yelled as I ran behind her.

"I'm going to find Chance. I think I know where he is."

"Codie, I don't think that's a good idea. You don't think he might beat you up again? Please don't go. Alex is going to kill me if you leave before he got back."

"Tell him when you woke up that I was gone."

"I can't tell him that. I already said you were in the bed sleep. Just stay here until he comes back, then go. I don't want to be in any trouble if you leave before he gets back," I explained.

"Okay, Siam. I will wait until he gets back, but I'm out of here immediately after he walks in the door."

"I don't understand why you have to go find Chance. He seems like he is a bad man. I don't think he will accept the fact about you pregnant today. Just give him some time to think and go from there."

"He's really not a bad person. He was just drunk and I told him about the baby at the wrong time. Maybe today, he will have a better judgment than last night."

"I really don't think so, but that's on you. I don't want you to go to be honest. I like talking to you. Your presence makes me happy."

"Oh, Siam, I love talking to you too, but I have to go find Chance. If I talk to him again and he still doesn't want the baby, then I will leave him alone. I won't pressure him to love me or his child. I promise I will be back," she stated with those big blue eyes.

"Promise me that you will come back here. Don't go to your mother's house. Come back here or at least call me. Text me, something, letting me know that you're alright."

"I promise to keep you updated."

"You're going to have me stressed out, worrying about you and your brother."

"Don't stress out, Siam. We don't mean to stress you."

"I can't tell." We laughed as she packed her items and headed to the front door. She put the two bags down and in walks Alex. He had this crazy look on his face. You could tell that he had been up all night without sleep.

"Where in the hell are you two about to go off to?" he asked as soon as he saw the two bags by the door.

"I'm leaving, Alex, but I will be back," Codie replied as she picked up the bags.

"Where are you going?"

"I'm going to mama's house and talk with her." She lied.

"She's going to find Chance," I blurted out as she looked at me with a disappointing look.

"Siam."

"I don't want to see you hurt. I feel like if you find him that he will hurt you again. I have dealt with too many cases like that," I added as I held her hand.

"You're not going to find that dirty bastard. When I eat and get some rest, I'm going back out to find him. Put your bags back down," he ordered as he tried to take them out of her hands.

"I'm not staying here, Alex. I'm going to find Chance and you can't stop me."

"I can and I will stop you. Do you want me to call mother and father? I will tell them everything that's going on. I'm serious, Codie."

"Don't you dare threaten me."

"I will do whatever I want. If you do see Chance, then I will tell them everything."

"Alex, don't do this to me. Please. I promise that I will return. I already told Siam that I would keep her updated on everything."

"Codie, go sit down and relax, because you're not going out this door," Alex demanded as he gave her a slight push and locked the door.

"You can't keep me hostage here, Alex. You know what, go ahead and tell mama. I don't care," Codie spoke as she grabbed the bags back from Alex.

"Do you really want to risk your life going to find him? What if you don't make it back?" he softly spoke. It made me think about what Codie had told me about Emily.

"I just want to see if he really wants the baby or not," she mumbled. I looked at the expression on Alex's face. *She made me promise not to tell and here she is, telling it.*

"Baby. What baby?"

"I'm pregnant with Chance's baby."

"How far along are you?"

"About six weeks. That's why I need to go see if this is what he wants, if he really wants me and his baby out of his life for good? And, if he says yes, then you will never have to worry about me and him again," she stated as she stopped tugging with him over the bags. Alex released the bags to

Codie.

"Go ahead and do that, because I don't want this to come up again if he says he doesn't want you or the baby. How long have you known that you're pregnant?"

"I've only known a week. Just let me do this and promise you won't tell mama and father."

"I promise, but you better come back."

"Thank you, Alex," Codie said as she kissed him on the cheek and then, gave me a huge hug.

"Text me everything please," I stated as I released her.

"I promise, Siam," she replied as she opened the door and walked out. Alex held the door, looking at Codie get into the car. I stared at his face and a tear rolled down. He immediately wiped it away, hoping that I wouldn't see it. Closing the door, he stated, "I don't feel right, letting her go."

"I know you don't, but she has to do this. I don't feel right either."

"I love you, Siam," he said, changing the subject.

"I love you too, Alex," I replied.

Alex took a shower and got in the bed, falling asleep quickly. I sat there by the door and watched him sleep. Walking over to the nightstand, I saw that Codie had texted me:

I think I know where he is. Alex didn't go to the pub. It's a bar outside of town that his brother owns.

Me:

Are you going there?

Codie:

Yes, I'm going there first. I'll let you know.

Me:

Be careful. Love you.

Codie:

I will. Love you too.

I held the phone, hoping that she would text me back and say that she changed her mind and not going to find Chance. But I knew that was a lost cause. She seemed like she was determined to find him. I just hope that he doesn't hurt her again.

As I went to the living room and sat down on the couch, I decided to text my father back:

Hello Father. Love you.

Father:

Hey Siam. Glad that you're good and well. I hope to see you soon. When are you coming back down here?

Me:

I don't know when, but I hope soon. How are you and mother doing?

Father:

I'm good. Went to the doctor and he diagnosed me with diabetes. I'm taking insulin now.

Me:

Why didn't you tell me?

Father:

Because I knew you didn't have time for an old man like me. Plus, I didn't want to burden you with bad news.

Me:

Father, that's not funny. You are my concern. Have you learned to take your insulin yet or is mother teaching you and giving you shots?

311

Father:

You know your mother is giving me shots. I don't think I have the nerve to do it myself.

Me:

Please take care of yourself. I love you.

Father:

I will. I love you too. Keep in touch.

Me:

I promise to keep in touch.

After we texted, I put the phone down next to me and decided to take a nap while Alex was sleeping. When Codie comes back, we will probably be up all night talking about what happened when she found Chance.

Feeling kisses on my forehead, I woke up. Alex was standing there with a hard on. He began tugging at my jeans and pulling my pants down. He grabbed my panties and tossed them across the room, climbed on top and slid his cock in slowly. I opened my legs, inviting all of him inside me. I slid down a little on the couch as he began fucking me missionary style. We stroked and stroked at each other until he busted a nut. He pulled out his cock and shot cum on my stomach, all the way up by my neck.

After he came, he re-entered me and began stroking again. Thrust after thrust, he moaned louder than he's ever moaned before. He continued to stroke and moan until he busted another nut. I didn't even get a chance to cum. But as long as he was happy, it didn't matter.

"Damn, princess, you felt so good," he stated as he leaned up off of me and stood there holding his cock, hoping not to drop any remaining cum on the floor.

"I'm glad you're happy, sir."

"I woke up hard. You were on my mind and I couldn't find you. The next time I go to sleep, you need to lay in the bed with me until I wake up. Don't forget when I go to sleep, you go to sleep." He changed that quickly.

"Yes, sir," I replied as I jumped up to run get him a small towel.

"Thank you," he stated as I ran back in the room with him a small towel.

"You're welcome, sir," I answered.

313

"I'm hungry. Let's see what we have here in the kitchen to eat on," he spoke as he threw the small towel on the floor and, I immediately picked it up. I picked up my cell phone to check it quickly for Codie, but there was no messages from her. A message appeared from Zoey, but I didn't have to time to read it because Alex turned around quickly to see what I was doing.

"Have you heard from Codie yet?"

"No sir, I haven't heard from her."

"You're calling me sir now?" he asked looking seriously at me.

"No, master."

"Sounds more like it. You're acting like you have forgotten the rules. Don't think this dominant/submissive relationship is supposed to happen when you want it to happen. You want to see the real Alex Tremblay, then you shall have him," he sounded off like a drill sergeant.

"Yes, master."

"Who has texted your phone?"

"My father texted me saying that he had diabetes and Zoey just texted me, but I didn't read what she had to say," I replied with a little nervousness.

"Zoey texted you? Read it," he ordered.

Looking at my phone, it read:

Hey boo, holler at me.

"That's it?" he remarked.

"Yes, master, that's it." I handed him the phone and he read the messages for himself.

"I don't need to read it. I trust your word. What do you want to eat?"

"Hamburgers and French fries. I haven't had that in such a long time."

"Good. Me too, now get in here and cook it for us," he stated as he walked out the room. I hurried and put the dirty small towel away then came back to cook. I didn't bother to put on any pants after he'd fucked me twice. I walked around with just my shirt, bra, and socks on.

I ran dishwater in the sink and thoroughly washed my

hands in the other part of the sink. After washing up, I began preparing the burgers and putting the French fries into the oven. He didn't like me cooking much and grease popping up on his stove. I put a lid over the burgers as they simmered. The house reaped of onions.

I began cutting up the lettuce, tomatoes, and red onions for the burgers. Suddenly, my phone began vibrating on the counter. I ran over to it and looked at it. Codie texted:

I found Chance and he doesn't want anything to do with me or the baby. I asked him was he sure and he said yes. He wants me out of his life forever if I kept the baby.

Me:

Well, come back here like you promised. I'm happy that you are okay. Are you still with him?

Codie:

No, I'm not with him. I just texted Alex and I called mama. She told me to come home. I hope you don't mind, but I would like to go see mama. But I promise, I will be back over there soon.

Me:

I understand, Codie. Just be careful. Love you.

Codie:

Love you too.

I walked back over to the burgers and took them out.
Putting them on the strainer, I turned off the stove. The
French fries had about ten more minutes to go. Alex walked
back into the kitchen. I saw him out the corner of my eyes. I
knew the rules where for me to bow to him whenever he
entered the room, but I just pretended that I didn't see him.

Suddenly, Alex grabbed me from behind, pushed me
against the counter. His left hand had me under the neck,
slightly choking me as he pushed his cock against me. His
right hand guided his cock to my pussy and entered me. My
insides began to burn as he choked me more and more. I felt
like I couldn't breathe, but it felt good. He moved up and
down inside me and I busted a nut real quick from him damn
near shutting off my breathing. Alex let go of my neck and
put me what you call a full-nelson. He shoved his cock so far
up my pussy, I thought my heart moved. As he thrust in me
harder, he came in my pussy, filling me up. His cum ran
down my thighs as he continued to move in and out of me.
Easing up on his grip, his cock went limp and he fell
backwards against the island. I turned around and jumped to
my knees, servicing his cock with my lips. He was limp, but
I kept pulling and pulling, trying to get him up again, but

failed. He grabbed me by the arms and spoke, "That's enough, princess, I'm hungry." He smiled.

"Me too." I smiled back.

We cleaned up, then ate our hamburgers and French fries.

"Codie texted me and told me that she was alright. I see she knew exactly where to find Chance. I did go to his brother's pub, but he wasn't there last night."

"She texted me too. She was coming back over here, but changed her mind. She said she was going to your mother's house and talk with her."

"Do you really believe that Codie is going to mother's house? She is probably still with Chance. She just doesn't want us to worry. I'm going to text mother to see," he stated as he left the table to go get his phone.

Coming back in, he spoke, "I lied, she is over there. Mother just confirmed it."

"I'm glad she is over there and not with Chance."

"If I had found him, I wouldn't be sitting at this table with you right now. I would probably be dead with him or God knows what else."

"I'm happy that you didn't find him. I don't want to lose you, master. I want to be with you forever," I said, noticing that he used God in a sentence. That's a first.

"I don't want to lose you either. That's why I haven't decided to give you what you want, like I said before. If this dominant/submissive lifestyle what you want, then okay. Don't go crying back to Georgia to your parents talking about I did you wrong and shit."

"I won't, master. I am a strong woman, I can handle myself."

"We will see if you are a strong woman. Since Codie isn't coming back tonight, I have a little treat for you."

"Codie won't be back tonight?" I said with a disappointed voice.

"No, she won't. I told her to come back tomorrow, because I wanted to spend a little time with you." He finished his two burgers and fries, but I still had food left.

"What kind of treat do you have for me?" I asked.

"Don't worry about that. Once you have finished eating, I will help you pack a night bag. You will need to soak too before we leave."

"Yes, master. Will you stay with me?"

"No, I won't be staying with you. Kale will take care of you while I am gone."

"You're leaving me? I thought you said you wouldn't leave me again alone by myself."

"I did promise you that. I will let Kale know. She is going to be very mad at me. I told her that I would leave you for a night."

"Is Kale a woman or a man?"

"Kale is a woman. She lives not that far from here. She has two female submissive living with her. I promise you that they won't hurt you. Kale is very gentle."

"Oh okay," I replied as I continued to eat my food.

As soon as I soaked in the tub and packed my bags, we were off to Kale's house. If Alex promised to leave me alone, they must be going to service me. Or, am I going to service all three of them. I had fun eating pussy before, but I'd rather have it done to me, than me doing it to them. All kinds of thoughts came across my mind.

Kale's house was about four blocks over. "See, I told you that it wasn't far. Do you still want me to stay?" he asked.

"Can you please stay for a little while until I am comfortable with them? If you say they won't hurt me then I trust you; they won't hurt me."

"Good girl. I'm glad you have courage."

"Yes, master, I do."

SIAM'S THOUGHTS

As we pulled up in the driveway, I was very nervous. Alex is leaving me with three lesbians all night. There is no telling what is all going to go on this house tonight. This was one of my dreams and that's to be licked and sucked by many lesbians. Some of the porn I had watched back in Georgia made me so fucking hot. Women took their time and licked with passion. The way their tongues moved in and out slowly. Teasing the clit with their tongues. Putting their fingers in the pussy as they licked. Finger fucking and bumping pussies. That night I gently rubbed pussies with this other girl was so freaking hot. I got so excited just thinking about those girls. I was ready to be a full-blown lesbian tonight.

DOUBLE HEADED DILDO

CHAPTER 16

We entered the house and a black lady in her mid-thirties came to the door. She had big hips and a small waist. She was a light-skinned female with long pretty hair.

"Welcome to my palace," she invited us as we walked in.

"Hey, my love. I've missed you."

"I've missed you too, darling. Who do we have here?"

"This is Siam. The one I was telling you about a couple of days ago."

"Siam, the girl that you're so in love with?" she remarked, as she looked me up and down like I was a piece of meat. I wanted to give her that stare back, but instead I put my head down.

"Yes, she is. I am giving her to you for tonight."

"We would love to have her for tonight. Benton, Allie, come and get Siam's bag." She demanded as two girls ran into the room.

"Hello, Allie and Benton." Alex spoke as he grabbed each one's hand and kissed it.

"Hello, master Alex," the cute Asian girl replied as she blushed. Her name was Allie. I was a little jealous at first, at how she blushed at Alex. I looked over to mistress Kale and she was staring at me, trying to study the expression on my face. Allie didn't have much of a chest. In fact, she was almost flat chested with a little booty.

"Hello, master Alex," this beautiful mocha-looking girl replied. She was skinny with big breasts. Her name was Benton. She had a much bigger butt than Allie's.

"Girls, this is Siam, she will be our guest for tonight. We must treat her right," mistress Kale ordered as she looked at me and licked her lips. I smiled at her. I didn't know whether to call her mistress, master, ma'am, or what.

The girls grabbed my bag and took me off into another room. I looked back at Alex and waved at him. He smiled at me and exit the door. I was letting him know that I was going to be all right. After meeting them, I didn't think they were there to harm me.

"Hey Siam, I'm Allie," she spoke with such a screechy voice. It was kind of annoying, but it was only for one night.

"Hello Allie, nice to meet you. And you must be

Benton?" I turned to the black female. She shrugged her nose up at me and just threw up her hand.

"Yeah, she's Benton. She's just a little salty right now, but if she doesn't get it together, I will report her to mistress Kale. I don't think Benton wants that, do she?" Allie threatened as she looked at Benton with that "don't fuck with me look" or I will tell on your ass.

"Yes, I'm Benton," she replied, sticking out her hand and still looking salty.

"Now, that we're off to a good start, let us show you where the play room will be," Allie stated as she grabbed me by the hand and led me upstairs.

We walked into this big room, looking like a studio. There were lots of different color pillows on the floor, along with big thick covers. They had a big crystal ball hanging from the ceiling. When it moved around, it put off a sparkle all over the room. Benton turned off the light and the room was purplish hue from some type of light. I took everything in as Allie still held my hand, walking with me. She took me over to this sex toy called the Inflatable Fuck Lounger. I knew that, because Alex had one in Pillars Dungeon.

"All of these toys won't be used on you tonight. We don't want to scare our guest off with so much play time," Allie stated.

"I think she will be alright," Benton interrupted as she smiled at me and then stuck her hand between my legs. I had on a short skirt with no panties on. Her fingers parted my lips and she put a finger on my clit as she stared in my face.

"Benton, don't be so rude and rough with our guest," Allie remarked as she saw my reaction. Noticing I didn't move Benton's hand, she stuck her finger down there too, touching my clit.

"You're wet," Benton stated as she eased her finger in my pussy.

"Of course, I'm wet. You don't want me to be dry. I don't want to disappoint you too," I replied back as Allie walked behind me. She got down on her knees and began placing kisses all over my ass. Benton began kissing me in the mouth, moving her tongue in and out of my mouth.

"She tastes so sweet," Allie stated to Benton as she parted my ass and began licking my anus. Her tongue moving in and out, violating me.

"I want to taste too," Benton answered as she got on her knees and ran her tongue against my clit. "Sweet," she added.

"I want to lay her down," Allie said as she stood up and guided me over to the pillows all over the floor. Benton was still kneeling on the floor.

"Do you think we need to wait for mistress Kale?" Benton asked as she crawled over to us. Allie laid me down on the floor and turned me over on my side. She immediately went back to my ass and began licking. Benton took my pussy into her mouth. They both were servicing me when mistress Kale entered the room. She didn't say a word, but walked over to us and sat over my face. She pulled back her robe and her pussy was fat. Without saying a word, I began licking her fat pussy as she squeezed my breasts.

"You girls didn't wait for me," she commented. Both Benton and Allie stopped servicing me. They got together, getting on their knees and stood back. Mistress Kale let me lick her pussy for a few minutes then got up. I sat up and got into the position that Benton and Allie were in.

"We apologize mistress Kale, she was looking so

327

delicious," Allie apologized as she looked over to me.

"We apologize, mistress Kale, it won't happen again." Benton added behind Allie's comment.

"That's okay, bitches, it won't happen again. Go away," she said to them and they rushed out of the room.

"My girls know better than to start without me. I will have to teach them a lesson," she commented as she called them back in the room. They both came running. Mistress Kale picked up a flogger and walked over to them. She stepped in between them, separating the two. She walked to the back of them and let it rip. She began hitting Benton and Allie across the back as softly. She gave them about four licks a piece. I just looked at them. My pussy had gotten wetter, wishing I was feeling the pain. Mistress Kale walked over to me and began teasing my breasts with the flogger and slightly hitting my back. Deep down, I think she wanted to punish me too. Instead, she sat in a chair that was in the room. After she was seated, Benton and Allie stood up. Benton went and strapped up with a big black strap-on. Allie finished taking my clothes off. Well, the little I had on anyway. She laid me flat on my back. Folding my knees to my chest, she sat on my thighs facing me. Benton walked and put her mouth on my pussy.

She licked and sucked my clit for a few minutes, then entered me. My pussy was wide the fuck open. She moved that cock in and out slowly. Allie massaged my breasts and Benton fucked me. She began shoving the cock inside me harder and harder. Letting out low sounds of moaning, I was feeling like I was about to explode. Benton stopped fucking me and Allie got down. She climbed on top of me and began licking me in the 69 style. Benton put the cock back in me as Allie continued to touch my clit, with her tongue massaging me. Allie didn't put her pussy in my face to lick, I guess because she was so short. Allie rose up and started massaging my clit as Benton kept fucking me. She fucked me slowly, not wanting to hit Allie in the face.

Benton stopped fucking and Allie motioned for me to get in a doggy style position. Benton entered my pussy as Allie got under me and began eating my pussy. I massaged Allie's pussy as she ate mine. She was indeed short, I laughed to myself. After a few minutes in that position, Benton took off the strap-on and gave it to Allie. She strapped up with the cock and put it in my mouth. Benton stuck her tongue in my ass and then slid a finger in me. I moaned out as she took advantage of me.

Switching positions, Allie got behind me and began fucking for a few seconds. She wasn't back there long. The two girls began nibbling and sucking on each of my breasts. I looked over at mistress Kale and she was sitting on the Inflator Fuck chair, with the dildo on the machine stuck in her pussy. She was watching us and fucking it. I definitely wanted to try that chair. As they sucked my breasts, Allie had her hand massaging my pussy. She spit on my pussy and played more. Benton got up and sat on my face. She put that big ass down and started grinding. Allie had begun fucking me again. I almost couldn't breathe because Benton was so rough. She grind that pussy on my face. I licked and sucked until I felt her pussy cum. Her cum slid down my face. She got up and began licking my face, eating her cum off my face. Damn, that was hot.

Allie finished fucking then started licking my pussy. I began to feel sensitive and exploded in her face. I actually squirted everywhere. Benton jumped down by Allie and they both took turns licking my cum and then Benton licked Allie's face. These girls were non-stop. Allie laid on top of me, rubbing the dick between my legs. I humped at her, wanting her to start fucking me again. Benton tapped Allie on the shoulder and they got up. They grabbed me by the arm and guided me over to Mistress Kale.

"It's time for me to play with this pussy," she spoke as she moved the dildo out of her pussy. Mistress Kale laid flat on the Inflator Fuck Chair. They motioned for me to get on top of her, and I did that. Allie grabbed me by the hips and guided me backwards until I felt the dildo on the end of the pole. She put some oil on my ass and inserted a finger. She moved in and out, then I felt the dildo at my ass. I backed up, taking the dildo into my ass. Mistress Kale grabbed my pussy lips and began sucking me hard. She wasn't soft at all. She pulled and bit down on me, making me sore. I didn't stop her, but continued to let her be rough. After I couldn't take it anymore, I eased up from her mouth. Allie moved me from the dildo and I stood up, barely moving.

Mistress Kale put on the strap-on and charged my pussy. She fucked me rough as the other two played with each other. They had a double-headed dildo. Getting into the doggy style, they fucked each other. I was in pain with mistress Kale. She wasn't gentle but killing my pussy. She jumped up and flipped me over quickly. She rushed my pussy from the back and rammed hard. Benton and Allie looked at me. They knew I was in pain. This mistress Kale was no joke.

"Come over here, Benton, and show this girl how to take this cock," mistress Kale instructed Benton. She moved me out of the way and spread her legs like an eagle. Mistress Kale pushed into her pussy and went to work. She fucked Benton so hard, I kind of felt sorry for her. Allie was rubbing mistress Kale's back. After a few minutes, mistress Kale stopped. She took off the strap-on and both girls began eating her pussy until she exploded; her squirt was all in their faces. They both licked up the cum and she walked out. She didn't play with us anymore.

Benton and Allie guided me over to a purple-looking couch in the room. Allie put on the strap-on as Benton laid on the couch, then pulling me over her. I put my pussy to her mouth and she began massaging me as Allie entered my pussy softly. Benton ate my pussy as I licked her, while Allie fucked me. Benton massaged my sore pussy. They serviced me so that I wouldn't be as sore before I left. After a long while with soft fucking, we fell asleep. I had never felt so tired in my life.

The next morning came and Allie was up first. I opened my eyes to her kissing on my breasts. I smiled as her.

Reaching for her pussy, I massaged her as she continued to kiss my breasts. She motioned for me to get up. I moved to the other side of the pillows with her. Pulling me down on the pillows, she went between my legs, gently caressing my swollen clit. She stuck a small glass dildo in my pussy and licked my clit. After I came in her mouth, I then returned the favor until she came.

After that little excitement, Benton woke up and mistress Kale walked into the room.

"Did you enjoy last night?" Mistress Kale asked as she walked over to me and stood directly in front of me.

"Yes, mistress Kale, I did." I responded back.

"Make sure you give a good report to master Alex when you return."

"I definitely will do that. Benton and Allie showed me a good time. Everything was great," I replied.

"I'm sure it was. We usually do more than what we did, but master Alex said that you weren't that experienced, so we held back. Right girls?" she directed towards Allie and Benton.

"Yes, mistress Kale," they both responded back.

"You're dismissed. Clean this place up," mistress Kale ordered as she grabbed me by the hand and led me out of the room. We continued through the house and entered another room. Allie came running behind us. Mistress Kale turned around quickly with an evil look on her face.

"Her clothes," she spoke as she placed them on the floor with her head down and walked off.

"Thank you," I responded as I picked up my clothes as Allie disappeared about into the room.

"You will need those. Master Alex will be here soon to pick you up," she stated as she continued to guide me into this room. "Lay down on the bed and let me examine your pussy."

"Yes, Mistress Kale."

"You look mighty swollen down there," she stated as I laid down and she looked at my pussy. She poked here and pulled there. It was very sensitive until she stuck her tongue in me, licking my pussy.

Suddenly the door opens and in walks Alex, naked. I felt

kind of embarrassed at first, then he walked over. mistress Kale immediately stopped licking me and took his cock into her mouth. She began spitting and rubbing him. He was very hard and ready to fuck, but I didn't know if my pussy could take anymore. Alex lay on the bed next to me as mistress Kale mounted him backwards. She sat on his cock, fucking him. She was a wild one. She didn't give his cock any mercy. I got up and tried to touch her breasts, but she pushed my hands away. She guided me towards her pussy. I touched her pussy as Alex moved violently under her. She was giving it back even more. The two were crazy fucking. Mistress Kale acted like she hadn't had cock in years.

After a while of them fucking, mistress Kale got up. She pushed me onto the bed on my stomach. "Get in the doggy style."

"Yes, mistress Kale," I replied as Alex stood up.

Alex put his hand on my pussy and spoke, "Your pussy is swollen. You must have worked her overtime."

"You said you wanted her treated right, so they fucked the shit out of her. I bet she is happy and satisfied," mistress Kale replied.

Alex put spit on his hands and rubbed me until I began to get moist. He eased his cock into my pussy as I moaned out. Even my insides were sore. He stroked little by little, until I was fully wet. Mistress Kale stood on the bed, sitting on my back. She was a little heavier than I thought. I tried to peep around and Alex was kissing her on her back as he fucked me.

Finally, she got up and laid in front of me. I licked her pussy until she came, then Alex shot off in my pussy.

Mistress Kale picked up her clothes and disappeared again. Alex and I got dressed and went home. Damn, that was a wonderful night.

ALEX'S THOUGHTS

I wondered, how did Siam feel about last night. I hate that I left her alone, but after she waved goodbye to me, I figured that everything was great. She hadn't said a word to me since we entered the car. I wonder if she is embarrassed or too sore to talk. I want to hear every single detail that was done to her, even though, mistress Kale will send me a video. I bet she didn't know that she was videotaped. Siam would probably freak out.

CHAPTER 17

After taking a long, long bath, I walked into the bedroom and my cell phone was going off. Looking, it was Zoey:

Hey Siam. Please call me.

Me:

I can't right now, but I will later on. Can you text it to me or would you rather wait?

Zoey:

I can wait. I was just checking up on you. I miss your crazy ass. When are you coming back home? Or I could come visit?

Me:

I will call you later, big girl. I miss you too.

Putting the phone back on the dresser, I joined Alex in the living room. He was sitting on the couch, staring at some type of brochure. There was so much mail laying out that he had not opened.

As I entered the living room, he looked at me and I kneeled like I was supposed to. I was about to get back up, but he didn't acknowledge me. He just let me continue to

337

kneel on the floor. I just stayed there, even though my knees were hurting like a mutherfucker. So many thoughts began strolling through my head. *What if Zoey did come here? She would see me act like this or would he do this in front of her? I don't think it mattered because he did worse back at my apartment. He made me stand there and watch him fuck her. She would probably love that, fucking my big dick. I wonder would he fuck her more, since she could take the pounding like he wants. Zoey having a live-in man and her best friend in the same house would be a dream come true for her, but not me. I think I would get greedy, but then again, probably not as long as he let me fuck other men.*

Suddenly, Alex cleared his throat and spoke, "You can get up now."

"Yes, master," I replied as I got up slowly, because my pussy was feeling heavy and my knees hurt. I walked over to him and sat down on the floor next to him. My mind was telling me to get some sleep, but I couldn't sleep until he was asleep. That was the only thing I really didn't like about that situation. I wanted to sleep when I wanted to sleep, not when somebody else tells me to go to sleep, but I signed up for this shit.

"How was your night? I know Benton and Allie had a field day with you." He smiled as I peeped up at him.

"They were gentle and everything they did to me was great. I have no complaints about them two."

"And mistress Kale. You have complaints about her."

"No complaints really, she was just rough. I thought at one time she ripped my pussy," I said without smiling. Alex should have known that I was serious and didn't want to deal with her anymore. If she had put pain on any other part of my body, I would have been all right, but not my pussy.

"Mistress Kale is always rough. She doesn't know how to be soft and gentle."

"I noticed," I joked as I still didn't smile.

"It will be alright. And what about Mistress Kale and I sharing you. Did you like that?" he asked. "Look at me."

"Yes, master, I loved what you both did to me. It felt great. I guess I felt safe because you were there. I meant… I felt comfortable."

"They didn't make you feel comfortable?"

"Yes sir, they did except for Mistress Kale. I don't know what it was about her."

"Everyone says that about her. You just have to get used to her. She is a very nice and gentle person. We will visit her again, so be prepared for that. Plus, it shouldn't matter. That's why I set it up with her to let you see," he explained.

"Okay."

"Why do you sound disappointed? That wasn't pain enough for you?"

"Not really. That really wasn't the kind of pain that I was thinking about."

"I figured that by the look on your face. You don't hide disappointment well. I suggest that you start managing that, because you really are pissing me off. Your facial expressions are annoying," he said to me as he continued to look at this brochure. He continued, "Well, I guess since that wasn't the pain that you wanted, we will attend this party Thursday night. But Saturdays are the best ones."

"Party?"

"Yes, a party on Thursday night. You don't want to go?"

"Yes, sir, I will go where ever you want me to go."

"Good answer, princess."

"Can I ask what is the party about?" I asked.

"Master Barlow is hosting the party. He is a pain freak. He loves to hurt and I don't think it's the kind of hurt you want. He goes beyond the hard limits. Most people won't go to his parties, but I will take you. Once you see what type of person he really is, you will stop asking me to give you pain."

Can I ask you another question?"

"Yes, of course you can, princess."

"Why is it that you want to end our dominant/submissive relationship? When I met you, we both agreed on this. Seems like you wanted this more than me and now that I'm here, you are changing on me," I asked, hoping I didn't piss him off. It had been bothering me since the first time he mentioned about ending it.

"That's because I have fallen in love with you. It is my nature to control and be dominant, but you seem to delegated for that. I guess you are so used to being treated that way, it's imbedded in you."

"I haven't been treated that way. You are actually the second man I have ever dealt with."

"What happened to the first one?"

"He didn't do like I wanted. He wouldn't give me the pain and pleasure I needed. He was too nice for me. And then, when I met you and you were dominant the first day, I fell in love with you."

"You fell in love with being dominated, not me," he retorted with his eyebrow raised.

"I fell in love with you and the fact of you being dominate."

"It doesn't matter now, you're here," he smarted off.

"Yes, master, I am here."

"It's sad that you passed up being in love because you wanted to be dominated. That's why I am giving you what you want."

"Why is it sad, master?"

"Because being in love is the most beautiful thing in the world."

"Oh okay," I replied as I put my head down, looking at the floor.

"Enough about that garbage because it seems like you're not interested. There you go again with that facial expression."

"I apologize, master. I didn't realize that I was doing it."

"Sure, princess. Don't try to play me like a fool. Anyway, master Barlow's Naughty Fuckoffee Sex Party will be something that interests you," he assured.

"Naughty Fuckoffee Sex Party," I repeated as I looked up at him. We both smiled at each other.

"Sit up here on the couch with me and let me explain it to you. There are rules and things you have to abide by."

"Rules?"

"Yes, every party has rules, princess. What did you think when I said Naughty Fuckoffee Sex Party?" he asked.

I smiled at him and said, "I thought it was just like an orgy."

"No, ma'am. There are parties like that though, but this

343

one is different. Maybe you don't need to attend this one first. Here is another one from Domme Jonica and Cuckold Jared. This one is called Strawberries & Champagne Poly Play Party."

"Strawberries & Champagne Poly Play Party," I repeated again.

"A poly play party is a unique type of party. It's mainly focused on making love, rather than casual sex, involving people who are polyamorous towards long-term relationships."

"Okay, I think I understand what you're talking about," I giggled, hoping he would elaborate more for me.

"This means like vanilla sex. It may or may not involve the BDSM community, fucking missionary style," he laughed.

"Really? Vanilla sex?"

"Yes, vanilla sex. Let me guess; you don't know what that means."

"Of course, I know exactly what that means. It's just plain ordinary sex. No BDSM involved." I smiled.

"I figured you knew, as much as you say you stay on the internet learning everything." He laughed too.

"I didn't stay on the internet all day and night, just most days when I wasn't working so hard."

"Well, thanks to me, you don't have to work hard anymore. I promise to take care of you."

"I thank God for bringing you into my life. I'm so happy that I decided to get on the internet that day or I wouldn't have met you."

"I'm glad you did too. So, do you want to go to the Strawberries & Champagne Poly Play Party first, then go to master Barlow's Naughty Fuckoffee Sex Party? That way you will experience a little of both."

"Yes, master, I would love to go to both."

"Good, because I have to respond by one p.m. The Strawberries & Champagne Poly Play Party is tonight. Let me respond back to Domme Jonica and Cuckold Jared. I will be right back to go over the rules and stuff," Alex stated as he kissed me on the forehead and I smiled up at him.

As he walked out of the room, I was thinking, *the party*

tonight might be fun, but I'm more interested in Master Barlow's party. It seems like it's going to be very exciting. And this Domme Jonica's party, sounds like people just fucking and getting their rocks off. No excitement or anything. I don't know if I really want to go, but I will see what it's all about. Apparently, Alex has been to one of these parties before. He seems to know a lot about all of this stuff.

As Alex was walking back into the room, he blurted out, "Penny for your thoughts."

"I was just thinking, how long have you been in this lifestyle? You're only thirty years old," I asked, suspicious.

"I have been in this lifestyle for about ten years now."

"Ten years. So, that means you were twenty?"

"Something like that, but I think I was eighteen."

"Who started you with this BDSM lifestyle?"

"My father started me."

"Your father? The one at your house now with your mother?"

"Yes, princess. The one at the house with my mother."

"Wow. I didn't see that coming. Your mother seems like she is the one running everything."

"That's because they play only in the bedroom, not a twenty-four seven relationship like you and I."

"I'm surprised. Does Codie know about it?"

"Of course not."

"Why did your father tell you about it and not her?" I wondered.

"Because he wanted me to be like him. Codie is sensitive and she probably wouldn't understand. She is the hardheaded type. Not trying to listen to any man, especially not being dominated by one." He laughed.

"I know what you mean."

"Well, let's move on to the rules that we must follow at the party, because we have to prepare. There are six rules:

#1 No video cameras or cellphones are allowed.

#2 Must get verbal consent to touch anyone.

#3 Respect people's personal space.

#4 Cleanliness is a MUST. Hygiene is vital.

#5 Bring your OWN lubrication, condoms provided.

#6 Practice Safe Sex at all times.

"The rules are very simple. We can follow them with no problem," I stated.

"Yes, the rules are very simple. The thing they enforce at these parties is to make sure that touching or making love is consensual."

"Of course, it must be consensual."

"A lot of men take advantage of that. It's a lot of problems concerning giving permission, but we won't have to worry about that problem. Domme Jonica and Cuckold Jared only invited five couples beside themselves. I know all of them when I played before with..." he trailed off. I already knew what he was about to say.

"You went with Emily," I continued for him. He just looked at me and down at the brochure. I added, "If it's hard for you, we don't have to go. I mean, I don't want it to bring back painful memories."

"I'm good, princess. I want you to go and experience it. Everyone should experience a poly play party. At Domme

Jonica's poly play party, everyone in the room gets a chance to make love to a different partner. It's usually no longer than ten minutes each with a partner, then afterwards, we all talk about how we felt with each partner," Alex explained as he held the brochure open, looking inside.

"Do you have to talk about your experience with each partner?"

"No, you don't, but that's what these parties are about. Make love and then talk about it. You will see what I'm talking about. It's all about making love, no rough sex, whips, canes, or anything dealing with BDSM. I am sure that you will enjoy it. It's all about exploring your body. Different people do things differently. If there is something you loved, talk about it. Even if it was something you didn't like, you talk about it."

"Seems like a lot of talking afterwards."

"It's talking before and after making love, which we call a munch."

"A munch."

"Yes, a munch. Like I said, it's basically a casual social

gathering for people involved in or interested in the BDSM community. We are already in it. I just want you to experience a poly play party."

"Yes master, I'm ready to go see."

"Good. The invitation also says BYOB, which means bring your own booze, there will be snacks, appetizers and non-alcohol drinks, like sodas or flavored water."

"Okay."

"You might like it. I enjoyed it every time I went. It's been a little over a year now since I have gone though. I'm surprised Domme Jonica had sent me one. Once you're in the group, she likes for you to keep participating," Alex chuckled.

"That's only right because the people already in the group, you already know them and don't have to get familiar with other couples," I added.

"True. Well, tonight you will see everything. But I bet you are more into knowing about Master Barlow's Naughty Fuckoffee Sex Party."

"I guess so," I giggled. "Why do you say that?"

"Because princess, if you like pain, then Master Barlow's party is the one you would be interested in. Common sense to see that."

"You're right. So, the difference in the two parties is one is focused on making love, and the other is focused on BDSM."

"Something like that." He laughed. "Well, princess, if we want to go let's eat. You do your chores, and take a soaking. I will get a shower. It's important to be smelling good, but not with strong cologne or perfume. There will be too many bodies in one room for all that. They will have the air on, but it will get hot. Steamy bodies going at each other," Alex explained as he got up and walked towards the kitchen. I jumped up and followed behind.

After we ate, I did my chores, soaked in the tub, and then we were off to the Strawberries & Champagne Poly Play Party, hosted by Domme Jonica and Cuckold Jared.

Arriving, we had on trench coats. We parked in a garage. The elevator went directly to their floor. Walking to the end of the hall, a young girl maybe in her twenties was standing at the door to greet guests.

351

"Welcome Master Alex and guest, Siam," she greeted. I nodded my head, smiling. Alex greeted her with a hug and we went in.

"Well, if it isn't Master Alex, he's not lost after all," a woman with blue streaks in her blonde hair called out.

"Hello to you too, Jonica," Alex greeted as he gave her a hug and she just stood there.

"Alex," a man yelled out across the room. Alex took his index finger and tapped Mistress Jonica on her nose, then turned to greet the man yelling across the room.

"Jared, what's up?"

"I haven't seen you in such a long time. I'm so glad you decided to join us tonight. And who is this lovely lady?" Cuckold Jared asked as he walked over to me and grabbed my hand. Mistress Jonica still hadn't said a word to me. She just stared at Alex until he acknowledged her again.

"This is Siam," Alex introduced. Jared kissed my hand and then pulled Jonica next to him.

"Hello, Siam, you're a very pretty chocolate baby," Jared stated as he pushed Jonica towards me.

"Hey Siam, nice to meet you. I'm glad someone has brought Alex back around here. He just up and disappeared on us," she stated as she held out her hand to shake mine. I shook her hand and she pulled me up to her and gave me a big hug. The way she was acting, I thought she was mad at me too, but I guess not. I hugged her back.

"That's much better, Jonica," Alex blurted out as he hugged her again and she hugged him back, this time with a smile. We had to take off our shoes at the door and give Jonica our coats. At first, I was kind of nervous, because Alex had me dressed in my plaid play-suit.

"Now that's over, let's join the rest," Jared instructed as Alex held my hand and we walked into this room. It was set up very nice. There was a lovely fragrance in the air. White flowers were all over the place, with three couches and two big chairs like the bondage sex chair Alex had back at Pillars Dungeon. I didn't feel uncomfortable anymore after I walked in and saw the other ladies' outfits. All the men were in blue jeans and white shirts.

"Everyone, this is our good friend, Alex, and his girlfriend, Siam," Jonica introduced as she hit Alex on the arm. Everyone spoke as we waved back. "It's introduction time," she added. I looked around the room and there was another black lady in the room. I didn't think about that at first but I'm happy that I'm not the only black woman in the room.

"To start off, everyone should know that I'm your host, Jonica, and this is my husband, Jared. Let's start on this side and introduce ourselves to Siam."

"I'm Paul, and this is my wife, Angela."

"David, and my wife, Julie."

"Ken, and this is my wife, Becca."

"I'm the handsome Ted, and my wife, Paula."

"Great, all the introductions are over with and now let the party begin," Jared screamed out as Jonica punched him in the arm lightly.

"That's not how it works, stop playing," she replied as she tapped him on the butt. He jumped, while sticking out his tongue in a licking motion. "Everyone should know the routine. All the ladies grab a number from that side of the room, then the men from this side of the room. That's whom you will start out with. After that, we all will exchange partners in the room, until everyone has made love to each other. It's simple, we are here to explore our sexuality. It's all about making love to each other."

"No fucking the dog shit out of someone," Jared jumped in as Jonica shook her head.

"Only you would say something like that," she added.

"I know, only my horny ass," he blurted out again, as we all got up and went over to a table and pulled numbers. I had gotten number 4 and so did Ted. Alex was paired up with Julie. The partners began talking to each other over drinks. All the men brought bottles. Ted shared a bottle of Engraved Dom Perignon champagne with me. I never tasted it before and it was kind of bitter. After talking to each other for about ten minutes, then it was time to head to another room.

"Let's head to the Paris Room," Jonica invited.

"It's show time," Jared joked again.

"You and these not funny jokes," Jonica shot back.

"They're funny as hell, you don't have a sense of humor," Jared replied as he grabbed her ass, while we all walked with our first go around partners. Ted wasn't my type, but I had to deal with it. He was my height, had a small mustache and beard, with red hair. He had muscles. I'm the only one that doesn't like men with facial hair, but a couple glasses of Dom Perignon champagne and I forgot all about Ted's beard and mustache.

Before going into the room, we had to take our clothes off and leave them at the door. Usually, I would feel a little uncomfortable, but I wasn't. Maybe it was because of the wine that relaxed me. Upon entering the room, there were blankets and pillows in six different spots. Ted walked me over to the first area and guided me towards the blankets and pillows. He began kissing on my neck and fondling with my nipples. My hands went straight to his cock, caressing him and pulling him to a full erection. He was about six inches. That was enough, but I was hoping I could feel him after Alex's big cock had been going in and out of me.

After a few minutes, Ted lay flat on the blanket and I got on top of him. He wanted me in the sixty-nine position. He took my pussy quickly, with his beard and mustache tickling me. I swallowed his six inches deep into my mouth and could feel him at the back of my throat. I lifted my head as slob eased down his cock. Rubbing it with my fingers, I swallowed him again and again. He whispered, "Let's make love before you make me ejaculate."

Climbing on top of me, putting on the condom, and entering my pussy, I thought I was going to cum. After stroking each other, what sounded like a cuckoo clock sounded off. Ted got off top of me and the men walked to the next woman. Looking up, I saw Paul standing over me. He immediately mounted me and began stroking. His dick was a little bigger than Ted's. I could feel him digging deeper into me like he was hungry. He kissed on my neck too and sucked on my ears. His tongue going in and out of my ears was making me so hot.

"Fuck me back," Paul whispered in my ear and I lifted my hips to every stroke. He flipped me over and began taking me from the back. Sliding into my wet pussy, he bit me softly on the nape of my neck. As we stroked, I heard a woman scream out. Looking across from us was Angela and Ken. He was eating her pussy and she exploded. Afterwards, he began making love to her. It was more like fucking to me. I couldn't wait until it was my turn with him.

Almost close to our time to end, Paul pulled out quickly. There was a small white towel laying on the floor. He sat up and I noticed he had cum. The condom was hanging from his cock. He took the white towel and wrapped it into it. He went to the front door and put the white towel into a black bag. He took another condom from the small table at the door and headed back to me. His cock was still limp, so I took him as he stood in front of me. I pulled and pulled at his cock until he was hard again. He put on the condom, but the cuckoo clock went off. He looked at me and shook his head.

After Paul, there was Ken. He was a much smaller man. His cock was very small too, but his licking pussy game was tight. I guess he had to be good somewhere, since his cock was so small. He did such a good job that I came in his mouth over and over. I busted three nuts in his mouth. He continued to lick me until I was shaking. I kept trying to grab his cock but he pushed my hand away each time. I guess he was finished. I was so excited about fucking Ken that he disappointed me. I wanted to feel his small dick inside me.

Finally, it was David's turn. He directed me to get on my knees. He licked my pussy from the back for a few minutes, then entered me. It was soft and gentle but once he got in, he was like a jack rabbit. I thought we were supposed to be making love. David stroked and stroked until I lay flat on the blanket. He continued to fuck me hard. Seems like all you could hear was his cock slapping against my pussy. I looked around and I saw Alex next to me. He didn't look over at us. He was so busy giving Becca his big cock. She was humping back to him, taking it all in. I stopped focusing on David and watched Alex. He was kissing her all in the mouth, fondling her breasts and just making love, unlike this jack-rabbit, David. After a few minutes of him humping, he sat up over me and put his cock in my mouth. I began sucking him. I gagged a few times, because he was trying to push his cock deep into my throat. This wasn't making love at all.

After everything was over with, we all walked out of the room and grabbed our clothes. It was two couples in the shower at a time. There was no foreplay, no sex whatsoever in the shower. After we all finished, we sat down and munched. Everyone discussed the difference in each partner. Alex looked at me and then he kept staring at Becca. I didn't like the way he was looking at her. In a way, I was a little jealous. That was a no-no, concerning jealousy at parties like that. After they stared at each other for a few seconds, she looked over at me. I just looked at her and Alex looked at me. He gave me a slight nudge, breaking my stare at Becca.

After talking about the likes and dislikes of everything, Alex and I helped Jonica and Jared clean up as everyone else went home.

"Thank you all for helping us," Jonica said as she looked at me.

"You're welcome," I replied as Alex grabbed my hand and guided me; to put on my trench coat.

"You know I don't mind helping you clean up, Jonica. You just need to stop being such a bitch at times," Alex chuckled as he walked over to Jonica.

"And you need to stop being an ass, Alex. You know women don't like men being an ass," she snapped back as she grabbed his cock through his pants. He didn't flinch, but smiled as Jared walked in.

"Jonica, stop being all horny and shit. I'm going to fuck the shit out of you just as soon as they leave out that door," Jared said as he popped her on her ass.

"Why wait? I don't have on any panties, you can take me down," she said as she bent over right there and sure enough, she didn't have on any panties under that small ass skirt she had on, almost showing her pussy anyway.

Jared pulled out his dick and pushed in her pussy. She screamed out as they began fucking each other.

"Bye, you two crazy kids," Alex stated as he grabbed me by the hand and we walked out the door. I looked back one last time and Jared was staring at me. I knew then that he wanted to fuck me. *Maybe next time, Jared. Maybe next time,* I said to myself.

"How did you like the poly play party? Alex asked as he drove us home.

"It was nice. Jonica and Jared are clowns," I joked.

"They were good tonight."

"Jonica seemed liked she was mad at you."

"I told you she was mad because I stopped coming and I stopped fucking her. It seemed like she was addicted to me. Each time I make love to her, it seems like my body just comes alive and out of control," he smiled.

"Really. So, I don't do that to you?"

"Are you seriously asking me a question like that?"

"Yes, I'm seriously asking you a question like that. Do I make your body come alive and out of control?"

"Enough of this nonsense, princess. You make me feel awesome, but I know what kind of relationship we have. So, I'm giving you what you want," he explained.

I would have rather him say, "No, you don't make my body come alive and out of control." But instead he is trying to sugarcoat the shit. For some reason, I was fucking jealous.

"If she makes you feel that way, I can only imagine what that Becca girl does to you. I saw you two staring at each other like you two were in love. What's up with that?" I snapped as I folded my arms.

"Are you jealous, princess?"

"No, I'm not jealous. I'm just asking you a question."

"Nothing is up with me and Becca, besides she was my girlfriend back in high school."

"Really?"

"Yes, really. I was just making love to her, just like the rest of the women when I attended the parties. I thought it was going to be the same people I was used too but these people are new to me, except for Becca and Ken. Jonica use to be in love with me back in the day too, but I didn't want her," Alex explained as he pulled into the driveway.

"I knew it was something the way Becca and Jonica looked at you."

"It's nothing, baby. You made love to other men at the party and it looked like you were enjoying it, so don't come at me like that. If I knew you were going to be jealous of other women, then I wouldn't have brought you into this lifestyle."

"I'm not jealous about other women, just Becca and Jonica. Girls that were in love with you at one time."

"You shouldn't be jealous, because we have fucked other people before in each other's presence. I thought it would bother you more that everyone was married, except for us. You're too busy worried about another woman I fucked. Get your ass out of my car," he snapped as he got out and slammed the car door. I sat there for a few minutes, then got out.

The thought did cross my mind at first, when they

introduced each other at the poly play party. But he had a valid point, all of them were married, except for us. But the fact of the matter was, I wasn't ready for marriage.

After that night, Saturday finally showed up. I was very excited about attending master Barlow's Naughty Fuckoffee Sex Party. Alex thought I had forgotten about our conversation, but I needed more clarity on Jonica and Becca. He would never announce a safe day, because I wanted to tell him exactly how I felt. I didn't care what he said, I wasn't jealous.

I was sitting on the bed, not wanting to go in there with Alex. Ever since that night of the Strawberries & Champagne Poly Play Party, I didn't want him touching me. And apparently, he felt the same, because he hadn't fucked me either. "Princess, get in here," Alex yelled out.

Running down the hall and into the living room, "Yes, master?" I got on my knees as I entered the room and bowed my head.

"Master Barlow's Naughty Fuckoffee Sex Party is tonight and I wanted to share with you the type of rooms they will have there. Let me know if you're interested in any of them.

The way you have been acting, I shouldn't let you go anywhere," he stated.

My heart fell to the floor. I hope he doesn't fucking start tripping now, I want to go to this party. *Damn, Siam, you're fucking up*, I thought.

"Do you think you deserve to go?" he asked.

"Yes sir, I deserve to go," I replied. I knew he was thinking that I was going to say no. I told the truth, fuck yeah, I wanted to go.

"I don't fucking think you deserve to go. You have been acting like a bitch for the last few days. You really didn't think that I would notice how you acted towards me? Staying away from me and shit. I've been in the game longer than you think I have."

"Yes, master."

"Don't fucking 'Yes, master' me. I should kick your ass down on the floor and see if you like that kind of pain," he threatened. I hate it, but if he did do that, I was going to fight back. I was already pissed off and right now, anything would set me off. But I didn't act up because I was too far from friends and family. Shit, I just thought about it, I forgot to text my mother, my father, and Zoey. Damn it, Siam.

Alex added, "One of Master Barlow's room consists of bestiality. Do you know what that mean? Wait, I forgot; you should know since you have searched the internet."

"Yes, master, I know what bestiality is," I answered.

"Explain it to me. What is it? I want to make sure you know what it means. I just might throw your ass in there with them," he threatened.

"Bestiality is when a person intentionally engages in sexual contact such as penetration or intercourse with an animal," I replied with a smirk on my face. He probably didn't think I knew that.

"I knew your smart ass knew that. The second room is the bondage room. These are professionals tying people up the correct way. There is a correct way to perform bondage. Did you know that too?" he sarcastically spoke.

"Yes, master, I knew that."

"Good. The third room is the caning, whipping, and flogging room. And I know you know what that is. And if

366

you don't get that chip off your shoulder, you will be caned. Then again, maybe not because that's what you like. That's what you want me to do. Come to think about it, maybe I should not give you what you want. Maybe your ass will straighten up and do right," Alex threatened again.

"Yes, master, whatever you give me, I will accept," I whispered hoping his ass wouldn't do that, because I hated to leave him here in Canada.

"I know it's what I give you. That's my problem, I've been giving you what you want. Anyway, the fourth room is homosexuality, which is sex with men."

"Yes, master," I blurted out before he could explain it to me, even though I already knew that.

"Let me fucking finish before you answer."

"Yes, master. I apologize."

"Like I was saying, the fourth room is homosexuality, with three men doing a scene. There are probably two scenes going on at one time. People can walk in and watch. One man is the middle man. He will have a dick in his ass and one in his mouth. I wonder would you get off to that," he snapped at the end.

"Yes, master," I replied, but my thoughts were, *you mean you might get off on three men fucking each other.*

"You probably would get off. The fifth room is the massage room. Do you know what that is?"

"I guess someone giving out massages."

"The massage room is when the women or men give massages to the body or genital area, getting them ready before play or foreplay."

"Yes, master, I understand much better now," I mumbled, hoping that my attitude go away. It was hard, but I was working on it. I had to go see this master Barlow. My interest was piqued.

"Glad you do, and the last room is the pain games room. That's what you want. Explain it to me what the pain games room is," Alex ordered.

"Pain games is pain or the threat of pain that releases a rush of endorphins into the body. Endorphins are responsible for the sensation of pleasure in the body. That's why some people like a little side of pain with pleasure, but it's also extremely dangerous. There is usually spanking, hair pulling, choking, body clamps, blindfold, restraining someone, and so on. Things that I desire," I explained, as my pussy immediately got wet and moist.

"Are you wet right now explaining the pain games?" Alex asked.

"Yes, master, I am very wet."

"Good, because you're not going to master Barlow's party tonight."

"What?"

"Don't fucking yell at me. You expect me to reward you and you act like this towards me? It doesn't work like that, princess."

"Master, don't do this to me. I promise, I will be good. Please, master, I want to go," I begged as I looked up at him.

"Put your head back down. Who in the hell do you think you are? I give the orders, not you. I own you; you don't fucking own me. I said that we are not going and that is final," he screamed as he threw the brochure on the floor and tears formed into my eyes. I was really looking forward to tonight.

"Master, please forgive me. I won't act like a bitch again. Please let me go." I begged as he jumped up and grabbed me by the hair. He pulled me onto the floor.

"Is this the kind of pain you want to feel, Siam? You want a mutherfucker to be rude and nasty to you? You wanted this shit, now take it."

"Alex, please don't do this. I want to go to the party," I managed to get out as I yelled from the pain of my hair being pulled. He had me wrapped up tight into his hands.

"Fuck what you're talking about. You won't be seeing Master Barlow tonight," he screamed again as he took me into Pillar's Dungeon and grabbed rope. He tied me up and left me right there on the floor.

"Alex, please."

"And you called me by my name twice. I told you to address me as master in the house. You can only call me Alex on our safe days, but you know that already," he spoke as he looked down at me tied up. He got the ball gag harness/blindfold and placed it on my face. I laid still as he put it on my face. My mouth was sealed with me unable to express myself.

Alex had hogtied me. My feet were connected to my legs. I couldn't believe he wouldn't take me to Master Barlow's Sex Party. But instead, my attitude and acting like a bitch has ended with me tied up by myself in a room alone. Alex slammed the door and I stayed there half the night.

ALEX'S THOUGHTS

Damn, I can't believe I tied and locked Siam into Pillars Dungeon. She shouldn't have fucking pissed me off. I knew she wanted to go to Master Barlow's Sex Party. After her being an ass, she didn't deserve to go. Her ass sleeping on the edge of the bed, trying to get away from me. Staying in the bathroom acting like her stomach is hurting, not talking to me, and eating fast so she could leave the table. I was tired of her attitude, acting like a fucking brat. I knew that she was jealous. That's the only reason she acted like that.

Maybe I should keep punishing her like she is now. I try to give her what she wants, but I'm not doing the job. I don't want to go into beast mode on her like I did tonight. Siam is beginning to make me think that she doesn't know the difference between abuse and being dominated. My mind is telling me that she wants a man to inflict physical, mental, and emotional harm on her. Acts inflicted on a person is without their freely given consent. And being dominated is

371

governing or exercising one's will, influence, or control over a person in a consensual, pleasurable of power.

I think I need to have a serious conversation about it. Maybe I should go get her up from there. And then again, fuck it. Let her stay there until she is still and can't move. I bet she will feel pain in the morning.

CHAPTER 18

Early that morning, Alez came to get me. I was sound asleep on the floor. After he untied me, I just lay there for a few seconds and then tried to move. Alex snatched me up real quick. My legs were like Jell-O. Trying to stand up straight, I had to put my hand on his shoulder to balance myself. Alex grabbed my face, "Are you finished acting stupid or do I need to tie your ass back up?"

"I'm finished, master. Please forgive me," I managed to get out. I was thirsty and felt very tired.

"You better be fucking finished, because I'm not trying to keep putting up with your shit. You don't act like you want to be a submissive. You told me a lie. You really don't want this."

"Yes, master, I do want to be your submissive."

"I'm seriously thinking about auctioning you for charity. Do you know what that means, Siam?

"I think I know what it means, master. I'm not sure right now, I can't seem to think," I blurted out.

"Auctioning you for charity means the women are silent,

373

naked, and chained. They are put on a display while buyers scrutinize the merchandise, commenting, and possibly touching them. Later, each woman is displayed one at a time for the actual auctioning. The biographies of the women are read aloud and they go to the highest bidder," Alex explained to me. I had never read about auctioning for charity. I was scared to death.

"Please don't send me away. Why would you do that to me?" I replied as I began crying. I fell to my knees and Alex didn't move. He just watched me cry. Putting my hands to my face, I cried harder. I couldn't believe that he was talking about giving me away.

"Get your ass up and let's go to bed. It's two o'clock in the morning. You lucky I'm letting you go now and not later. I figured your body would be locked up soon," Alex demanded, as I rose to my feet and put my head down. He grabbed me by the hand and pulled me to the bathroom. He added, "Get in the shower and clean yourself up first. Don't come out this mutherfucker until you have gotten yourself together."

"Yes, master."

"You want rough, I'll give you that," he said as he walked out and slammed the door.

"Yes, master," I stated and turned on the shower. I was going to bathe this time, but I'm sure he wants me in and out. I washed myself slowly and tried not to get my hair wet. I didn't want to be up half the night trying to get this thick hair dry.

"You aren't finished yet?" I heard Alex yell as he opened the bathroom door and rushed over to the shower.

"Yes, master, I'm finished."

"You need to make it quick, because I don't have all night staying up with your ass. Hurry up and let's go," he ordered as he stood there and watched me dry off. I dried off quickly and went to the bedroom. He had laid out some pajamas for me, so I hurriedly put them on and went to bed. Alex lay next to me without touching me. I cried to myself, hoping that he didn't hear me. I kept sniffing. It really hurt me how he did me. That shit wasn't the sexual kind of pain I wanted to feel.

After about two weeks, I had gotten myself together and did everything Alex asked me to do.

"I'm glad that you've had a change of heart to be submissive like we agreed," Alex stated as we were walking back from the gym. It was looking like it was about to rain, but we weren't in a hurry. The breeze felt so right.

"I apologize again, master, for making you feel like I didn't want to be your submissive." It's been like the one-hundredth time I said it to him. I just didn't want him to auction me off to another dominant. If anything, send my black ass back home to my mother and father.

"You've been doing the right thing, princess. I just want to apologize to you for saying that I would auction you for charity. I shouldn't have said that to you."

"I think that's something dealing with Rule number 16: I am free to leave my Master at any time without the fear of permanently losing him."

"The rules aren't for me, they are for you."

"I'm saying that I should be comfortable saying anything expressing myself to you, without the fear of you leaving me. You threatened to leave me. I thought you were my boyfriend first and my dominant second," I expressed as he continued to walk beside me, listening to everything carefully.

"I am your man first. Boyfriend is more for the teenagers."

"You really don't make me feel like it. That night I was very emotional and you threatened to leave me, just like that. We agreed that it would never come down to this."

"It won't come down to that. I said that I apologize for that. Can you just get over it?" Alex spoke harshly as he looked at me with that stone face. I hadn't really noticed that he was still doing it until now.

"Yes, master."

"But I do have a surprise for you and I hope that you like it," he stated.

"What surprise?" I looked at him with a smile on my face. I haven't had a surprise in such a long time.

"I will tell you when I get to the house," he replied.

"Let's go," I stated as I took off running towards the house. The only reason I took off, was because the house was in my sight. Alex took off running right behind me. My legs were hurting a little, but I tried. Alex beat me to the house.

"You're not as fast as me," Alex boasted.

"I thought I could get you."

"You're going to need more training than that to beat me," he laughed.

"I see that. I just knew you were tired."

"Not by a long shot." We laughed as we entered the house.

I walked straight to the bedroom to check my cell phone. Mother had texted:

Hey Siam, call me, it's your father. He's sick.

I didn't text her back, I picked up the phone and called her immediately. I had forgotten that I had to ask for permission to use the cell phone. That's why it had been on the dresser all that time.

"Hello Siam," her sweet voice answered.

"Mother, what's wrong with father?"

"He's in the hospital. He fell out and the doctors couldn't

wake him up. They say that he almost went into a diabetic coma. His blood sugar was six hundred and ninety-nine."

"Mother, that's way too high. How is he now?"

"He's lying in bed right now asleep. We're still at the hospital. Siam, you need to come home. Your father needs you," mother stated and I could almost see the frown on her face as she said that.

"I will be home soon, mother. We just don't have the money for me to travel like that," I said, not even knowing how much money we really had. All I knew was that we didn't suffer for anything.

"I understand that, baby. I will keep you updated on your father."

"Is Charles or Dean there?" I asked, hoping that my brothers had come to see him.

"I called the both of them. Charles rushed back from Aruba and is here, but Dean refuses to come see your father. He is still upset with him," she replied. My father and my brother, Dean had fallen out. Dean told father a couple of years ago, that he was marrying Malik, another man. My father was so furious, he disowned Dean. They hadn't talked to each other in years. Mother still talks to Dean though. Father thinks she is still in communication with him, but he doesn't know for sure.

"I figured Dean wasn't going to come, but at least Charles is there. I'm surprised he's not there," I stated.

"I will try my best to come home. Please let father know that I love him dearly and I hope he gets well soon."

"I will do that. You know I love you, baby."

"Yes, ma'am, I do know that. I love you dearly too, Mother."

"If you need money to come home, I will send you money. You don't have a job up there yet?" she asked.

"No ma'am, I don't have a job. Alex works and take care of all the bills."

"You should be working to help that man out."

"I do want to work, but he said just take care of the house and that he will take care of the bills. I don't want to go against any of his wishes, mother," I stated.

"I understand, but you really need a job so that you can have your own money," she added.

"Mother, don't worry about that right now."

"I have to worry because you can't come home right now. I have the money if you need it. Do I need to send you any money?" she asked.

"No mother, you don't need to send me any money. Just take care of Father until I can come home. Love you."

"Love you too, Siam. And remember what I said, I will send the money for you to come home if you want to."

"I know, mother. Love you, bye," I said as I hung up the cell phone. I stared at the wall for a few minutes, until I heard Alex clear his throat. Looking over at the door, he stood there with that stone look on his face again. I immediately got on my knees and bowed down.

"Get up and come over here," he ordered.

"Yes master."

"So, you told your mother that you don't have any money to come home to visit. Why did you lie?"

"I didn't lie, master. I don't have any money. The only card I have is my bank card that she has. All my money is back in Georgia. You told me that I didn't need any money once I came here."

"I didn't like the fact that you told your mother that you couldn't come home. I stood right here and heard the entire conversation."

"I did not lie. I told her the truth. How do I know if you can send me home or not? I don't have a clue about any finances you have or anything of that sort," I stated.

"You should have called me in here and asked me before you ran off at the mouth telling lies. Furthermore, why did you have your phone anyway?"

"I just looked at it to see if I had any messages from my mother or father. You said I could check it, just in case they were trying to reach me."

"I did say that but did you ask for permission to use it?"

"No, sir, I did not. Once I saw that my father was in the hospital, I just had a reaction. That is the only father I have."

"I understand that and I forgive you this time. Next time,

let me know what is going on before you start telling our business. You know I don't like that," he replied.

"I apologize, sir. Please forgive me."

"You just keep apologizing over and over. It's getting annoying. Go take your shower," he ordered as he picked up my phone. I looked back at him and he was either texting or going through my phone.

"Yes, master."

After we both had a shower, we ate, and I checked my cell phone again. I saw where Alex had texted my mother:

Hey mother, Alex said we have the money for me to travel home. Love you.

Mother:

Thank God. Love you too.

I looked at the ceiling and whispered, "Thank you, God."

As I walked into the living room where Alex residing in the recliner, he stated, "Do you want to know what your surprise is?"

"Yes, master, I want to know. Tell me," I said with much

excitement.

"Well, master Barlow is having another Naughty Fuckoffee Sex Party 2 and we're invited. I know I didn't let you go to the last one, but we will go to this one." He smiled and I jumped up, running over to him and kissing him passionately. Then, I kneeled beside his recliner.

"Thank you, Master. Thank you so much."

"I figured you would be excited. The party is tonight. That's why I wanted to come on home and get you prepared.

It starts at four p.m. and ends at midnight."

"Four p.m. is a couple of hours away from now. I have to get my hair done, pedicure, manicure and other stuff," I said in a panic.

"Calm down, Princess. Your nails and toes are fine for right now. You can go get them retouched up next week some time, but we do have to get that hair done," He chuckled as he pulled back my hair gently.

"Yes, I need this thick stuff done."

"Have you thought of a hairstyle that you want done?"

"I would like something simple like the Shirley Temple curls. It's not going to take me all day. I'm too excited." I laughed as I stood up and swung myself around.

"Calm down, Princess, and get your stuff together so I can drop you off at the beauty shop. Maria already knows that you're coming in."

"You're the best," I yelled out as I hugged him and kissed him again.

"You can have your cell phone. I know you want to keep up with your father since he is in the hospital."

"Thank you so much."

"You're welcome. Now, go get your things."

Alex drove me to Maria's and she hooked me up with the Shirley Temple curls I liked. My hair was long and thick enough for it. Alex didn't like me wearing make-up. I didn't care to much for it either since the Mary Kay broke out my face years ago.

Getting back home, I bathed again, and got dressed. Alex had picked out an all-black Gothic outfit for me. It had two, black heart-shaped dots with black strings hanging to cover my nipples. I had on a short dress, with the panties saying "spank me", and long boots just above my knees. My nipples were trying to pierce through those heart-shaped dots. Alex was dressed in black pants with a few chains hanging from them. He had a hooded sleeveless shirt. He put on a piece of jewelry, which was a black cross. He put the hood over his head and it almost covered his face.

We were off to Master Barlow's party. "Does he have the same rooms there as last time?" I asked.

"I believe he does. I know it's the bestiality room, bondage room, whipping room, homosexuality room, massage room and the pain games room." He replied as he looked down at my breasts then put his eyes back on the highway. "Do you have your trench coat to wear until we get on the inside?"

"Yes, master, I have it."

"And do you have your collar?"

"Yes, master, I have my collar," I answered, feeling real good about my outfit, even though my breasts were hanging out.

"You need to put it on now. I thought I told you to put it on before we left the house," he stated.

"No, sir, you just told me get it and I did, but I will do as you instruct me."

"Great. Do it."

I put on the black collar with spikes. Alex added, "You look beautiful."

"Thank you, sir, and you look delicious." I smiled back. Alex smiled at me and we drove on to Master Barlow's Naughty Fuckoffee Sex Party 2.

Before I stepped out of the car, I put on my trench coat and buttoned it up. Stepping out of the car, Alex walked over and tightened the collar around my neck. He spoke, "Do you know what this collar means by you wearing it at the party?"

"It means that a collared submissive should not be approached to play under any circumstances," I answered.

"Good girl. You have really done your homework. And before we go in, do you remember the rules for this party?"

"Yes master I remember the rules. Don't disturb people

who are playing. This is a very important rule for me to remember. I don't need to interrupt a scene. If I have any questions, wait until they leave before asking. Also, I need to keep my voice down in play areas. May be music or it may not be music playing. And, no touching without permission or no touching myself. And mostly, leave other people toys alone," I explained as I looked at him with a big smile on my face. I remembered that when he had thrown the brochure on the floor the first time and I looked at it the next day.

"No wanking," he replied.

"That means no touching yourself, right?" I answered.

"Yes, it does. I was just making sure that you were on your game," he said.

"Will there be food here?"

"Are you hungry?"

"No, master, I'm just asking."

"There will be areas for eating, drinking, smoking, and engaging in sex. You don't have to worry about engaging in sex or talking to anyone anyway. Don't say a word unless I tell you to."

"Yes, master," I said as my legs began to feel like Jell-O. I wanted to go in and Alex was still talking.

After a few minutes, we walked to this building. A big, tall black man let us in the building. He didn't say a word but nodded his head. Alex walked over to this red-haired white woman sitting at the table.

"Good evening. Welcome to Master Barlow's Naughty Fuckoffee Sex Party, Part 2. Do you have your identification for the guest list?" she politely stated as Alex handed her his identification and mine. She gave them back to him. "It will be fifty dollars for a couple," she added.

Alex handed her two twenties and one ten. "Is that it?"

"No alcohol and bring your own toy bag."

"We won't be needing all that," Alex said as she stamped our hands and we headed in to the party.

As soon as we walked in, it was kind of dark. There were red lights everywhere. Looking straight ahead, I could see a stage. I began walking and Alex stopped me. He connected a leash on the front of the collar I was wearing. He had a tight hold on me.

"Stay behind me. If you walk one step in front of me, I will pull you down right here in front of everyone. Is that clear?"

"Yes, master," I whispered to him still feeling excitement about being there. Alex directed me towards the stage. I could see a group of people standing up watching. There was this big wooden-looking stand with ropes hanging from it. There was this guy standing there tying up this girl. He called it the *Ball Tie*. The ball tie is a person put into a fetal position and is tied up tightly into a ball. The knees are brought up to the chest and constrained to remain there with rope. This position can restrict breathing.

The man on stage then began pouring drops of hot wax all over her body. Drip after drip, she would scream out loud. Watching her scream, Alex looked at my facial expression. I looked at him and smiled. After turning back around, I saw a few men gawking at me. Alex pulled me along and we went to another scene dealing with bondage. This was a black man and a white woman engaging in *Breast Bondage*. This was a position involved in tying a rope around a woman's breasts, causing them to bulge outward. Usually the same rope is used to tie up both breasts so the harness is held together at the front. The black man in this scene then began flogging her breasts and upper body. She was turning so red. I was imagining that it was my breasts being beaten. Damn, I wanted to feel it. I moved closer to Alex, letting him know that I was very excited.

Moving on to the next scene, they had the *Frogtie Bondage*, *G-String Bondage* that I wasn't really caring for, and the *Head bondage*. It was so much stuff going on just with bondage. I didn't want to see the *Hogtie Bondage* either. Alex had already taught me about that one. I had no fucking idea what the *Shrimp Tie Bondage* was, but had to find out once I got home and look it up on the Internet. The *Rope Harness* wasn't a favorite either. Neither was the *Suspension Bondage* or *Over Arm Tie Bondage*.

I did find the *Reverse Prayer Bondage Position* very interesting. It involved restraining a person's arms by binding them behind their back with the hands between the shoulder blades, with the fingers of both hands straight, extended, and the palms of their hands touching each other. After a long period of time, this position will become painful and cramps will set in. I saw one video where some people were in bondage friction. People in this position sometimes are forced to have their elbows touching, turning their body into a form of elbow bondage. I don't see how it's done without dislocating the shoulder.

I had enough looking at bondage until Alex showed me one more and that was the *Strappado Bondage*. It did indeed have my attention. Alex and I had to definitely try this position. It's when a person's arms are bound behind their back, then attached with a rope or chain that runs from the wrists to a secure position above the head. The man had this lady's arm hanging up from an iron beam from the ceiling. Her arms were lifted up high behind her until she was forced to bend forward. Her legs were separated with a spreader bar. This was a must try.

Moving along to another part of the building, we ran across the bestiality room. Alex walked through the door and I tried to brace myself, letting him know that I didn't want to go in, but he pulled me hard.

"Don't forget what I said. You move when I move," he whispered in my ear.

"Yes, master."

We walked in and the first thing I saw was a woman

having sex with a dog. I just put my head down and closed my eyes. I guess Alex got the hint and we walked around. Opening my eyes because I thought we left out of the room, I saw another girl with a horse. I almost vomited on myself.

"Are you alright?" Alex asked as he whispered in my ear again.

"No, master. I feel sick to my stomach. Can we please go?" I asked as I looked up at him.

Moving on through the house, Alex brought me to the pain games room. Now this is what I had wanted to see. My mind had been on this for weeks. I wanted to know what really goes on in these kinds of rooms.

As we walked into the room, I noticed there were several *Dungeon Masters,* known as a DM. A DM is a person who is charge with supervising a play area or dungeon at a BDSM party. The DM makes sure that all play scenes are safe and if for any reason the DM thinks it has become unsafe, the scene will have to stop immediately. The primary responsibility for the DM is to ensure the physical safety of all participants engaging in the BDSM play. That was one of the things that I had liked about those types of parties. They believe in safety.

I saw a person doing the *Wallflower Patrol* too, before we entered the pain games room. A Wallflower Patrol is people going around and talking to shy people, clinging to the corners to make sure they are not scared to death or lost. If I hadn't had Alex, I would have been scared to death. I probably would have left after seeing just a little bit of the bestiality room.

Moving through the pain games room, I saw this tall, muscular man with a small goatee. He had golden blonde hair just like Alex, but longer. He kept his hair in a ponytail. His eyebrows even looked blonde from the angle I was looking. "That's Master Barlow," Alex whispered as I stared at him.

"He's looks younger than I expected."

"I think he's twenty-seven," Alex answered.

"He is young," I blurted out, hoping that he would notice me. I wanted to see what all the talk was about.

Alex moved along, going to another pain game in the room. There was this mistress who had a man tied up with his hands behind his back and a spreader bar on his legs. She was cursing him out and spitting on him. All he was saying was "Yes ma'am" to this or "Yes ma'am" to that. She started hitting him with a leather paddle. He screamed out with much pleasure. I wanted to be in that position, feeling his arousal. It looked like he had already came multiple times. Paddling after several orgasms results in an extreme endorphin rush. People don't know that shit, but I read it on the internet. You could see his cum on the floor. I was thinking he had to be rushing, with all that cum on the floor. It was like a puddle of milk. After a few minutes, his legs began shaking uncontrollably. The mistress immediately stopped and untied him. He was about to fall on the floor, until she caught him and helped him to the floor. That scene was over with.

Alex continued on down the hall to another scene. A big framed man grabbed this tiny, small framed woman by the neck and began fucking her roughly. His left hand was choking her. I knew it had to feel good, because I liked a hand to my throat choking me; it was intensely arousing. I would be ready to submit instantly to anybody.

The big framed man twisted her hair into his hand and pulled her hair back, putting her head in a bind. He shoved cock in her pussy hard as she counted slowly from 1 to 20. I bet that was some intense shit. He took his hand from around her neck and began beating her ass cheek until it was red hot. Taking his cock out of her quickly, she squirted. He began cursing at her, saying she didn't have permission to cum. He picked up a whip and began whipping her ass. Just looking at it gave me chills. My pussy was so wet that I thought I felt it running down my leg.

Alex doubled back to find Master Barlow. He must have known that I wanted to see him again. I didn't get a chance to see him in action. As we walked up, he had another scene that was about to start.

He had a brunette sitting in this bondage chair. She slid down to the edge of the chair and opened her legs wide. Two other female companions tied her legs back. Her feet were almost to her face. She looked to be in *Torture Bondage*. The restrained person is purposefully tied or chained in an uncomfortable or painful position. If the person is tied up long enough, it can be used as torture bondage.

One of the female companions began putting clothespins on the restrained girl's breasts. Let me remind you that her breasts are already in a tight bondage. She placed a clothespin on each side of the breast. The girl screamed out as master Barlow began hitting her with a cane. Caning is very common in the BDSM community. It is used in which the dominant is repeated striking the submissive with a long flexible cane, usually on the ass. But, this girl was getting her punishment on her legs and pussy. The idea behind caning isn't to hurt the person or submissive, but to straddle the line between pleasure and pain.

As Alex and I looked on, Master Barlow repeatedly caned the restrained girl. He had on a black shirt with no underwear or pants. The other companion had gotten down on her knees and sucking his cock. He had about ten inches. She had slobbed all on his cock and it was rolling down her shin. She was in a *Bondage Rope Harness*. This harness is a rope dress. It involves multiple passes of rope from front to back around the body to build up a diamond-shaped rope starting from a rope halter and moving down the body.

The younger companion who was sucking his cock, licked his balls and sucked a little more. Master Barlow then walked away and retrieved a golden packaged condom from a lady standing back in the crowd. He looked at the package carefully as the younger girl stayed on her knees and went over, licking the restrained girl's pussy. As she ate her pussy, the other female companion looking on began caning her. She licked and licked as her ass cheeks were being beaten. The restrained girl moaned out and her pussy was being licked. She did have red marks all over her legs and pussy from master Barlow's cane. It didn't seem to faze her any, because she was enjoying getting that pussy licked. There were seats to actually sit down and watch this scene.

Master Barlow had moved back on stage. The younger girl continued to eat pussy, while he put on the condom and stroked his cock until he was fully ready. He moved the younger girl out of the way and inserted his cock into the pussy. He moved in and out slowly as she screamed out with pleasure. My legs had gotten a little weak and I almost fell. Alex looked at me and we took a seat. Master Barlow was choking the restrained girl and slapping her across the face. I could imagine that she was already in pain from the position she was in, the clothespins, and the nipples and the rope bondage. Her face was so red from the slapping and choking. At one time, I thought she was going to pass out with the chokehold he had on her.

Putting his arms on the table she was tied to, he got on his tiptoes and fucked her hard. She was screaming out with pleasure as he dug deeper. He began hitting her on the legs. The chair was rocking back and forward and I thought it was going to snap. Her head rocked back and forth as he slapped her across the face letting her to take his cock and shut up.

Finally, her pussy exploded with cum squirting everywhere. The older lady came from behind master Barlow and began hitting her pussy with the cane. After about three licks, he entered her again, fucking like a wild man. The older lady went above the restrained girl's head and began choking her as her face turned red.

After the older lady moved and began giving a guy in the crowd some head, master Barlow took both of his hands and choked the restrained girl as he pounded her harder. She began crying out until she exploded again. He began hitting her pussy with his hand, then licking her pussy.

The girl couldn't cum anymore, so master Barlow caned her a few more times. He pulled the clothespins off her breasts and began massaging them. She screamed out. Other people got up and began rubbing her breasts as Master Barlow continued to fuck her, then he exploded.

"How do you like that?" Alex whispered.

"I love it," I replied.

"Do you think you can handle it?"

"I don't know, but I would sure try it."

"I figured you would say that," Alex said as he took off my collar.

"What are you doing?" I asked.

"I'm seeing if you could really handle it," he stated as he got up and instructed me to sit there. He left for a few minutes, then returned.

They untied the restrained girl and a big black man carried her out of the room. The other two companions who were with Master Barlow immediately began cleaning up. A few other people pitched in to help.

Master Barlow returned to the room and walked over to me. He didn't ask any questions, but snatched me up. I looked at Alex and he gave me the nod to go ahead. Tonight, I better put on my big girl panties. The two companions of master Barlow's undressed me. I was standing there naked in front of a room full of people. They tied my hands up over my head. Then tied one ankle and pulled it up towards my arms. They tied my thigh to the rope the older companion placed around my neck. I had one leg standing on the floor. The older companion then put a gag ball harness in my mouth and tied me. She then began putting clothespins on my inner thigh. That shit was hurting and I moaned loudly. She put clothespins on my nipples too. More people gathered in the room. Master Barlow walked over to me and began hitting my pussy with his hand. He was very harsh, not that soft shit Alex has given me. This lick stung me. He rushed his dick into my pussy and began fucking. He grabbed me by the neck, putting my head downwards as he fucked.

The older companion was on the side of me rubbing my clamped breasts. She rubbed my pussy too as Master Barlow put the pounding on me. Master Barlow then put a hand on my shoulder and the other on my waist and fucked, until he stopped while laughing. He moved out of the way and another guy walked in. He began playing with my pussy with his fingers and rubbing it all in my face. Then he began ravishing my pussy.

I began crying and the younger companion walked over and wiped my face. The older companion had a massager and held it to my clit while the guy slowed down, giving me all of his cock. After he moved back, she spit on her hand and rubbed my clit. Master Barlow came back over, pulling on the clothespins on my nipples. I screamed out with pain but I was trapped. I looked around for Alex, but he was gone. I didn't have no safe word or no safe signal.

The older companion began taking the clothespins off me and fuck me all mighty, that shit hurt so bad. Master Barlow began hitting me on my legs with the cane. The other man who was fucking me had them to untie my leg from the ceiling. It felt like I didn't have any feeling in that mutherfucker. They tied both of my legs together and I was just leaning forward. The clothespins coming off my legs gave me so much pleasure. That was the only thing that kept my pussy wet.

Leaning forward, master Barlow got behind me and pounded my pussy. It was amazing that he was still hard. The older lady came over and started flogging my big breasts. She wasn't playing. Master Barlow grabbed my breasts and pulled real hard as he fucked me, then she began flogging me again. They were giving me the works.

Fucking me over and over while beating me with their hands and caning me, I was tired as fuck. Untying me, I was falling, but someone caught me. I looked up and it was Alex. He lifted me in his arms and walked out. He sat me down on a chair at the door and put on my trench coat. Not able to walk, he picked me up and carried me to the car. Another person opened the car door.

"Thank you," Alex said as he shut my car door and I fell over. I couldn't move at all. My body was like it was in shock. Alex jumped in the car, not saying a word all the way home.

SIAM'S THOUGHTS

On the way home, I couldn't believe that I didn't have enough strength to lift my own fucking head up. My body was in so much pain. My hands and legs were trembling. But that was because of the ropes. My pussy was very sore from the beatings and caning, master Barlow pushing dick in me like he couldn't get enough, and this other man fucking me like he couldn't get enough. I didn't remember if either man got a nut. I know I did several times. My body had never felt anything like that, but that's what I crave from Alex. He sees now that I'm serious about this pleasure and pain. That's all we had talked about when I was back in Georgia and he was in Canada. I guess he was full of hot air, not knowing if I could really come or not.

My mind was on master Barlow. I loved the way he did his girls. Maybe one day, Alex will let me be a part of his

403

team. I would love to feel that pain every day. Well, not every day, but every other day.

Getting up the strength, I looked over at Alex and smiled. He smiled back at me. I wanted to ask him what he was thinking about. He stared back down the highway and it was as if he wasn't in the car. His body was here, but his mind was gone. Maybe he was thinking about the events that happened tonight. Either way, this is the pain I had been craving. Alex, it's show time!

CHAPTER 19

Getting home that night, Alex did *Aftercare*. This technique is very important for everyone, not just for those new to the scene. Many people's feelings, emotions, and thoughts are tested. Their limits and boundaries are too. Aftercare can be a gentle and slow process from the psychological standpoint of euphoria that BDSM often creates. My intense erotic and psychological event was expressed by my silence in the car and then once I got home, I cried like a baby as Alex gave me a bath. The agony of the clothespins is what really hurt the most. And, the caning was a little damaging. I had huge whelps on me.

Alex rubbed me down with some type of oil after my bath. He gave me water and food, then put me to sleep. He held me all night. This went on for a couple of days until I was back on my feet again moving around like it never happened.

"Hey princess, today is a safe day. Are you ready to talk about what happened about master Barlow's Naughty Fuckoffee Sex Party 2? Or would you rather talk about something else?" Alex asked as he fixed up a bowl of fruit and we shared it.

"It's whatever you want to talk about, master," I replied.

"Princess, it's a safe day. You can express whatever you want. Are you sure that you're okay?"

"Yes, sir, I'm good."

"You just don't seem the same since the other night. Did you like the way Master Barlow did you?"

"I loved it. I just wished you had warned me that you were going to throw me to the dogs like that. I think you were trying to punish me or something. Perhaps show me that I wasn't ready for the real punishment that men like him do to women," I replied as I continued to eat more strawberries.

"It wasn't a punishment, princess. You said that you wanted to feel pain and I wanted to see exactly what type of pain. I wanted to see how far you really wanted to go," Alex shot back.

"Well, you did a very good job, because I loved it. I need you to do me like that. Punish when you fuck me, just like that."

"What did you think of Master Barlow?"

"He has my attention. I really like him."

"I can tell that you really like him. When you talk about him or I mention his name, you have a sparkle in your eyes," he explained as he put his head down. He added, "I figured once you experienced the real pain that masochists go through, the physical pain and humiliation in front of strangers, you wouldn't want that full time."

"Well, you're wrong. Thank you for showing me that, because that's exactly what I want. My body craves it," I spoke out.

"How does your body crave it and you've only done one scene?"

"My body has been craving the gratification of physical pain and humiliation from you. When you first told me that, I became addicted to you. I wanted you that badly. If only you knew, how much I wanted you."

"And what about now? Do you still want me like that?"

"Of course, I do. I just want you to give me the same physical pain and humiliation that master Barlow gave me a couple of days ago. I would really like to experience being one of his girls. I want that right now."

"Why? I can give you what you want. You don't have to go to master Barlow for that type of shit." Alex spoke with a little whimper in his voice. I couldn't help but to look at him. The expression on his face told me that he was a little jealous of master Barlow. Well, he should be, because I had been trying to think of ways to tell him that I'm leaving him. But first, I needed to contact master Barlow to see if he wanted me. I loved Alex, but I had to go. This wasn't the life he promised me in the beginning.

After eating breakfast, I checked my phone and saw a few text messages from **Mother**:

Hey Siam, call me.

Mother:

Hey Siam. Your father is still in the hospital. Charles has made it up here with us. I told him that you had moved to Canada.

Mother:

Please call to check on your father.

I looked and there was a long ass paragraph from **Zoey**. It read:

I guess you don't know how to call nobody. Don't make me come to Canada and beat your fucking ass. You need to hit me up.

I replied to Mother first because if I didn't, she would think something was wrong with me. She knows how close Father and I are:

Hello mother. Love you. Hope all is well. How is father doing and I'm sorry I didn't answer your text last night, was busy.

I didn't want to tell her that I was still recovering from an ass whipping or caning. She would really come and drag my ass back to Georgia. A few minutes later, she replied:

I know you're busy, but it's not like you to not check on your father. You have me worried.

Me:

Mother, don't start that again. Stop worrying about me. I'm wonderful. How is father?

Mother:

He is great. He is up talking noise early this morning. He is anxious and ready to get up out of here. How are you?

Me:

I'm wonderful. I feel so much better this morning. I wasn't feeling well.

Mother:

What's wrong? Are you pregnant?

Me:

No mother, I'm not pregnant. I am taking my birth control pills every day. Alex reminds me every single day.

Mother:

I'm just checking. Love you.

Me:

Love you too and let Father know that I love him as well. I will be home soon.

She didn't reply back and then I texted **Zoey**:

Girl, you are not coming to Canada. You wish. LOL

I waited for a few minutes, but there was no reply. I put down my phone and began my daily chores, cleaning up the house, while Alex worked in his home office. Even if I did go to master Barlow, I didn't have any money. How was I going to get money? I didn't want to show up at his door broke. Then, I remembered; Alex had a little of money put away in his bottom drawer. I don't think he ever counts it. He uses it for cash emergencies.

For the first time, I thought about stealing from Alex. *That was wrong and if I did take it, I would be able to give it back as soon as I could. Or maybe I should just ask him for some money? I will take one hundred dollars, so that way he wouldn't know that it was missing. Maybe he would, that's a lot of money. I should just get twenty; that would be enough.*

My phone started buzzing. It was **Zoey**:

Since you been in Canada, you have been MIA. And I will come up there.

Me:

Relax girl. I'm texting you now.

Zoey:

How do I know it's not Alex texting me, pretending it's you?

Me:

Okay Phat Cakes, really.

Zoey:

Okay, it's you. Why have you not called me? You acting brand new up there.

Me:

Stop it. Alex has me very busy.

Zoey:

411

I bet, giving you all that dick lol

Me:

Is that all you think about, Phat Cakes? What did you want anyway?

Zoey:

I wanted to check up on you and see what has been going on since you cannot call.

Me:

So much has been going on lately.

Zoey:

Excuses, excuses. You must have a job now?

Me:

No. Alex doesn't want me to work. Why?

Zoey:

I was seeing why you so busy.

Me:

Stop it, Phat Cakes. Love you.

Zoey:

Don't try to end the conversation

Me:

I have to go. Hit you up later

Zoey:

You said that months ago. Love you too.

I laughed to myself at Zoey as I continued through the house cleaning up. And then, there it was, master Barlow's Naughty Fuckoffee Sex Party 2 brochure. I began looking through it quickly before Alex walked in the room. He had it bad, sneaking up on you when you weren't paying attention. I saw a phone number and email address. Since I had my phone in my hand, I took a picture of the information. Placing the brochure on one of the coffee tables, I finished cleaning up the living room because I was in a rush to send off an email. I was going to send a text message, but I wasn't for sure if it was his cell phone or not. It stated plain as day, cell phone number for Master Barlow. I prefer the email. I didn't want Alex to see a text message. He didn't know my email address; only the one I had given him when we first started talking. I had about three email addresses.

After my chores were done. I went to the bathroom and sat on the toilet. I sent Master Barlow a detailed email:

Attention Master Barlow:

This letter is long overdue and you have been on my mind for weeks now. So, I thought it was time for me to put pen to paper and let you know how I feel. I don't know if you remember me, but I'm the black female that Alex Tremblay brought to your party a couple of days ago. I loved how you made my body feel and I want more. I want to be one of your companions. Is this possible?

I have no problem submitting myself to you or anyone of your companions. You have helped me to turn my dreams into reality in so many areas of my life. I can't believe that it's been a few days and I crave you. I want you in my life. Is this possible?

Please feel free to email me back.

Siam

I hit the send button, then erased it from my sent files. I didn't want Alex knowing that I contacted master Barlow. I waited patiently for hours, but no response. I just hope I sent it to the right email. I walked through the house and into the kitchen, grabbing a peach to snack on.

"Hello, princess. I'm finished with my work," Alex called out as I almost jumped out of my skin.

"Goodness, you startled me."

"Why is that? You and I are the only two in the house. What have you been up to that has you jumpy?" he asked.

"I did my chores and then grabbed a snack. That's about it." I replied as I looked at his naked chest. Those gym shorts were showing the print of his dick. I looked at him up and down, like I was ready to jump him.

"Can I have a bite of your peach?" he asked as he stepped closer to me and I smelled his cologne. My body was reacting some kind of way.

"Yes, master, you can have anything you desire."

"I'm happy you think that way," Alex blurted out as he bit my peach and began chewing slowly. I watched his lips and then my eyes connected to his eyes. He grabbed me and began kissing me passionately. I kissed him back as I pushed my body closer to his. Alex put his hands between my thighs and lifted me off the ground by my ass. He walked to the bedroom as I continued to kiss him. I tried to put every inch of my tongue down his throat. Tossing me on the bed, he took off his gym shorts. He had on no underwear. He started undressing me and finally, my nakedness was exposed. As he looked down at me, I moaned out in ecstasy, wanting him to take my body.

"Make love to me, master. Please," I begged as he stood there, stroking his cock.

"As you wish," he replied as he crawled between my legs and slowly entered my gem. I called out with pleasure as we stroked harder at each other. All I could think about was how master Barlow was fucking me. It made me throw my pussy back even more to Alex. I busted a nut, then we came together. Collapsing on the bed, Alex stated, "You're like an animal. That's the Siam I know. The one that's making love to me like she wants me."

"I will always want you, master."

"I know you will," he said as he brushed my hair back from my face. My pussy was still aching, so I straddled Alex and began sucking his cock, getting aroused for round two. He immediately became hard. I got on top of him and rode like a cowgirl. There weren't many times that I was on top. As he pushed up in my pussy, I stroked downward to meet him. I rocked my hips slowly to his beat. When he speeded up, so did I, until we exploded together. Alex grabbed my breasts and squeezed.

He tossed me on the bed on my stomach and mounted me from the back. We were laying down and I just kept throwing that pussy back the way he liked it. My thoughts were on the girl who was tied up with the clothespins on her breasts. Master Barlow was having his way with her, as his older companion rubbed her breasts.

I lifted my ass into the air and let him go as deep as he wanted, without holding his legs like I usually do. I put my hands above my head and Alex took advantage of that. He gave me the pounding of my life. I didn't think he was ever going to bust a nut. He fucked me for so long that my insides were a little sore after we finished.

"That's exactly what I like," he stated.

"You like it when I let myself go and you just fuck me as hard and as long as you want?"

"Yes, princess. I don't want you to be tied up or having to punish you all the time to make your body act like that. Your body accepted me for me and that's why I delivered that cock to you like I did."

"That's good to know."

"When I said that Becca and Jonica makes my body comes alive and out of control, that's exactly what I meant. You accomplished it and didn't even know it. It's not all about the twenty-four seven relationship we have. You were open and gave me, you."

"I've always given you, me." I replied, hoping this conversation didn't kill my drive. I wanted to feel more even though I was sore.

"You have given me more on my terms, now yours. When I walked in the kitchen, I looked into your eyes and could tell that you wanted me to make love to you. The way you held your head, your body language, and that appetite; I haven't seen that in a while on your face for me," he stated as he held my face.

"I didn't know that."

"You're not happy here with me. Tell me the truth, princess. I won't be mad. Heartbroken, but not mad."

"I'm happy with you, master."

"Stop calling me that on our safe day. Remember, you can call me by my first name," he smiled.

"Yes, I remember," I giggled.

"I hope that you are happy with me. It would kill me if you weren't happy," he shot back.

The first thing that came to my mind was guilt from sending Master Barlow that letter. Alex was more in love with me than I was with him at that moment. Over the past months, he just wasn't doing it for me. I didn't want to break his heart. *Damn it, Siam.*

We had a safe day all that week. Alex made love to me every single day. I gave him what he wanted. We were like mad dogs as each other. Kisses all over his body and mine. Exploring each other's body like we had never done before. That poly play party did come into play in our lives. I learned a few things while listening to those ladies and men talk. Then I thought back to Becca's speech about each man. When it came to Alex, she was passionate. She told how her body responded to his and the explosion it gave her. I applied what she said to Alex and it brought me that raging animal every time. Who knew that listening to another woman tell how she made love to your man worked?

After about three weeks of giving Alex his non

dominant/submissive relationship request, Master Barlow finally hit me back via email:

Hello Siam:

Thank you for contacting me. I do remember you. How could I forget such a sweet mocha pussy as yours. Alex did a good job when he let me fuck you. I had never fucked a black girl before in my life. You have been on my mind and I do want you as one of my companions. Contact me for details.

And, how would you get away?

Barlow

"He replied back," I whispered to myself and I hit the reply button immediately:

Master Barlow:

Thank you, Sir, for responding. I have been waiting for your email. When do you want me to leave? I'm ready to submit to you. My cell number is 555-555-6783.

Siam

I sat there for a few minutes and there was no reply. I heard Alex moving around in the front, so I took my cell phone with me into the living room. I texted Mother real quick to play it off:

Hello, First Lady. How is Father?

Mother:

He is great and out of the hospital. He is disappointed that you haven't called or texted him.

I didn't text her back; instead, I called my father.

"Well, if it isn't my strange daughter from Canada. Anna, she is alive," My father screamed through the phone.

"Hello, father. How are you doing?"

"I am great. I should be asking you how are you doing, since you can't call your parents or even come visit," he shot back. I rolled my eyes, hoping he would be quiet about that. At least I'm calling now.

"I am wonderful, father. I've just been a little busy lately, but I haven't forgotten about you all," I replied.

"What is this your mother tells me; you don't have the money to come back home?" he stated and as soon as he did, a text message popped up on my phone. I quickly looked around for Alex and glimpsed at it. It was from an unknown number. It just read: *Siam.*

"Father, I can come home, that's not a problem. I was

telling mother that I wasn't for sure if he had the money, but Alex assured me that he had plenty of money. If I want to come home, then it was no issue," I shot back as I was anxious to reply to the text message. I bet it's master Barlow.

"Well, if he doesn't have the money, I will send you some money so you can come home. Why did you leave your bankcard with your mother anyway? I don't think it's safe not to have any money on you. This man hasn't given you any money?"

"Yes, father. He gives me money to go shopping, get my hair, nails done and anything else that I want. He hasn't denied me anything. To change the subject, how is your health? Are you doing better with your blood sugar?" I asked, hoping he wouldn't go on and on and on.

"My blood sugar is great. I've gotten it under control. Your mother threatened to beat me if I didn't."

"Well, maybe I should threaten to beat you too. I need for you to be okay," I replied as I walked back to the bedroom.

"I'm okay, Siam."

"Promise me that you will take care of yourself. Promise

422

me, father."

"I promise to take care of myself, if you promise to come home soon. And stay more than a week with us. I didn't get any time with you the last time. I wanted you and your mother to enjoy yourself," he added.

"I know, father. I promise I will come home soon. But I have to go. I promise to text you later."

"I will see because lately, you have been breaking your promises. It's hard to believe you," he snapped back.

"I promise, father. Have to go. Love you both."

"Love you too, Siam."

I hung up the phone quickly before my father said anything else to me. I looked at the text message again and quickly replied: *Master Barlow.*

Barlow:

Yes. Are you ready?

Me:

Yes, I'm ready. Give me about fifteen minutes and I will head out the door. I don't have a car here so I don't know how I would get back to your place.

Barlow:

Don't worry about that. I will send Jewel to come and pick you up. She is one of my companions.

Me:

Do you need the address?

Barlow:

No, I don't. I know where Alex lives. We used to be old friends.

Me:

Okay, let her know that I will be walking because Alex is here now.

Barlow:

Don't worry about him. I will handle that.

After that, I began packing my two small bags that I had brought with me to Canada. I only grabbed the stuff that I came with, and to get my hygiene stuff. My heart was racing fast, hoping that Alex didn't walk in on me. I was planning on telling him that I was leaving on my way out the door. That way, he wouldn't be able to stop me.

After packing, I walked through the house slowly with fear in my heart. My palms were sweaty and my face felt hot.

How in the hell was I going to tell Alex that I was leaving him to be with Master Barlow?

A few minutes of walking through the house and I couldn't find Alex anywhere. I even looked in *Pillars Dungeon*. He was nowhere to be found. Rushing back to the bedroom, I took one hundred dollars of his money from the bottom drawer and rushed out of the house. Looking at the driveway, his car was gone. I walked fast down the street.

Me:

Alex is gone, but I'm walking down the street anyway. I don't want to run into him.

Barlow:

That's okay. I have talked to him already.

My heart stopped right there. I didn't know what to think or text back. Starting back walking, a car approached me. It looked like master Barlow's older companion. "Get in," she ordered as she rolled down the window.

"Thank you, ma'am, for picking me up."

"Thank you for wanting to join us. Master Barlow is going to love having you. We haven't had a black girl. You're going to be a lot of fun." She laughed as we drove

425

back to master Barlow's place in silence.

Walking through the doors, we were at a different location. Looks like we were downtown.

"By the way, my name is Jewel," she added as we rode up the elevator.

"I'm Siam."

"I know who you are, young lady. This is the only advice that I'm going to give you. Take heed of it, do everything that Barlow wants you to do. Don't tell him no or he'll toss you out in the street so fast."

"I plan on doing everything he tells me."

"You mean everything *we* tell you. You're the rookie at this and we are the bosses. Don't forget that either," she spoke as the elevator doors opened.

We walked down a hall then turned left. At the end of the left turn was Master Barlow's condo. Jewel opened the door and there stood Alex. My heart dropped.

"Alex, what are you doing here?" I whispered as I stopped in my tracks. Jewel pushed me on into the room.

"I should be asking you the same question. Barlow told me that you contacted him. He said you would leave me and come here today. I didn't believe him until now, as I'm standing here looking at you in the flesh," he stated harshly as he looked at me with disappointment.

"You weren't giving me what I wanted. You knew what I wanted when I came here. The deal was that we have a dominant/submissive relationship twenty-four seven and I felt like you lied to me. Once I came here, you seemed different. You just wanted a regular vanilla relationship and I'm not built for that," I tried to explain as best as I could.

"Plain old vanilla relationship. Are you fucking serious, Siam? All the shit that I have done for you. I brought you here to Canada and gave you the life you wanted."

"That's old. I don't want to be with you anymore like that. I want to be with Master Barlow," I replied and as soon as I did, Alex slapped me across the face, sending me to the ground.

"Stop it, Alex. Don't beat up my treasure because she chooses me over you," Master Barlow interrupted as he helped me off the ground. I held my face and never looked up at Alex again.

"You have done it again, Barlow."

"Done what, Alex? You brought her to me, I didn't bring her to you. You should be happy that your leftovers want me. I will treat her well," Barlow stated as he ordered security to escort Alex out of his home.

"Siam, come back home with me. Please."

"Alex saying please," Barlow remarked. He added, "You must really love this one. Don't worry, I will take good care of her."

"Siam, just come back home and I will fix everything."

I walked away from Master Barlow's side and spoke out, "Remember Rule number 16: I am free to leave my Master at any time, without the fear of permanently losing him."

Before he could respond, security had tossed him out the door. I smiled and turned around to Master Barlow. Before I could place my eyes on him, he slapped me across the face very hard. I fell to the ground again. He angrily spoke, "Don't you ever walk from my side, talking to another man. Once you become my property, you are mine. And you shall address me as Dom Barlow, nothing else."

He walked off and Jewel walked off too, leaving me on the floor. The younger companion rushed over to me and said, "I'm Tina. Let me help you up."

"Thank you, Tina," I replied as I gathered myself from off the floor and she showed me to this room. After unpacking, Tina immediately began telling the rules. The do's and don'ts for Dom Barlow's home. She showed me videos of all the torture that I would have to go through to be able to hit the floor with him at the sex parties.

Two weeks had gone by and I was really beginning to miss Alex. Dom Barlow was indeed a fucking crazy man. He was nothing like I saw at the party. He was controlling, abusive, and sick. I really saw just how sick he was from the inside. He had two pit bull dogs in the house with us. I was scared of them, but they didn't harm me. There were times when he was on the couch playing with himself and the dogs would walk up and began licking his cock. He would let them, then ask one of us to suck him off. It made me sick to my stomach, but that's where I wanted to be.

One Thursday evening, Dom Barlow had a private setting.

I was the girl being tied up that night. Dom Barlow and Jewel had me in the *Strappado Bondage*. They beat me with floggers and canes. My back, my thighs, and my calves were on fire. I felt hot all over my body. Jewel flogged my pussy as everyone watched at the private party. Tina licked me as she flogged more. Then Dom Barlow fucked me hard. He walked around pulling on himself as other men entered me. Some were soft fucking and others were hard fucking. Afterwards, Dom Barlow comes back and began beating on my pussy with his hands as I screamed out. He ordered Jewel to put a gag over my mouth. She did so. After being beat for over an hour, I was exhausted. The sad part about it was that once they finished torturing me, they left me right there on the floor. There was no aftercare or anything. Tina helped me after they went to sleep. She was the nicest one of them all.

I learned later that Dom Barlow and Jewel were husband and wife. I never knew that all the time I was there.

After that event, the next week rolled around and I was in public being humiliated. I thought that was something I would like, but it was embarrassing as fuck. Jewel and Tina were walking on each side of me fully dressed, while I was naked with a pink collar around my neck and my breasts in bondage. Jewel had the leash in her hand that was connected to me and a spreader bar. As we walked in this park around dusk, men gathered to see what was going on. People were everywhere, but luckily, I didn't see any children. I would have run away from there immediately. Jewel and Tina both had canes, hitting me everywhere. Tina would hit me across my breasts every once in a while, to see me squirm. She was once in that place.

After walking for what seemed like miles, Jewel stopped me as men gathered around. She connected the spreader bar to my ankles, flogging my pussy and watching the men rub themselves. They began taking out their cocks and pulling on them. Jewel pulled me along as they followed like buzzards. We continued to walk as the men pulled and poked at me. Jewel and Tina were still hitting me with the canes. My body was on fire. Jewel ordered me to sit down and she pushed my head into the ground. One of the men grabbed me from the behind and guided me back up on my legs. Jewel placed the heel of her shoe on my head, pushing me into the ground. This strange man was about to fuck me, but Jewel stopped him and gave him a condom. He tore it off quickly and began boning me. He was anxious to get the pussy. I did like the way he fucked me. What I didn't like was my face in the ground.

Jewel pulled him up and guided the next man. He grabbed his condom and fucked me. There were maybe fifteen men out there in the park I counted, not including the ones that had walked up, looking onto the scene.

After all them got their turn, Jewel pulled me up by the neck and walked me back home. I was spitting grass from the side of my mouth. My face was dirty and sore. My body was damn near about to collapse from exhaustion. Tina held me close to her and I just laid my head onto her shoulders.

Getting home, Dom Barlow saw how nasty and beaten up I was. Tina took off the breast bondage and eased me onto the floor. Dom Barlow ordered me to come to the couch. I crawled over to him and he jumped behind me and began fucking wildly. My body was so exhausted and sore that I bent over with my face on the couch as he pounded away. Once he was ready to explode, he stood up over me and nutted in my hair. He tossed me to the floor and I just laid there, not being able to move.

A few days went by and I was just sick to my stomach. They fed me little and fucked me every single day. I finally

432

decided that it was time for me to get out of there before Dom Barlow and Jewel killed me. Jewel had me out that day while Dom Barlow and Tina left town to take care of another sex show. She dressed me like a school girl and walked me to the back of the building where there was a little green space. She had this wand in her hand. She was about to conduct *Electro-Play*. This is a technique using electrical stimulation to the nerves of the body, using a power source for purposes of sexual stimulation, tickling or torturing.

Jewel tapping me lightly on the thighs with it and I screamed out. She had set it up with about three men, who were outside waiting on us. She would tap me with the electro-play wand and I would jump around. It didn't feel good at all to be shock. I liked pain, but this wasn't one of them.

Pushing me to the ground, Jewel ordered me to begin sucking cocks. So, I had to take each one into my mouth as she hit me lightly on the thighs and lower calves. After a few minutes, the men helped her tie me into a *Ball Tie*. My ass was hanging out. She said go ahead and left me out there with them. Looking up to her, one of the men got behind me and ravished my ass. He didn't use any type of lubricant. I screamed, but another man put his hand over my mouth. I couldn't move because I was tied up like a dumb ass. The man fucked my ass until he came, then the next and the next. I don't know what happened after that because I fainted, falling to the ground and hitting my head on the brick wall.

ALEX'S THOUGHTS

I couldn't believe that Siam had left me for Barlow's crazy ass. How could she say that she loved me but yet, it was so easy for her to leave me for another man? Siam's parents had been calling me over and over. I decided to answer the phone and told her parents the truth, that she deserted me for another man. I explained to them that I tried to call and text her but she wouldn't answer me. She didn't respond to anything, then again, Barlow probably took away her phone. That's how cruel and mean he was. That sick bastard believed in fucking animals and shit. How could she be attracted to a sick fuck like that? I had to figure out a plan to get her back. This wasn't over yet with Barlow. I loved Siam so much that I thought about taking my life if she didn't come back home. My mother and Codie told me to go find her and bring her home. The truth was, I knew where she was, Barlow wasn't going to let me come near her. He never liked me after our friendship was over. He had done Emily the same way. She was leaving me that day she died to go be with Barlow too. I should have dragged Siam out of there.

But, it was too late. Her parents had sent the police to my house a couple of times. They had threatened to come up here, because they hadn't heard from her. I didn't know what to do. I have been stressed out for almost two months. And not a word from her. Damn, I hope she is okay.

CHAPTER 20

Waking up, I looked around the room and didn't recognize anything. There were two paintings on the wall. One was of a bushel of yellow daisies and the other one, of a single red rose. Looking at myself, I had an IV drip in my hand. It was hooked up on the backside of my hand. I tried to remember what took place before I ended up here.

I remember Jewel had me ball tied with three guys and they were fucking me in my ass. That's all that I remembered. As I sat there and tried to remember more, the hospital door opened and in stepped a skinny blonde-haired nurse, with a pointed nose.

"Hey young lady, I'm happy that you're awake," she greeted me.

"Where am I, what hospital?"

"You're at Rockyview General Hospital."

"Why am I in the hospital? Where is the Jewel, the lady that was with me?" I asked as I tried to get up.

"Please, lay down young lady, you're still not well," she spoke as she walked over to me. She added, "There was a lady who dropped you off and left. She gave me these two bags here. I tried to get some information on you. She just told us that when you fainted, you hit your head on this brick wall," she explained.

"I hit my head," I remarked as I felt my head. There was a knot indeed on the side of my head.

"You didn't have any identification on you. She just said your name was Siam Wilson. Is that true? Your name is Siam?" she asked.

"Yes, that's my name. I don't have any identification on me because my ex-boyfriend, Alex has it."

"I know he does. I called your emergency contact and she is on her way up here. She told me that Alex has it," she replied as if she knew who Alex was.

"Who was my emergency contact? I didn't know that I had one," I remarked.

"I looked at the cell phone you had in the bag and saw that mother Della is your emergency contact."

"How do you know mother Della?"

437

"She is my mother-in-law. I'm married to her son, John," she answered.

"Alex told me that you all were in Toronto."

"We were in Toronto. We moved here about six months ago."

"Okay. Did mother Della answer the phone?"

"Yes, she did. She is here now. I told her to give you a little time to wake up and then she can come in."

"Is she upset?"

"No, she's not upset. And by the way, I'm Auburn."

"Good. You didn't call Alex, did you?" I asked.

"No, I didn't call him, only mother Della."

"Great. All I need is him looking at me with disappointment. I need to call my mother and go home. Alex probably never wants to see me again."

"It doesn't look like that judging from your phone," she replied as she reached on top of the bag and pulled the cell phone out. I looked through the cell phone and saw that Alex had left so many messages. My parents, Zoey, and a few unknown numbers were in my phone.

"I didn't know that everyone was trying to get in contact with me. I should be ashamed of myself. All these people were concerned about me," I stated as the tears fell down my cheeks.

"Don't cry. The good thing is that you can be discharged today, but after we make sure the baby is fine."

"What baby?"

"You're pregnant."

"I'm not pregnant. I take my pill every single day. I haven't missed any days."

"Well, something happened because you're pregnant. You're three and a half months pregnant, almost four from the looks of the baby. And you really didn't know that you were pregnant?" she asked, looking concerned.

"No, I didn't know. I thought I was feeling sick because of the things going on around me. And not eating enough. I felt tired all the time, but I figured it was exhaustion," I explained as I felt my stomach.

"You do need rest. You were dehydrated too, that's why you have the IV drip in your hand. You haven't felt the baby move at all?"

"I figured that was just gas."

"Well, your gas is growing and moving around. I'm going to let mother Della know that she can come in. Sorry that we had to meet this way, but congrats, sweetie," she stated as she walked out the door.

I looked down at my stomach and began rubbing it. There is no way that I was pregnant. All the fucking I had been doing, I could have killed my baby. Then, I started thinking, which man could be the father. I used condoms with everyone, except for Alex. But then again, a condom could have broken. All kinds of thoughts raced through my mind as mother Della peeped in the door.

"Hello there," she smiled as she walked in the door, looking like new money.

"Hello, mother Della," I said as I put my head down in shame. I didn't want this sweet lady seeing me like this.

"How are you feeling?"

440

"I'm feeling great, ready to get out of here. I'm going back to Georgia. I have brought too much shame to Alex," I blurted out.

"Why are you going back to Georgia?"

"Because I'm embarrassed about all of this stupidity I have brought upon myself."

"Things will be alright. There is no need in being embarrassed. We have all done some things that we aren't proud of," she remarked.

"True, but they didn't come all the way to Canada just to embarrass themselves like I did. Alex must really hate me."

"I don't think that he hates you. Does Alex know that you're pregnant?"

"How did you find out?" I asked, but realized it had to have been Auburn. I added, "Never mind."

"Alex will be devastated if you leave and you're pregnant with his baby. It will be like the Emily incident all over again. I'm afraid it will send him over the edge."

"Technically, I have already left him. I know he has told

441

you that. He doesn't want me back after the things I have done. I'm going to take my shame and go home to my parents."

"He does want you. You can tell him everything once he gets here."

"You called him?"

"Yes, I did. He needs to be here with you. We don't turn our back on family. You're carrying his child, so I consider you family."

"We're not married."

"Maybe one day you will be married. If I know Alex correctly, he will ask you to marry him before the baby is born. That's how I raised him. We don't turn our back on family."

"That's not possible because I'm going home."

"You're not going anywhere," Alex interrupted as he forced the door open and marched over to the bed. He hugged me tightly and I hugged him back. I began to cry uncontrollably. He started crying too. I heard mother Della whimpering and she was crying too. Touching him sent a relief through my body. I felt protected and safe. I just broke down like a double barrel shotgun. I laid out just crying my eyes out. *Damn it, Siam.*

"I'm so sorry, Alex, please forgive me. Please forgive me. I have shamed you," I sniffed.

"Don't apologize for anything, princess. This is all my fault. I should have stopped you from leaving. I was scared that you would end up like Emily if I stopped you. I didn't want to be the cause of you being hurt or dying. Damn it, princess," Alex remarked as he held me tighter.

"I want to go home. Please take me home. I don't deserve to be with you. I'm so embarrassed for leaving you like I did for some stupid shit," I announced as I dried my eyes and looked up at him.

"We can go home, Princess, and I will take care of you. Damn it. I still can't believe that I let you leave me like that. I should have put up a fight."

"I'm talking about home in Georgia. I can't be here anymore with this shame. Do you realize what that man did to me? You shouldn't want anyone like me. I'm no good for you. I felt so humiliated and degraded. That man is a very sick individual," I stated as more tears rolled down my face.

"I tried to call you and text you. I don't ever want to lose you again. And now, that you're carrying my baby, I will never let go. Mother tells me that you're three and a half months pregnant."

"How do you know it's your baby?" I asked. There were so many men and even though they used condoms, it crossed my mind again.

"It's my baby, Princess. I counted up the time and it all adds up," he remarked as he placed his hand over my stomach.

"I don't understand how I could be pregnant, because I haven't missed my period. It's got to be a mistake. I've been taking my birth control pills every day," I assured.

"You have been still bleeding?" he asked.

"Yes, I have. Is that normal?" I asked.

"I will go ask Auburn and see, but I am sure it is normal. Most women stop bleeding while others continue their period," mother Della blurted out as she walked out the door.

444

"Princess, what happened to you?"

"It was terrible. This girl, Jewel, was shocking me with the electro-play wand thing. She took me to three men and tied me up. They were having their way with me and I remember looking up to the sky and after that, I don't remember anything. Auburn said Jewel told her that I fainted and busted my head on this brick wall."

"Princess…"

"I didn't ask for it. She ordered me to do it. And I couldn't have my cell phone until after three months. That's why I didn't get all the texts and calls from everyone. My parents are going to kill me."

"I'm not trying to speak bad about you, but you could have killed our baby. If I had known you were pregnant, you wouldn't have left like that. I blame myself for all of the fucked-up shit."

"I didn't know that I was pregnant."

"I know, Princess. After you get out of the hospital, I am going to take care of you. I'm not sending you back to Georgia. Your parents have sent the police to my door,

445

thinking I was lying about you running off with another man."

"You told my parents that? Oh, my God, they're really going to kill me now. I am too embarrassed to even talk to them now," I remarked.

"I didn't have a choice after the police showed up at my door. What did you expect me to do? I just told the truth, which was, you ran off with another man."

"You did right. It's all my fault. That's why I'm going home," I remarked.

"You're not going home to Georgia, Siam. I refuse to let you leave with my baby. If you tell me right now that you don't love me, I will let you go," he stated as he looked at me and tears rolled down his face. He was very emotional right now and so was I. There is no way in hell I could lie to him.

"You know I love you, Alex. I just left with master Barlow because I wanted to experience the pain. I didn't know he was a sick bastard like that. I've never stopped loving you and wanting to be with you. You crossed my mind every single day. I figured you called me a loss and found someone else. There were days that I prayed that you

446

came to get me, but you never showed up."

"Fuck. Why would I just get over you like that? I'm not cold-hearted, princess, like you think I am. I fucking love you so deeply. I'm willing to do anything you want me to do right now. I can't lose you. I refuse to let you go, Siam. Right now, I just can't lose you."

"I didn't say you were cold-hearted. I don't know what I was thinking, but I do know that I don't ever want to experience that again with master Barlow."

"You will never have to experience anything like that with me. I love you too deeply. Please rethink about going back to Georgia. We love each other and that's all that matters. We have a baby on the way Siam, a baby." He smiled as he kissed me on the cheeks.

"Yes, we do have a baby on the way. Maybe I should stay here and raise our child. Your mother said earlier that she considered me as family. It felt good to hear her say that," I stated as placed my hand on Alex's cheek.

"You should. I love you more than my own life. I promise to give you whatever you need and more. Just tell me that we can mend things and love each other like when we first met. I refuse to lose you, Siam," Alex announced.

"Yes Alex, I'm ready to mend things and be in love like before. I was stupid to leave you like that. I was being selfish and not thinking how you would feel about losing me. All I want now is for you to love me unconditionally and never letting me go. You best to believe me when I say that I will never, ever leave you again."

"So, does that mean you will stay here and we raise our child here together?"

"Yes Alex. I want to stay here and we raise our child together. Promise me that you will never leave me."

"Siam, I promise you that I will never leave you, because I want you to be my wife. Will you marry me?" he asked, without blinking an eyelid.

"You don't have a ring."

Mother Della had walked back into the room and we both looked at her without me answering the question. Alex looked at me again and asked again, "Siam Wilson, will you marry me?"

"Alex," I said as I looked at him and Mother Della pulled

out a small black box out of her purse. I was hesitating, because I wanted him to have a ring when he asked me. Not just throwing out words.

Alex grabbed it quickly and asked, "This is my third time, Siam Wilson, will you marry me?"

"Yes, Alex Tremblay, I will marry you," I replied as we hugged each other tight. Alex placed this big ass princess cut ring on my finger. The diamonds were shining so bright.

"You scared me there for a minute. I didn't think you were going to say yes." He pointed at my nose.

"I'm sorry, I was trying to say that you needed a ring for me to believe you wanted to marry me. I didn't think you were serious, just throwing out words to me," I replied.

"You need to stop playing. You just wanted me to sweat." We both laughed and mother Della came over hugging us both.

"Congrats to you both," she stated.

Later on that day, I was released from the hospital. Once I walked through the door of the house, there was family standing there to greet me; my parents, Alex's parents, Zoey, my brother Charles, Alex's brothers, John and Jack, and Codie.

I sat on the floor crying with joy. Everyone was there to love me. They all cared about me so much that they traveled there to be with me. Flowers and balloons covered the living room.

Alex picked me up off the floor and called out to everyone, "Ms. Siam Wilson agreed to marry me. Her being in the hospital for a week made me realize that I needed her in my life forever and I couldn't live my life without her. Even though, I had to ask her three times before she gave me a yes."

Everyone came up and gave me hugs and kisses. I was so overjoyed to see my parents there that I just cried and cried. That was the happiest moment I could experience right there. Even though, I met Alex on the internet, as my father would say, I had found true love. So many emotions and heartbreaks I had to experience to see that Alex had true love for me. In the end, he was willing to give me whatever I wanted, including his last name.

EPILOGUE

After that day, Siam and Alex became inseparable. They married on September 23, and their handsome baby boy was born October 28. His name was Alex Thompson Tremblay II. They remained in Calgary, Canada.

Siam and Alex continued their dominant/submissive relationship. They only played in the bedroom and Alex did give Siam the pain she sought, but only with him in the privacy of their home. Their life in the BDSM world still continued strong.

Alex did give Siam permission to play with Master Barlow once a month. She tried to stay away, but Siam still craved him deeply. She just couldn't get enough of Master Barlow and his wicked ways`.

www.ingramcontent.com/pod-product-compliance
Lightning Source LLC
Chambersburg PA
CBHW010829250626
47157CB00010B/3215